TOM'S APOCALYPSE

Theresa Dale

Paper Doll Publishing

CONTENTS

Apocalypse

Source: Dictionary.com

uh-pok-uh-lips

noun

- any of a class of Jewish or Christian writings that appeared from about 200 b.c. to a.d. 350 and were assumed to make revelations of the ultimate divine purpose.

- a prophetic revelation, especially concerning a cataclysm in which the forces of good permanently triumph over the forces of evil.

- any revelation or prophecy.

- **any universal or widespread destruction or disaster.**

What if the man who's supposed to save the world

Has a notebook full

Of suicide notes

Alternating with grocery lists?

As though his life is only as important

As the ingredients for

A sandwich?

Can he save himself in time

To save

The world?

For

All the unlikely heroes

Who

Save the world every day.

For

Those of us who are trying

Even

When it's the harder thing to do.

And finally, for

The part in each of us

That

Is counting down.

CHAPTER 1 – EARTH

The cliché of it all makes me want to scream.

I lay dying on my sofa, unsure if I was dying for certain, but seemingly at the mercy of flashes of my life playing on a loop in a mind that as yet refused to let go. Refusing because of the cliché; you know the one. About how, on our deathbeds, we regret the things we held off doing because we thought we had more time.

My list of held-off things was short, but represented the weight on my shoulders that had not only pounded me down into a fractured, hateful shadow of a human being, but had proliferated and spawned in the form of a myriad network of regrets – decisions made in anger, actions taken before the realization of their impact succeeded in halting them. And yet I carried on in that way until every link I had to joy and every chance I had at salvation were corrupted.

And by that time, folks, one is so completely dismayed by their circumstances that changing them seems an insurmountable set of tasks.

Hell, by the time the virus got me, I'd lost sight of the very possibility.

I'm sure my neighbors – what was left of them – whispered behind closed doors at the injustice of my longevity, especially considering those who'd been taken far too young. Or those with productive places in society, when I'd been a con or ex-con since the age of fourteen. Or the children. The innocent ones – while I hadn't been able to boast that title since before I could even talk to say the words. After all, I fit perfectly into the "high-risk" category: males over sixty-five with pre-existing conditions, especially diabetes (check!), hypertension (check!) and/or limited support (double check, but that one was by choice, making it all the worse).

Which brings us back to my poorly lit bungalow, neatly tended, but odd, I'm sure, with its cluttered mantles against bare walls, stacked with months of mail atop dusty fly-fishing accoutrements. No framed photos of family proudly displayed, no hint at the comportment of its single inhabitant, and besides the hand-tied flies, which clearly hadn't been used, nay *touched,* in years, no indication of the preferences or personal style of the man himself. Nothing to tell the story of his life.

The life of me: Thomas Wall.

But maybe the motorized cart just inside the door helps to explain that. Or, if one was so inclined, they could go through the piles of mail to find an assortment of bills and subscriptions. To start to put a picture together, you know? Spending habits, hobbies, perhaps a hint at the target market I belonged to. And somewhere in there was a lone, unopened note from one Louise-Anne Wall. Unopened because it seemed too thin. Because it was a reply to the solitary attempt I'd made to reach out and it had taken six months to arrive in my mailbox.

Unopened because I was afraid.

I can say that now, but if you'd asked me then, I'd have claimed a different, more believable reason: that I hadn't opened it because I didn't care.

Oh, and now that I think of it, there was one more item in the house that might lend some insight into my mind, and it sat casually by the bread box on the kitchen counter. It was a nearly full notebook, and I kept it there because I used it to make grocery lists. But it served one other purpose, and for that, I'd take it to the table. I'd skim the last note to see if it would suffice, but it never did. I never could find a pleasing justification for killing myself, so each time I decided on it, I found myself writing a new one.

And that little notebook summed my existence up pretty well: alternating suicide notes and grocery lists to illustrate the clashing goals of sustenance... and surrender.

CHAPTER 2 – AIR

It was her I thought of last; little Louise-Anne in my arms. I don't know if that final memory was of one specific time or an amalgamation of all the times I'd held her – it didn't matter in the end, though. I'd only held her a few times, and I don't think I took the time to really see her much at all. I was just thankful in those last few moments, when the breath rattled in my throat and the room begun to dim at the edges of my vision, that there was a time when I *did* see her. That I'd formed a memory that could take me through the last seconds. Her pudgy, satin-soft skin and her clouded, navy-eyed stare. Her tiny fist clutched around my right index finger, her peachy colouring clashing with my callused, nicotine-stained skin. And the weight of her in my arms, totally trusting and entirely dependent. It terrified me. But at the same time, she was so warm, so soft, such a perfectly contained little bundle that I found myself wishing I'd never have to let her go.

And finally, as my eyes darkened further and I felt myself begin to separate from the pain, I immersed myself in her scent – sweet, yet heady. Something completely unique to newborns, I think. That's what carried me off; that perfect scent on impossibly smooth, cool air.

And that's when I realized the complete absence of the pain that had turned achingly insistent and coldly numb in alternating patterns. It'd become such an intrinsic part of the tapestry of my life that I'd forgotten how to recognize it as a separate thing. When it had worsened – especially in my legs - and I had started to fall, Doc Joe had declared me in need of the cart.

There were other pains, of course: the daily agony of badly-healed broken knuckles, the anguish of an arthritic spine which refused to be quelled with anything the doc prescribed, and for which I'd developed a semi-reliable drinking scheme so I could at least care less about the pain.

I was perhaps inappropriately proud of my perfectly-scheduled, if not controlled, alcoholism.

But it's a tedious subject, pain is. It's very hard to care about the pain of another, I find. Besides pitying them, what else can one do except listen to them complain? It was why I'd stopped going over to the club to play darts. Once I became dependent on the cart, it served as an ever-present reminder that I was sick, and suddenly everyone wanted to talk about their own aches and pains. And those of their family and friends. And neighbors and some old lady on the news. Ad nauseum. And unfailingly it all boiled down to a common and reliable subject: the unpleasantness of aging.

And while I hated the pitying looks of strangers and friends alike, having to paste one on for others was worse.

But then the apocalypse happened. Still was happening when I finally kicked off, but by then millions - billions! - had died and the lingering sick promised to do the same. Still, rumours of a virus-resistant group abounded. I'd even wondered if I was one of the "lucky" few before the symptoms started showing up - even held on to the possibility for the first week or so. After all, symptoms varied from person to person. The virus clung to each of us uniquely, see, except for one thing: as far as I could tell, every person who would die from what experts called "Metastatic Ankylosing Retrograde Spondylosis 2021, or MARS-21" developed an extreme version of something like lockjaw. That particular development always, always meant walking around with a jaw frozen open, maw stretched wide for the flies and weather and other viruses. And it stayed that way until you either got well (unusual at that stage) or died.

It started in the spine; the vertebrae built up and fused to varying degrees, and then it would move on to other joints and cause a plethora of issues, right from further fusing bones to dissolving bone, to rubberizing it. Some had weeping sores, others had bony protrusions like spikes or horns. Most had facial deformities to add to the unpleasant visage their lockjaw created.

The truth was, though we learned more about it as it ate greedily away at the human population, we were ages away from understanding the hows or whys. And of course, that only became further exacerbated as health-care workers and research scientists fell victim themselves.

In any case, I wasn't mortified when my back lost some flexibility. It had gone out many times before, and the transition to the cart was easy to blame.

But then it never improved, and then my left elbow grew something that looked like a jagged horn, and I knew.

The jaw was last for me – a blessing, for certain, though I don't know why I deserved anything of the like. But it was the worst of it; I'd have gladly dissolved into a pile of jelly over the pain of having my jaw stretched and frozen to the edge of its limit. Of being starved but unable to eat, of tasting every smell, of choking on liquids and waking every time I'd managed to get to sleep because my pillow was soaked with saliva and my mouth was as dry and stiff as Play-Doh left out overnight.

I could go on. There were so many more inconveniences. But my own suffering will not be the focus of this story. I want to tell you what happened afterward.

CHAPTER 3 – FIRE

It sounds strange to say it, but I found death rather anticlimactic.

And it was odd; it was only after I'd succumbed that I wondered if an IV of fluids and peritoneal nutrition (PTN was how the experts had figured out how to keep MARS sufferers alive, but still only some recovered; the rest merely had a prolonged death) would have saved me. It was usually the ones with irrevocable damage – noodle-like bones were a sure-fire prediction of impending demise – that died regardless of treatment.

But it took even less time to remember that the agony of recovery would only have served to return me to the miseries of daily life. Which, after all, was why I'd chosen to fade away on my sofa, instead.

But then, something odd happened. Or didn't happen, if you want to get technical.

I stayed.

My body died. I felt it wind down to a grating stop. But I lingered within it. For several moments I allowed myself to be overwhelmed by the emotions that followed – relief, then joy, then anger, then disbelief. I'd say it all happened rather quickly, but time was immediately different, so I don't know for sure.

And then, like a toddler coming out of a fit, I slowly came around to the fact that I was still exactly where I'd started, and I took in my surroundings, dazed.

And that's when I got a little nervous.

Where was the whisking of my spirit to the fabled tunnel? To the gates? The light in the darkness? The beckoning destination for the soul? I was far from a religious man; I wouldn't even have defined myself as spiritual in any sense of the word, but I'd watched documentaries and read stories. You didn't have to believe in God to go somewhere *else* when you died. Near-death experiences were reported by people of all faiths and backgrounds, all ages and levels of intelligence.

You could say it was something I'd counted on as an oft-suicidal alcoholic whiling away the last of his days alone.

But there was none of that.

Rather, I seemed stuck.

I could still *feel* my body, but it was different. It wasn't *me.* It was heavy and strange and cumbersome and oh, God, it was *done.* If I'd have been shopping for a used (corporeal) vehicle, I'd have passed that one by without a thought.

Just as I was coming around to realize just how damaged my earthly body was, though, I came the realization that, though I hadn't moved, I was not tethered to that shell any longer. And in the beginning, that was frightening.

It was my foot that separated, first. The purplish one that Doc Joe had termed "the one that'll make you into an amputee, Tom," ha-ha, shoulder clap and all that bullshit. Hilarious.

And I guess it seemed logical to check that foot out first, because it had been the thing that had been dying the longest. So, I lifted it without thinking, really. I was still considering my predicament as a whole and assuming I was stuck in my defunct body; contemplating, really, the possibility that this would be my own very special brand of Hell. So, when my foot raised above my physical self, I recoiled in shock. Which had two immediate consequences:

First, I made a sound that was more an echo of breath than the yell it would have been, had I been using my vocal cords. I automatically equated it to being eerie. Ghostly, even. The reaction struck me as a little stupid and a little funny, too.

Second, I went ahead and recoiled the rest of myself right on out of my body, but backwards. And after a very confusing moment of disorientation, I realized I had landed myself inside the couch, amongst the layers of springs and foam.

Horrified, I projected myself forward, ending up hovering in the middle of the room, my back to my old self.

And I turned around to see.

The combination of those movements would be the easiest I'd have controlling where I went on the earthly plane after I'd left my body. Ever.

But I digress.

My current state of being, the nuances of which are still a vast mystery to me, paled while I took a look at the shell of who I'd been for the first time.

In short, I looked like shit.

How had I managed to get so fat? And *greasy?* OK; the last few days of my illness could probably have been blamed for much of the horrors of my final state, but at the time, I wasn't feeling particularly logical.

True to its impact in life, the lockjaw was the worst of the horrors. I suddenly knew why dentists had always felt compelled to lecture me on oral care basics. But it was worse than bad teeth; it was a jaw opened too wide for too long, stretching my face into a grotesque mask. My eyes had rolled upward, leaving scant half-moons of colour over bloodshot white, and the lower lids pulled down with the force of my frozen, gape-mouthed, silent scream.

I'd have been offended by it under any circumstance, but the fact that that *thing* had been *me* until very recently made it the worst of circumstances.

I wanted to scream but hadn't an inkling how.

So, I decided *not* to see. And was immediately confronted with the new fact that I had no eyelids to close. No *eyes*, even. *How was I even seeing what I saw?*

And thus began the overwhelm of knowing nothing about the stage of life/death/life I'd transitioned into.

I know now that it was all purposeful; all intended. I needed to be overwhelmed. I needed to face the fear. To feel alone, even here.

And again, I cannot tell you how long I lingered in that panic. But I can say that being in my living room with no hint at change, unable to look away from the increasingly horrifying pile of a thing that had been *me* was torturous. I wonder, often, at the fact that I'm not still there. I know that would have been what I deserved. I don't know why it's not what happened.

But I never, ever take what *did* happen for granted.

And what happened was that, in my throes of agony and the depths of my suffering, there was a voice, and then suddenly I wasn't in the living room anymore.

And, impossible as it seemed, I was told it wasn't my time to die.

CHAPTER 4 – SEED

"That's impossible."

There was laughter.

In that moment, that was all there was. I saw nothing. Felt nothing. There was no light and no gravity, no pain...wait. No *physical* pain. Can you believe that it was in that moment that I learned that there are far worse versions of pain than physical?

It's true. And though my bodily woes had vanished, my relief was short-lived, because I'd brought everything else with me. The weight of my wrongs, my regrets, the awareness of the pain I'd caused others... it was all solidly in place. And worse, without my physical agonies, it was all there was. That and the echoing laughter I was immersed in.

"This can't be it," I mumbled, realizing I was able to speak without the strange, breathy accompaniment I'd had in my living room.

"Can't be *what?*"

Anger surged. "*This!* I'm dead, right? I thought – I thought it'd be *different.*"

"It is. It is different for *everyone.*"

A gravelly growl ripped through my consciousness and I realized it was my own. "Why do I still *feel* this way?"

"You feel the burden of your wrongs, Thomas Wall - loved one, son, friend – because you are not yet finished your work on earth."

If I'd had a mind, it would have been blown. "*What?*"

"You are not finished. You will go back."

"*No!*" Fear and rage overwhelmed me. Death was something I'd coveted for so long. Granted, I'd hoped for more of a release than *this* death seemed to allow, but the prospect of going back was far worse.

"You *must.* You will have more leeway to choose later, Thomas, but for now, I must insist that you agree."

Sadness overtook me. I'd never experienced emotion in such a raw way. It was torturous. "Why?"

"Because we need your help. The dying ones. The last wave of the virus is upon the people of the physical plane. You must help them. It is your work."

"What? You want me to help the dying? *How?*" I wanted to laugh. I think I *was* crying. I couldn't be sure without tears.

"You are one of the privileged few for whom the levels are not yet determined. So, you walk between the lines of the living and the dead until you decide. You can navigate the dying through the planes. And you must, for your own life. Your own destination."

It was too much. I had so many questions. I was so angry – and confused, and disappointed – yet I seemed trapped in my own silence.

"This will be difficult, Thomas."

"What if I say no?"

"That would be the cruellest fate of all. Do you remember feeling *stuck,* Thomas?"

Visions of my life passed before me as if on a movie reel: me dying on my couch, me sitting in the motorized cart for the first time, the doctor announcing the utter uselessness of my left foot, getting the letter from Louise-Anne and stuffing it somewhere into the middle of the dusty pile of unread mail, crying on a cot in prison, laying numb on the cold floor in solitary, getting kidney-punched in the showers, then sodomized by my assailant as the others cheered him on, knocking an angel-faced little boy out with the butt of my gun so he'd be quiet while I robbed his parents, so much more, so much to regret. So much of what I'd worked *not* to acknowledge every day of my life.

Until finally, there was just me, in diapers, watching my foster father – one of many – strike my foster mother with a left hook, breaking her jaw and rendering her unconscious before he whirled and struck the high-chair I practically lived in during waking hours, sending it (and me) flying into the wall.

The *thud* of impact that sent everything into darkness.

Yes. I remembered feeling stuck.

"It will be worse here," that voice – neither male, nor female, but gentle in that moment – blew over me like a cool breeze. Impossibly smooth, like when I'd first left my living room.

I imagined returning to that place – to that body and all of its aches and pains. "How?"

"You are only given one vehicle for each life, Thomas.

Now I laughed. "But – the virus! It's ruined me!"

"It hasn't ruined *you*, Thomas." There was a hint of a pause, during which I prepared myself for some lesson on the layers of oneself. But the voice carried on without elaborating. There was the tiniest of sighs when it started again, though. "Ah, but worry not; your body will be restored. Somewhat."

Call me cynical, but neither choice appealed.

"Are you ready, Thomas?"

"No! I – what am I supposed to do? Just go around finding dying neighbors? Hold out a hand and say, 'Hey, you've seen me around – I'm that angry alcoholic from down the street, remember? Yeah. Well, congratulations! I'm here to *help you die!*'"

There was a silence.

I floundered in it. "Seriously!" I called.

"You do not see your privilege, Thomas? Not even now?"

The words struck a chord in me, but it wasn't understanding. It was fear.

I'd heard those words from nearly every authority figure in my life. I'd hated them, because I couldn't grasp what the fuck they were trying to say... any of them.

"Let me instill one point of knowledge in you before you return, Thomas Wall. Your insistence that you are the victim is very dangerous and has made a victim of many. You have many victims, Thomas, and you have *always* had a choice."

"Did you even *see* that last little bit of my little life story, there? Did I have a choice then?"

"You had a choice, Thomas, of whether you'd use that uncontrollable event as the reasoning behind every act of anger or hatred you have done."

I made a disapproving sound. "Guess I didn't realize that *as an infant!*"

"Its validity as an *excuse* faded as you grew; as you realized your free will."

The anger was raging and hot without a gut to roil within or a jaw to clench against it. "Seems like a pretty valid excuse to me."

"You must realize it is not. Nothing is."

"Why not?" I laughed cynically.

Silence again. I knew I was being stupid, but when had that ever stopped me?

"Use this gift well, Thomas."

I was not ready to go; not even close. I'm sure I could have wallowed there forever. It was disappointing, but not unfamiliar. But time was up, I guess, because I was whisked back. And, for those of you who haven't experienced it, I'll say the process of re-entering one's (very dead) body is far more difficult than leaving it.

But, as I endured the torturous reconnection of tendon to energy, vessel to wisp, the voice came once more.

"Do not squander the second chance that many would give anything to have," it said.

And some time later, sitting up for the first time, again, in a body that *had* been *somewhat* restored (including the unlocking of the jaw, which, to be honest, would have satisfied on its own), I answered it.

"This is fucked up," is what I said.

CHAPTER 5 – SOIL

I learned quickly that going back didn't mean just picking up where I'd left off. Nothing – not just my body - was the same after that.

I proved it by standing and walking to the kitchen without much trouble, other than being stiff at the joints and having a mouth that was as dry as the desert. But as I said, the immense relief of having my jaw move at the hinge and then to close was overpowering; it took me weeks to fully realize the extent of the changes to my physical self. But I realized it all too late; I knew my body was not *me.* If I'd known that in life – ah, but I won't dwell in the what-ifs. They'd fill a book of their own.

But if you'd asked me then to give you any details about what had happened in that time between life and death and life again, I wouldn't have been able to put it into words.

That's taken time, too.

I remember running the tap while I got a clean glass from the cupboard, then the anticipation of slaking my thirst for the first time in days. Then the following confusion as the liquid sat like a bubble in my mouth, refusing to sink in, then spraying all over the window above the sink at my first attempt to swallow it.

Clearly, this is going to take time.

I eyed the glass with determination, working my mouth and tongue to get the kinks out. Tried swallowing again and gagged, whatever mechanisms I'd tried to spark into action gluing together in my throat. I coughed reflexively, then opened my mouth wide in an effort to pull apart whatever had knotted inside of me, then pulled in a gasping breath.

It occurred to me then that I hadn't breathed since returning to my body, and I stayed pitched over the sink for some time, just pulling and pushing air, mindfully. It was an exercise I'd scoffed at hippies and yogis for touting. Why think about *breathing?* Wasn't that one of the things we could trust our bodies to take care of? So, those moments over my sink were something of a revolutionary ilk for a grizzled, jaded old man. Yes, it had been forced, but in my dazed state, I hadn't the wherewithal to fight it. The deliciousness of breath filling my lungs. The feeling of life filtering back into my veins. After a while - once my hammering heart had slowed to a canter - I turned the tap on again. But that time, I leaned into the water, letting it run over my mouth. Closing my eyes to the sensation. Letting it do its work before I attempted to pull it in again.

I only swallowed after opening my mouth wide and letting the water run over my tongue and cheeks until they were less like rubber and more like live things. And then it happened on its own, some of the water hitting the back of my throat and the swallow coming organically. And it hurt still – there was the sensation of parts sticking together and then slowly pulling apart – but after the subsequent few attempts, it was heaven. I gulped and swallowed, the cool liquid soothing a throat that had felt aflame with thirst in the hours before I'd – well, I'd died. But it was too much, and suddenly it was all coming back in reverse.

I retched painfully, scant tears a relief on sandpaper cheeks. But when I was done, I didn't straighten up. I merely held my mouth to the flow of the tap, taking small sips with my eyes closed, willing it to stay down. To oil my joints, to feed my organs and lubricate my awakening muscles.

When I did stand, it was to realize the place had gone dim. I gazed through the spit-sprayed window with interest. I had no clue how long the entire ordeal had taken, but the sunset said less than a day.

I felt as though I'd been through a war.

I became overwhelmed with the desire to take full stock of myself. I remembered the full-length mirror I'd shoved in the closet after Claret – an appropriate name for the raging alcoholic of a companion I'd kept some years earlier – had finally left for the last time.

She'd died shortly after, or I'm sure she'd have come back; I was the only one who'd take her. I recalled hearing of her demise while throwing darts at the club; how her body had been found beneath one of the bridges that joined the provinces of Ontario and Quebec. The fellas knew Claret and I flirted with a relationship on and off, but as far as they'd known at the time, we'd long been "off ". Either way, they'd assumed I'd heard, and I didn't let on that I hadn't. And they discussed, for the good part of an hour, how the cops had labelled it a suicide at first, and then retracted the declaration, having learned from several corroborating witness statements that the woman was seen weaving her way across the bridge, drunk and singing at the top of her lungs.

So, it had been called an accident in the end, and I guessed it made sense. But the abruptness of it elicited a pervasive sort of shock in me for a long time after. We *had* been "off" as far as a relationship was considered, but in the past, that'd meant trying to guess when she'd be back – or when I'd go to her, begging. The fact that that wasn't going to happen – not ever – was a truth that required time to fully accept.

I shoved the thoughts aside as I retrieved the mirror and set it up. At first glance, I was a wasted version of the man I'd last peered at in that mirror. But then, it had been years.

I'd gained weight after the foot went purple and walking had become a chore. But surely, the sickness couldn't have whittled my limbs into apple tree branches so hastily – all knots and angles. Suddenly curious, I pulled the left leg of my flannel pants up and leaned toward the mirror. "Stupid," I muttered, resolving to look down at the leg itself, but what remained of the light allowed for nothing more than a confirmation that it was still there.

I crossed to the window, aware of the ease with which my foot took my weight. Noting the sensations of its sole as it touched the carpet, even through the sock. Oh, yes – it was different.

I opened the blind, then grunted, crossing to the doorway and reaching for the light switch; the increasing darkness did nothing to improve my vision.

And then I confirmed it: my foot had been "restored," too.

The smile that worked its way across my face pulled at tight, dry skin, but it was worth it. How many times had I wished to go back in time, before the foot had failed me? I'd considered it the last nail in the coffin, really. Or used it as an excuse for one, for shortly after, I saw the long list of intentions I'd had dwindle to nothing. Everything, over time, was replaced by pain and restrictions, the drink being arguably the most limiting of all.

It was revealing, though, that as I lost the drive to make things right with events of the past, to exercise more and eat better, to reach out to the family members that remained (though, to be honest, I hadn't any inkling of who remained and who'd already been taken by MARS - or other causes, for that matter), one hope remained: to see my daughter again.

Louise-Anne had remained as everything else fell around me to ruin.

I stood in front of the mirror again. Indeed, my clothes hung loosely on a frame I hadn't really seen since I was a teenager. The face, though, revealed my age. Death and disease had been unkind. I wondered at the vastly *unrestored* state of my face and settled on it being a low priority, all things considered. I leaned closer, touching my mouth with timid fingers. There were telltale wrinkles, papery and raw, where it had been stretched to its limits for so long.

I remembered my foot and stood back, lifting my pantleg again. I frowned at what I saw; despite the restored function and sensation, my lower leg hadn't lost much of its purple pallor.

I hurried to undress, bursting with the need to see my new, old self, and only scowled deeper at the state of my foot. It, too, was still an unpleasant shade of eggplant. I let it rest beside its partner and compared their sizes in the mirror. The swelling, at least, appeared to be entirely gone. Besides the colour, it felt and looked just like the other.

Maybe it's so I don't forget – I thought, but then scoffed at the thought. As chaotic as everything seemed in the moment, I was unwilling to theorize the meaning of the details.

I regarded my naked bottom half critically. My skin fairly hung off my bones.

I need to eat, I thought with some urgency. But I wasn't done. I pulled my shirt over my head in one smooth movement. The grimace I saw on my own face was an understandable reaction; my scant flesh drooped like pale bread dough. Even my nipples sagged. And I could see each rib. I turned to observe my spine in the same way, but groaned when presented with the sight of my ass – what was left of it. It may as well have been concave, hollow as it was. "Sad," I muttered as I turned again, then chuckled quietly. "Sad, but true."

I wrapped my bathrobe around myself, intent on a shower before I got dressed again. In *clean* clothes; I'd become all too aware of how I smelled as well as looked when I stripped down.

It was as though death still clung in the dark places of my body.

I did better than shower; I combed my hair and shaved my craggy face, resolving that my vanity – what little I'd had – had been demolished, but I could still make an effort.

But there was something else, too, and it was undeniable: I had *energy*. It had built as I'd moved about, as though my entire body was hovering over something. Anticipating whatever came next. I hadn't felt that way in years.

I ate some of the paltry selection of food that was still good in the fridge once I'd put clean clothes on my withered body, cinching my belt so much I'd sworn under my breath. And then, at a momentary loss, I sat there in the kitchen and looked around.

With fresh eyes, I saw so much of my surroundings as being sad.

I sat at the table, my eyes going to the window and travelling the empty streets and sidewalks under the pale glow of the streetlights. Realizing that I'd been given life just as many were losing theirs. Feeling an inkling of what that mysterious voice had worked to have me know – that I had a purpose, and it was a privilege.

But, where do I start?

Just the fact that I considered the question was new. So, I thought I'd start small and face one of my own monsters, first.

I crossed to the mantle between the kitchen and living room and picked up the stack of mail.

I wasn't aiming to take care of every bill; nobody had the staff or the funding to collect debts, and the majority of people weren't even working, so it wasn't really a priority for anyone, anymore. But I wanted to make a start. And when I got to the envelope from Louise-Anne, I aimed to hold it a minute before tucking it back into the pile. I knew I couldn't open it yet; maybe I couldn't even look at the name written in the upper left corner of the envelope, but I figured I had to make progress at home before I ventured out to figure out my new job. I needed to prove I could do something about the shit in my own life, first.

CHAPTER 6 – GERM

My physical self gained more than the promised restorations: there were other changes that popped up over time. Some for which I never learned the purpose – in fact, I questioned the wisdom of the one who'd returned me more than once. Cursed it once or twice, too.

But that first night, I recognized one of the more obvious changes: I needed much less sleep than I had in my first go around. When I'd finally sifted through the long-ignored pile of mail and sorted it, throwing away a considerable pile of junk in the end, the wall clock said it was three-thirty in the AM. *Way* past my bed time – and I was showing no signs of slowing. But I chalked it up to the events of the day before at first; it was an easy assumption. When, at five, I was still more bright-eyed and bushy-tailed than I could remember *ever* being, I considered other possibilities.

And if sleep was going to elude me, I was going to have a problem with boredom.

I'd medicated with drink in the past, as I've said, but when my gaze went habitually to the whiskey cupboard, an undeniable sense of rejection rolled over me. *Where'd that come from?* I thought with some trepidation. It hadn't felt like a reaction as much as an outward influence.

Alcohol had been an intrinsic part of my day-to-day routine for a very long time. Since the worsening of the diabetes and subsequent arrival of the cart, my need had only intensified.

I couldn't remember how I'd filled the time – or eased the pain, the apathy, the fact that my life's purpose (which was still elusive) was circling the drain and showed no signs of recovery – before my whiskey cupboard was carefully stocked.

With anxiety gnawing at me, I decided on an early-morning walk. It was forbidden to be out unless your task was essential, still – doctor's appointments, emergency room visits, and the occasional trip to the grocery store or pharmacy were all acceptable essential outings, but precious little else was – folks upheld the rule out of courtesy or requirement, now. Either you were sick, or you were in shock over losing so many that had been. In any case, my situation was different, and I was only starting to question my aptitude to navigate it.

Nobody enforced it anymore, anyway.

A surge of pleasure shot through me as I sidestepped the hated motorized cart and stepped out the door. *When was the last time I'd taken a walk?* I shook my head. My shoes crunched pleasantly on the gravelly pavement. *When was the last time I'd gone* outside? I reached the road and turned left automatically; it was the direction of everything, really. The gas station, the grocery store. The club where I'd played darts with the boys. I wondered how many of them were left.

I stopped in my tracks. I hadn't a clue.

I looked behind myself, in the direction I rarely went. Just houses there. Neighbors. And the daycare at the end of the street, where the secondary highway ran across the slowly ascending forest. Living so close to Gatineau Park had its advantages: well-maintained jogging, bike and ski trails, plenty of beaches, fishing spots, little shops and restaurants to stop at on your travels through the thick trees, and the famous lookoffs at the high vantage points, most heavily-visited in the fall when the leaves changed color. I wondered how many of those advantages were still accessible.

How many neighbors in that direction were left.

I cast my gaze along Wilfrid-Lavigne, which ran from my neighborhood at the top of the hill down to Principale, the town of Aylmer's main drag. There wasn't a soul besides me; no car lights, no bicycles pedaling along the bike path along Des Allumettiers, which cut across Wilfrid-Lavigne just beyond the gas station.

What if there isn't anyone? I tilted my head back, picking out the few stars I could see in the brightening sky. *What if it's just me?*

My stomach rolled unpleasantly.

Then, coming back to myself, I peered hopefully toward the gas station and was rewarded by the sight of the lit sign. *Thank God.* I sighed at the thought and started toward it, wondering anew at the sentiment.

I recognized the pimply teenager behind the counter, but I can't say I'd ever been so happy to see him.

"Holy shit," he smiled, his oily forehead shining under the fluorescents. "I thought you were dead."

I'd be lying if I told you that some of that old rage didn't curl my toes in my shoes. "Who says I'm not?" I smiled back.

The kid looked stunned for a long moment, then pointed at me as he smiled. "Good one."

"Any papers still printing?"

He looked dazed by the question. Maybe dazed was his resting expression; I didn't know. It was another thing that changed; I found myself looking at people more. Took me a while to grasp it, because I don't think I'd ever realized how hard I'd worked to avoid it. Maybe it was one of those things you gradually do out of habit, forgetting there's an alternative. Forgetting you're even doing it at all.

"Uh – oh, yeah!" the kid's eyes brightened. "They aren't the same – mostly just updates on MARS, you know?"

They'd been that way for nearly a year. "I haven't been out of sight *that* long," I said with a scowl. And the kid's eyes darkened. I took note of it with interest.

Funny how when you don't look at people, you don't know how you affect them, isn't it?

"Right," he gave himself a little shake, as if to slough off my dark look. "Well, they're right there," he gestured to the stand by the frozen treats.

I picked up a *Le Droit* – I'd passively learned enough French living on the Quebec side of the bridge to get the gist of its contents. I stopped short when I spotted the *Citizen* above it, then frowned at pimple-face. "Since when has the *Ottawa Citizen* been available for sale here?"

Had French Canadian politics changed so much in the wake of MARS-21?

"Oh, we've had that a while, now," he nodded. "Mr. Ackerson felt there was a demand for more of a 'national, or even global perspective,'" the kid air-quoted the last bit, his eyes rolling. "It's caused quite the scandal around here, let me tell you." He raised his eyebrows comically as he took the two papers I held out.

"I imagine."

He laughed. "Mr. Ackerson says he'll stop selling them when someone with authority tells him to, but not for -" he leaned toward me, which simultaneously struck me as comical (given that we seemed to be the only live humans in earshot... in town, even) and stupid (given that MARS-21 was proven to be transmissible by air and we'd all been "social distancing" our asses off for nearly two years.) "Joe Blow Frenchy!" he finished, giggling as he slapped a thigh.

I frowned. "You're French, right kid?" Under a certain age, residents in Aylmer unfailingly spoke English. It was part of the reason Ontarians defected here, coming to our side to raise their kids or retire with ease. But when considering who was native Quebecois, the accent was a dependable tell.

He laughed. "My parents were the separatists; me and my friends don't care much about all that shit."

"Don't say that too loud in here," I glanced around as he had.

He smirked; not even a shadow of a smile, and it had been my sole attempt at humour. "Doesn't matter when there's no one around," he muttered as he scanned the papers. "That's seven fifty, my man."

I recoiled. *"What?"*

Some of the glimmer returned to his eyes. "Yep. Mr. Ackerson is all about supply and demand. These babies sell out quick, drama or no," he jabbed a finger at the *Citizen.*

I scanned my card, then thought to look around.

"Sorry; did you want something else?" the kid gestured at the store behind me.

Something softened in me, then, and that was another change. I saw the kid's sincerity. He was that anxiety-inducing brand of jokester teenager, but he wasn't unkind. "Not many coming in these days, huh?"

He frowned slightly. "You gotta know that too, man."

"I'm sort of in the habit of keeping my head down," I picked up the papers and held them in front of my chest, feeling suddenly vulnerable.

He chuckled. "I know that. Anyway – yeah. It's too quiet, nowadays. Where've you been? Were you sick?"

"Yeah," I replied quickly, unwilling to ponder a response

that would convey the whole truth.

"With MARS, or -"

I held back a snide remark but said nothing.

The kid's confidence visibly wavered. "I mean, I've seen you in your wheelchair -"

"Cart," I corrected out of habit.

He nodded. "Right."

"You this observant of everyone?"

He wiped his palms on dirty jeans. "Sorry, man. I just – I sorta miss people."

I recalled the past-tense with which he'd referred to his folks. I'd assumed he'd moved out, but considered in that moment that they'd died. I found myself speechless, both as a result of my revelations and at the fact that I'd taken the time to make them, at all.

"Boss says I get too close to people. I don't even realize it though, you know?" He gazed absently out the windowed wall at the front of the store, then shrugged, meeting my eyes again. "I figure living in fear is worse than not living." He fixed a peaceful expression on his face.

I nodded. "You might just be right, there, kid."

"My name's Jeremy," he smiled.

"Tom," I replied, shocked again. I held the papers up. "Thanks for these."

He nodded and I scooted out of there, reeling. I'd spent the entirety of my life avoiding small talk. Hell, I'd worked around the assumption that people were fundamentally assholes for as long as I could remember... and a skinny, acne-ridden teenager with a hint of sadness behind his eyes was the one to make me question that?

I walked back toward my house quickly as the light took over, retrieving the day from the dark. Shining just like it always had, even though everything it touched was so different. So diminished.

It's not, though, I realized. I squinted, tracing the outlines of the trees above the houses and regarded the lush, bright-green grass that grew in the ditches. Without enough city workers, nature had gone untamed in favour of more urgent priorities. And it was teeming with life, the occasional apple tree sporting scores of shining fruit, just emerging from the blossoms, and previously-trimmed cedar hedges bursting forth unevenly with newfound freedom. I inhaled deeply through my nostrils. The air was fragrant, untainted by the usual levels of car exhaust.

Nature hadn't stopped when we had; quite the opposite.

I surprised myself again once I reached my side porch. Claret had brought some folding lawn chairs over at some point; I think we used them once or twice before they'd been folded last, and then she'd gone and they'd sat, reminding me of her absence each time I put off throwing them in the bin. And then she'd died and it felt wrong to think of throwing them away, so much like her life had been. And in that case, I'd failed to save her.

Saving the chairs may have been a paltry effort – meaningless, even – but I'd seemed unable to do anything else.

That early morning, though, I did. I reached for one of them and unfolded it. It creaked on rusty hinges, but held together when I sat. And I sat there for a while, doing nothing but feeling strange, like the world was ending and beginning at the same time, and somehow, I'd get to watch it happen.

And then I opened the paper and started working toward the back. After all, learning who was gone might be a good step toward learning who I could still help.

CHAPTER 7 – RAIN

I didn't manage to get to the obits before a headline caught my eye: MARS SUFFERERS CHOOSING TO DIE AT HOME screamed up at me from the *Citizen* as I flipped through the Gatineau paper. I wondered absently how I hadn't registered the front-page headline as soon as I'd seen the paper. The fact that the English paper was even there had probably precluded it. I dropped the local one and unfolded the one from across the bridge, my eyes instantly landing on the accompanying photo.

"Jed," I whispered as my heart sped up. Jed wasn't a friend; not like my darts buddies were, but he was a neighbor. I recognized him from the club, though he kept to himself, sitting at the bar and always bent over some greasy meal. And drinking a wide variety of things, but never, I noticed, the type that the boys and I nursed. We laughingly chalked up his bitter expression to the fact that he didn't drink, but I remembered the man before his bitterness seemed etched into his features. Back then, a lady walked the neighborhood with him, or pruned the hedges or weeded gardens, always lifting a hand with a smile to passers-by, squinting in the sun beneath a wide-brimmed hat.

Old Jed had never come to the club in those days. It was only when she was gone that I started seeing him there, eating probably the only hot meal of the day in his own little world.

And now he frowned up at me from a black and white feature in the English paper.

I read the story, despite the instant headache my

dyslexia caused. My guidance counselor would have enjoyed a self-satisfied grin at the frequent troubles reading caused me. "You should have accepted the help you were offered," she would've said.

But I hadn't, and I'd accepted that it was a choice made long ago and impossible to change.

The story wasn't just about Jed; it featured several MARS sufferers who frequented the large clinic on the Ottawa side for treatment, but who'd declined admissions to hospital, claiming they preferred to die at home than waste away under the watchful eyes of overworked strangers.

But it was Jed's quote that touched me: "My wife died in a hospital, despite her fear of that very thing. I've always regretted taking her there; it was selfish. I won't force her spirit to go there again; not for me. I will join her from home, if it comes to that."

I met the pixelated eyes of a man I'd only shared a courteous nod with when our paths crossed; touched the picture with some sense of understanding. And then my eyes widened with a realization: this was it. Here was my first assignment!

I peered into the street as the first car of the morning sped by. *Is it Jed? Is that who I'm supposed to see?* I asked voicelessly.

But there was no reply; no sign either way.

Irritated at being forced into an assignment with little direction, I stood, picking up the paper I'd dropped earlier. Once inside, having put the papers on the table for later, I looked toward the ceiling. "You're gonna have to give me something, here," I stated, my voice gruff. But I didn't wait for an answer; I headed to the couch and picked up the remote, clicking the TV on out of habit.

But there was nothing on. Literally. Despite the fact that television and internet services were guaranteed during the pandemic, static filled the screen and my ears, interrupted only by short pauses as I flipped aimlessly through the channels. I gritted my teeth as I punched the on/off button again, then threw the useless remote across the couch. It bounced and veered, landing on the carpet in front of the TV stand.

"Of course," I muttered. The old pessimism was alive and kicking.

But then I quieted. I leaned back into the cushions, my eyes going to the black screen. *I'm given my life back and I'm pissed the TV isn't working.* It was a sobering thought. But then I was squinting as I leaned forward again; there was something traced in the dust of the screen.

I leaned until I was falling, landing on my hands and knees and immediately crawling toward the TV.

Let it happen was what it said.

I sat back on my heels. Frowning. "Let *what* happen?" Was this the answer to my question about Jed? I looked toward the ceiling again. "Seriously?"

Silence answered.

Frustration fuelled me into standing and crossing to the kitchen. "Doesn't help much if it makes no fucking *sense!*" I said, my voice gaining volume until I was shouting.

I opened the whiskey cupboard so hard it bounced back. I recoiled as it seemed to gained speed on its own and slammed shut. My eyes widened. It hadn't bounced *that* hard. I hesitated, my hand in midair, then tried the door again, but that time it resisted. It was like the hinges had rusted over as I worked to pry it open, the fingertips of both fingers stinging in their effort.

And then suddenly, they were being pinched, the door squeezing shut against my efforts again. "What the hell?" I shouted, pulling my hands back and shaking them out. I turned on the spot, seeing red. "I *will* have a drink!" I bellowed, whirling back on the cupboard with a new fervour, but letting out a yell when I failed to prise it, even with a foot against the counter for leverage.

"Shit!"

I slammed a fist down on the counter. Bit back a resulting howl when my knuckle cracked, then crunched as though the joint was compressing broken glass. I cradled the hand, furious and in pain, and stalked off to the bathroom. But the mirrored cabinet above the sink held little in the way of a solution. I rifled through its contents nonetheless, grunting at the uselessness of band-aids and antibiotic creams. I settled on an elastic bandage and wrapped my hand hastily, still seeing red. Once I'd fastened it, I held it out in front of me. It was sloppy work. I wondered if I'd broken the knuckle. Surely, the crunch had meant I had. I wondered briefly if a doctor would do anything for it, aside from wrapping it as I had. "Splint it, maybe," I muttered, reaching to shut the mirror and then freezing once it snapped into place.

Another message had been traced onto the mirror, this time appearing as a barely visible fingermark that said, *Take care.*

I frowned until my vision doubled and I was scowling into my own eyes instead of the barely-there words. "Take care." Like the end of a note or part of a goodbye. But right after I'd damaged myself in a rage.

I watched as my expression cleared, a thread of shame whispering through me. Tried to find the message again, but it was gone.

I looked down at my hand, no longer angry, but still

frustrated and confused. "What do I do?" I whispered.

There were no messages to answer me that time, but a wave of exhaustion rolled over me. Finally.

I went to the bedroom and lay down, still cradling the bandaged hand. Still frowning, slightly.

I had to do *something*. I thought of Jed again and decided I'd knock on his door later in the afternoon. What was the worst that could happen?

After all, I'd been instructed to "let it happen," right? Go with the flow?

And there was one thing the events of the morning had told me for certain: I'd go mad if I didn't try.

CHAPTER 8 –
LOU-ANNE

At the height of the epidemic that had taken the lives of more than half the humans on the planet, the Good Hope Senior's Home had been devastated. Naturally fitting into the "high-risk" category, a mind-blowing ninety-nine of the hundred and six residents had contracted MARS-21. But – again because of the blanket "critical" status due to the high-risk factor - compared to the general population, the death rate was crushing. Seventy-six of the ninety-nine infected passed away.

Seventy-six.

Leaving twenty-three residents. Until eighty-six-year-old Frank Kirby choked on a mouthful of tuna-salad sandwich during a laughing fit at lunch, leaving twenty-two.

Kirby had always been one for pranks, and I personally like to think he's having the greatest laugh of his (after)life over the irony of his death. He'd been the first to contract the virus, you see, and it nearly took him more than once. He even got to the lockjaw stage...but the stubborn old coot refused to give in.

Until the tuna sandwich, of course.

It would be a vast understatement to say that work during that time was challenging. Losing so many – it was a nightmare! But then *we* started getting it, and the staff either left to isolate or be treated in hospital. We had worked hard to be able to boast a comfortable three-to-one resident to care staff ratio, with two full-time registered nurses on staff, and with the consequential drop in numbers on *both* sides, we maintained it, which, in the end, seemed even sadder.

Staff didn't die at the rate the residents did, but suddenly even those who weren't sick needed to care for loved ones that were. We lost our kitchen staff entirely, which relegated the owner's son, who had strictly been an office worker prior, to cook. It was one of the silver linings in my mind, though. Shy Carroll Krull no longer had the option to hide away from us all, and we delighted in learning his quirks and unique charms, which were so different than those of his father, the long-time owner/operator of the facility.

We lost care staff the quickest, which was far from surprising, but then there was Jan, the part-time yoga instructor, who left when two of her five children contracted the illness, and subsequently contracted it herself. And succumbed, to the immense grief of her husband and children, all of whom survived.

Dr. Jack, who was head of palliative care at the General, did rounds once a week, and still managed, despite having suffered with and surviving MARS-21 himself. He became a beacon for us; a sign of hope that we watched the front door for.

Beth, our senior nurse, died on duty. When the home was at the height of its suffering and she contracted the virus, she quarantined herself with the sick residents, moving the bulk of the seniors to the largest, westernmost wing for round-the-clock care. It was she who treated the sick, she who did the repetitive testing until she could release the precious few that lived.

She who sat with the dying as they succumbed, even though her own jaw stretched down behind her mask and froze in place, dragging her eyes into a frown.

She had help, of course. Medical staff from the hospital came daily to do assessments and prescribe treatments – and remaining staff on what became known as the "living wards" took care of supplies, meals, and family communications as Beth slogged through the hardest of it.

Mike, the night janitor, was the one who found her when she died, wrapped around Regina, our Sicilian ninety-four-year-old, who was the last on West Ward, and miraculously survived, as though Beth had poured the last of her living self into her final patient.

We still hadn't opened the wing. None of us wanted to face it; not even Marvin Krull, the owner. So much for being unfailingly stoic, as Carroll liked to call him.

In any case, we didn't need the beds.

There were six care staff left, myself included. And for a time, I seriously considered leaving. I had a family, too; a twelve-year-old daughter and a fifteen-year-old son, and my continuing exposure at work put them at risk, too. But then, their father was a paramedic, and they spent half their time with him...

In the end, the fact that I was the only RN left on staff decided it for me: I simply couldn't leave.

So, we were busy as always. But though the ratio was the same, our days were shaped differently. When the worst seemed to have passed, we spent our days doing reach-out in addition to regular care. Tracking down family for the remaining residents was priority number one, and let's just say that the pall of fear that had taken up residence over the wards failed to lessen as the threat of MARS-21 did. For during that time, the remaining folk were still learning of death within their own families.

I didn't spend a lot of time questioning the fact that I never got sick, but the moments when the thoughts snuck in were profound. Jessie and Mads were healthy throughout, too, as was my ex-husband Beck, which was something, exposed as the paramedics were to the worst of it. And he'd admitted to failing where protective protocol was concerned; in life-or-death emergencies, he'd acted before thinking. It had always been his way, and while it had, in a way, been the thing to break us apart, it had meant a very successful career as a paramedic for him.

But after things had settled in a manner of speaking, and they started talking about resistant folks and economic recovery, I questioned things a lot.

It was still like a nightmare, only more like waking up from one, only to realize I was still asleep and needed to wake up again. A nightmare within a nightmare – and there was nothing to indicate relief anytime soon.

I knew I was depressed; everyone was, after all. But I'd always been the type of girl who could find the good in things. Somehow, though, even the fact that my entire family had remained intact seemed strange rather than a blessing. Had me frightened, always, that our payment for the good fortune we'd had was still outstanding.

And there was another thing: I said my *entire* family had made it through, and for all intents and purposes, that was true. But there was one I still wondered about; one in the back of my mind who I both loathed and loved, despite everything.

My father.

He'd been a constant existence, at least in my mind, my entire life. When I'd fought with my mother, I clung to the idea that I could always find him. Whenever I failed, when I lost in love, and when life seemed cruel, there was still the possibility of him.

To me, the imagining of him being out there somewhere was the equivalent of hope. And when he actually reached out, it was like I'd been proven right! And like I had the choice, then. I had the power to decide.

And what had I done?

It hurt to think of it. And then MARS swept through the population, and a piece of me started mourning, because surely, it had taken him, for he'd never even replied to my note. And my note had demanded attention.

So, I'd lost hope even before hope proved its value, over and over. Every minute we all stayed well, even as the kids continued school - online through much of it - and going back and forth between Beck and I, I knew I should be grateful and nothing else. But I *had* lost something.

For it wasn't until I believed him dead that I finally accepted him as being lost to me. I'd willfully done that one thing that kept the door open: I hoped.

And the loss of hope is devastating, isn't it?

I think it's the worst of any blows. And it ate away at me, even when MARS did not, so I may as well have been sick, all that time. All that time when I wasn't, and everyone else was.

Until they weren't.

And suddenly, I was.

CHAPTER 9 – SPROUT

Even the heavy wood of Jed Baker's door seemed irritated, afflicted with knots that gave the impression of a scowl. I stood before it, hands trembling slightly at my sides, eyeing it with Jed's own frown in my mind, and froze.

What the hell am I doing?

That would become a common question during the last weeks of life in my body.

With no answers forthcoming, I raised a closed fist and knocked. There was an immediate answer; it was muffled, but I was pretty certain it was, "Go away!"

My first urge was to flip the bird at the door, but I turned to go, instead.

I stopped at the bottom of the porch stairs, sighing. I stuffed my hands in my pockets and peered up into the clouds, which were dark and heavy. The chill in the air pricked gooseflesh on my arms.

I'd *always* been a slave to impulse. It explained my police record, my jail time, and the fact that I had no relationships with family. Didn't even know them, truth be told.

But I'd died and I was back, and while I can't claim logic had always ruled me, I recognized that things had to change.

I thought of the realization, after leaving my body, that nothing was happening, and grimaced. Was that all that awaited? I found myself spreading my hands out and staring at them, front and back. *Maybe this is better than that.* I flexed my bandaged knuckle and winced at the answering pain. Wondered briefly if the deal on my "restoration" counted for my ability to heal, or had my benevolent host spent the entirety of the balance just to wake my physical self up again. I pried the edge of the bandage away and peered between it and my skin, which was a sickly shade of purplish brown.

A solid knock to the right startled me back to the present and I jumped, already yelling at the rude interruption. But the sound froze pretty quick in my throat when I caught sight of the mouth of a rifle aimed at me from the other side of a window.

Jed's stare was more familiar, though, and I made an effort to look past the gun and make contact with the man, raising my hands slowly. "Jed? It's alright, Jed; I'm just here to talk to ya!"

His frown deepened. I noted the fact that his mouth was shut and wondered at the status of his illness. I'd been expecting the gape-mouthed stare of a man on his deathbed after reading the newspaper article.

Jed seemed to search my eyes for more reasoning than I'd provided, but I kept my mouth shut, too. I'd learned the hard way that saying too little was less risky than saying too much.

Finally, he lowered the gun. The unobstructed view revealed more of the lesser man he'd become; his skin hung from his bones as mine had in the reflection I'd studied just a day earlier. His short-sleeved button-up shirt looked as though he'd neglected to change clothes in too long a span of time, and though his jaw had appeared shut, I could see then that he'd fashioned some sort of bandage vertically around his head, so his cheeks wrinkled further and his lips pooched just a bit. And he'd tied the material at the top of his head, achieving a comic resemblance to a dried-up old bunny rabbit. A really pissed off one.

I fought the smile that threatened, shouting, "What the hell're you doing?" instead.

He said something back; I watched, fascinated as his lips moved around clenched teeth. I put my hand to my ear, leaning dramatically toward the window.

He rolled his eyes and loped off in the direction of the door.

I was still debating the option of climbing the stairs again when the door opened slightly and Jed appeared in the crack. He held the gun in front of him, the barrel pointed at the ground. A clear *I'll use it if I have to,* if I'd ever seen one.

I cleared my throat. "H-hey, Jed," was all I could manage.

"Whaddyouwant?" he frowned, gesturing with the gun. I watched where he was aiming it carefully, my hands finding their way into the air again.

"I just – I read that article about you in the paper and thought I'd come check in on you."

"Aryashtoopid?"

I laughed. I couldn't help it.

"Gottadeathwsh?"

"Why in God's name have you tied your jaw shut, Jed?"

He pressed his lips together, seemingly at a loss.

I took a step forward, my eyes on the gun. "Surely, you know that contraption isn't going to prevent the lockjaw."

He stared hard at me, then in one swift motion, tore the bandage from his head. "Happy?" His eyes bored into me.

I moved from foot to foot.

"You look like shit; you sick, too?" His articulation had improved, but his attitude seemed to have worsened.

Temporarily flummoxed, I tried to form an answer. Unable to find the words, I shook my head, instead.

"Well you'd best stay where you are, then, because *I* am."

I nodded. "That's why I'm here, Jed." *That* felt right. Not to Jed, though. He raised the gun and my hands shot higher. "Whoa! I'm not here to hurt you, old man!"

"What happened to your cart?"

"Ah. Good; you recognize me. I wasn't sure -"

"Seen you often enough, but we ain't friends. T'way I see it, only reason a man with your past would come over here knowing I was sick would be to rifle through the shit I left behind."

Questions formed in my mind and demanded asking, but I shoved them down, shaking my head again. "I'm not here to rob you, Jed."

He adjusted his grip on the gun, pointing it right at my face. "Then what're you here for?"

I took two steps back. My conscience warred with my instincts. "I'm here to *help,* you old fool!"

Jed stepped onto the deck, his eyes riveted to mine. I, however, became distracted by the fact that the old guy was pantsless.

"Get off my property."

I pointed at his legs, poised to inform him of his state, but he reacted faster than I could speak, jerking the barrel to the right and pulling the trigger. A deafening shot rang through the air as the bullet whizzed inches past my ear. I ducked, my arms protectively around my head and my knees landing hard on the pavement before I knew what was happening.

"You deaf?"

I peeked between my arms. "What the *hell?*"

"Unless you got a cure fer this shit, I don' need your help, asshole!" the man bellowed, then disappeared into his house again, locking the door audibly behind himself.

I was stunned.

I think I stared after him for a full minute or two, my jaw agape and my heart racing. When I got up again, though, I was fuelled by rage rather than shock. I'd come to help the man, and he'd nearly shot me! I clenched my fists, my eyes on the door, still, and my feet itching to climb the stairs. I wanted to wrench the rifle out of his hands and break it over my thigh, just to frighten him. I wanted to call him on the attention-seeking article; accuse him of being a hypocrite, call him a few more choice names for chasing well-meaning visitors such as myself away.

I wanted to tell him again that no bandage would prevent his jaw from yawning open and locking in place, regardless of how tight he tied the knots.

But I didn't move.

I looked to the right and at the window he'd first appeared at, and he was there again, right up against it, that time. No gun. Just a man in filthy underwear staring daggers at me. Dialling his phone.

"What the...?" I muttered.

He begun talking into it, a look of self-satisfaction on his face.

"You know what, Jed?" I called.

He raised his eyebrows.

"*Fuck you!*"

I shook with anger as I headed back toward the road. I looked up at the sky. "What the hell was *that?*" I shouted.

"Is this just entertainment for you?" A siren wailed in the distance. I stopped in my tracks. "No, way." The cops didn't just drive out for nothing in the aftermath of the MARS-21 pandemic – could they truly be responding to Jed's call? I laughed at the ridiculousness of the thought.

But maybe they were ramping back up. Maybe things were coming back together.

As the siren grew closer, I knew I was right, and rather than continue toward my house, I waited, instead, seething silently at the circumstances. Cursing inwardly at the fact that my efforts, having been far out of my comfort zone *without* the addition of some existential intentions added in, had landed me exactly where I'd been so many times in my pathetic life: accepting the fact that I was about to be arrested.

CHAPTER 10 – LOAM

"Stick to the taped path, Wall," a gruff voice instructed from behind me.

I glanced backward. "I've already had MARS," I retorted, but he pushed me, that time. Officer Cromwell and I were not strangers – though I hadn't kept him very busy of late; a drunk and disorderly several years earlier had been my assumed swan song.

"The tape's not just for *your* benefit, shithead."

I gritted my teeth, focused on the empty chairs at his desk, and said nothing.

"We all thought you were dead," he laughed wryly as we sat, gesturing around the near-empty floor. "What's wrong?" he nodded toward my hands, and I discovered I was massaging my wrists where they would've been cuffed and stopped, tucking my fingers under my legs, then yelped at the resulting pain in my crushed knuckle.

Cromwell was laughing freely, then. "Old habits die hard," he wheezed, then nodded again. "What happened to your hand?"

I let it rest on my lap. "Got mad at a counter," I muttered.

He frowned, but moved on. "You gave old Jed, there, quite the scare, Wall. I thought you were done gracing us with your hijinks."

I scoffed. "Hijinx?"

He motioned me onward. "Answer the question."

"What was it, again?"

He leaned forward, and I saw something like fatigue in his eyes. Something like apathy, too. "Come on, Tom. I'm sure both of us have better things to do."

I sat back, considering. "I shouldn't be here, Cromwell. I saw Jed in the paper and went to check on 'im, is all."

He straightened, tapping the table as he shook his head. "He seems to think you went over there to loot the place."

I gestured with both hands, frustrated. "I gave him no reason to think that."

"You try the door handle?"

"No! I knocked on the door! Then when he didn't answer – well, now, that's not true; I think he shouted at me to go away –"

"You should have."

"I *did!*"

He frowned again.

"I started to, anyway, until he pointed a shotgun at me from the window!"

"Why would he do that?"

"I don't know! Same reason you've got me in here, I guess!"

"Your reputation precedes you, Tom. Always will."

I shook my head, scanning the room again. Even the window to the Captain's office revealed an empty chair behind the desk. "Maybe I'm trying to change that," I muttered, blood rushing to my face as though admitting the way I'd behaved pretty much my whole life was...well, it wasn't as – well received... OK, well-thought-out, either - as it could have been.

But the look of astonishment on Cromwell's face surprised me. I was *not* surprised when, after a few seconds, he burst out laughing.

I rubbed at my chin, working to harness the anger that was tracing the line of control and veering toward ballistic.

"I haven't had an occasion to laugh as you've given me today in far too long, Wall. Thanks for that, anyway."

"This is stupid."

"Ah," Cromwell wiped at his face with a bear-sized palm, then picked up his pen, but paused before pulling the appropriate form from his cabinet. The routine was familiar up until he hesitated. He met my eyes again. "You walk around the place?"

"Huh?"

"Jed's. At any time, did you walk around the house? Look in any windows, that type of thing?"

I rolled my eyes. "No."

He pressed his lips together. "What'd you say to him?"

"I said I'd seen the article and I was just there to talk."

"That it? Nothing about wanting to go inside?"

I shook my head vehemently. "No!"

He put the pen down.

I eyed the desk next to his. It's regular occupant had been a high spot of my past visits, and I was taken aback by that particular absence. "Did Rhonda get sick?"

He glanced toward the unusually tidy desk. "Nah; she's alive and kicking. Boss made us spread out, though. Her desk is by the windows, now," he gestured, but I found no occupied seats in that direction, either. "She's doing rounds," he added.

"I liked her," I said, noting the past tense of my words

and wondering at it.

"Like I said, she ain't dead."

I looked back at him, realizing my own use of past tense was for *me*, and feeling rather shocked at it. I *was* dead though, wasn't I? And the thought of not having said goodbye to the friendly, but cuttingly sarcastic lady cop that had joked with me even as Cromwell had lectured me, red-faced and sweaty, was sobering. I hadn't said goodbye to *anyone*. And worse, I'd chosen it. Given in with *relief*, hoping anyone interested would find my suicide note/grocery list booklet and get any answers they needed there.

And now, I was dead. And back again. And the only people I knew I'd see would be dying. And strangers, most likely.

"Can I get out of here, Cromwell?"

"Didn't you ever wonder what my first name was?"

I laughed, but the smile slid off my face when I saw the seriousness on his. "No – I mean, I guess I never imagined that would be appropriate."

He lowered his eyes.

"We aren't exactly *friends*," I added, suddenly aware of the pall in the air.

He shrugged. "Sometimes I wonder about all the rules and regulations, you know? Nowadays, everything's different. I mean, we keep going, day-to-day, doing the same things we always did...but I wonder if it all makes sense anymore."

For the second time that day, I was stunned.

He waved it all away, then rubbed at his eyes so hard it made me flinch.

"You OK, uh -?"

"Evan," he finished with his first name, then blew out a lungful of air as though he was giving in. "I don't believe you meant Jed any harm." He gestured toward the door. "You're free to go."

I stared at him, completely flummoxed.

"Go!" he turned to his computer.

I stood, then realized I was rubbing my wrists again with a sense of disbelief. He caught my eyes before I turned, though, and there was a sense of relief, somehow, at the thought that he'd go back to the old routine.

But instead he said, "Take care, Tom. Life is short, eh?"

I stuttered over words that wouldn't come, then simply nodded before turning and hightailing it out of there.

I immediately called for a cab upon reaching the road; it was going to rain and I'd had enough of walking for the day. When I got into the back seat, grateful for the plexiglass divider, I settled in with the thought of sleep in the forefront of my mind.

But no. It had been a hard day, and I needed something a little stronger than sleep to end it. And this time, I'd bring the axe in from the woodshed to accomplish it.

I was drinking whiskey that night if it killed me.

CHAPTER 11 – WORMS

I hustled inside, my eyes already going to the cabinet before remembering I'd wanted to get the axe.

Just in case.

Grunting in frustration, I went back out into the darkening night and headed for the wood shed. I was holding the axe over my shoulder when I went in again, and went straight to the cabinet, shoes still on.

I tried it once, on the offhand chance I didn't have to smash my kitchen up, and yelled in surprise when the door flew open. I'd pulled so hard I went stumbling backward, but the pain of catching the edge of the island with my right hip was immediately forgotten when I caught sight of the bottles. All lined up like soldiers ready to come to the rescue, the deep amber liquid shining gloriously in the light from the setting sun. The only thing missing was a choir of singing angels.

My mouth filled with saliva, but I hesitated, looking suspiciously toward the ceiling. "You taking pity on an old man, finally?" I crossed to the cabinet, dropping the axe on the way, and reached for one of the infantry. My fingers tingled and I pulled my left hand back, settling on using the already-broken hand. "Can't get much worse," I said under my breath.

But the door didn't slam back on me when I pulled the bottle out. I put it on the counter. Took a deep breath. *Maybe my guy – angel? Demon? Whatever – maybe it's asleep.* I unscrewed the cap, smacking my lips in anticipation. *Maybe he - it's - just got better things to do,* I reasoned further, and then lifted the bottle to my lips. The glass lip was cool and smooth. I scanned the place again, every cell on alert, then tilted the bottle.

The harsh, but heavenly nectar rolled over my tongue. It felt like salvation. I held it in my mouth, eyes closed for a moment, then swallowed. I relished the gentle burn of it in my gullet; the warm trail it left from mouth to stomach.

"Woo!" I hooted, holding the bottle high in triumph. And then I brought it back to my mouth and pulled hard, gulping shamelessly and flying high on the thrill of success – until my stomach made an odd noise. I lowered the bottle, frowning. Waited.

My stomach gurgled with a ferocity I'd never experienced. I blanched, and had the time to whisper "Oh, no," before reflexively bending at the waist and vomiting violently onto the kitchen floor.

The liquid, which had been so soothing going down, raged like fire in reverse, burning back on its path as though it were a match put to gas. Tears streamed as I watched the contents of my stomach splatter over the axe and splash up onto the lower cabinets. I hung from the waist for some time after the retching subsided, my middle still clenched in spasm and my eyes streaming tears.

"Shit!" I cried when I could manage a breath, and I stood myself up, though my lower back protested vigorously. I groaned, resting my forearms on the countertop and my head on the cold melamine between them.

"Jesus fucking *Christ.*" My voice was gravel being dragged through phlegm.

I realized I still had a hand around the offending bottle and pushed it away. I eyed the liquid as it sloshed. It had betrayed me. But I looked toward the ceiling, then. "Not so forgiving with repeat offences, are you?"

I wiped the sweat from my face, intentionally swallowing the rage that reared up. And then the *real* tears came. "This isn't going to work," I muttered pathetically into my palms. Then I slammed my hands down on the countertop. "I can't *do* this! I can't just fucking *be* a different person with the snap of your fingers!" I shouted. I straightened up and scowled at the mess on the floor. I'd actually felt proud of the late breakfast I'd made for myself – eggs, bacon, toast with jam and butter... I'd been *trying.*

"Fuck."

I cast a forlorn gaze around my bungalow again, but the glimmer of comfort I was seeking hid in the shadows. I hadn't even contemplated cleaning up. Instead, I shuffled toward the bedroom. I remembered my shoes halfway down the hallway and kicked them off, sending them flying in a satisfying burst of energy, one by one, toward the door.

I lay down, every inch of me begging for sleep, but proceeded to stare at the ceiling until it was too dark to see it. Then I sat up in defeat. "Not even that," I shook my head, but the rage had died. "OK," I sighed. "I get it. No booze." Images of the sickness I'd surely face in the absence of my greatest vice passed before my eyes. A momentary spasm of panic shot through me, but it was short-lived, because I instantly realized that I felt... fine. I hadn't successfully kept any alcohol in me since I'd come back to myself, but I was fine. Better than I could ever remember, actually.

Frowning, I felt along the bandage on my hand. No shock of pain arose. I squeezed a little harder, and yes, it hurt... but not like a crushed knuckle should.

I went to the bathroom, flicked on the light and unwrapped the bandage.

The purple-brown coloring had morphed to a more pleasant shade of yellow-blue.

Not only was I healing, but it was *fast.*

I sat hard on the lid of the toilet. I'd never been good at self-reflection; hell, I avoided it to the point of denial. But then, I'd never been given a second chance before.

It was an astonishing epiphany.

Why now?

Besides dialing down my typical path of mayhem and destruction in the last few years (and to be fair, it was largely because I'd become physically unable to accomplish it), I hadn't done much to garner any sort of redemption. And if the glimpse I'd gotten of the afterlife was any indication, my ultimate destination reflected that.

And yet, there I was. Better. Wondering what sort of state I would have been in, had life been different.

I'd always known there were alternative paths to take; there must have been. But they'd been elusive; veiled in the trees by my own path, and it was easier, I guess, to just keep moving forward, ignoring the blinders I could have ripped off.

I guess there was a bit of resentment there, too. I'd been handed a raw deal from the start; didn't I deserve something easy, for once? It didn't seem fair that the high road was so hard to find – so, out of some sort of spite, maybe, I'd refused to look for it.

But I was the only one who'd suffered the consequences.

I inhaled deeply, squeezing my eyes shut against more tears. How had it been so easy to believe I was only harming myself? Many had been affected by my decisions. I saw it clearly. And yet, I was still doing it! Just blundering forward by instinct, eyes straight ahead. But this time, a different path had been the only option; I'd been plucked up and dropped on it, for fuck's sake, and what had I done?

Despite everything, I'd sat in place, searching for the more familiar path of self-destruction.

Can't hurt to try something new, I mused. What had I to lose, anyway? That chance was all I had left.

And the letter.

Slowly, I lowered myself to squat in front of the cupboard under the sink. I pulled out a bucket and a sponge, then walked to the kitchen. Once I'd filled the bucket with soapy water and placed it on the floor, I absently reached for the sponge and found my notebook, instead. I very nearly turned back to my work, but something made me look. It was open, and not where I'd put it.

A sort of awe came over me as I read the message left for me, tingling in my chest and widening my eyes.

"Take care. Let it happen."

The same messages as before, but I saw them clearly, that time.

I cleaned up, then returned the axe to the shed. The cool night air was wonderful on my skin. Somehow new. And then I dumped the open bottle down the sink, and followed with the rest, emptying the cabinet one bottle by one, pushing the panic down as I did. And when it was empty, I put the notebook inside and closed the door.

But first, I wrote *thank you* under the message I'd been left. And then, I went to bed.

And slept.

CHAPTER 12 – JED

Seeing Tom Wall on my property affected me, Jedediah Baker, in two significant ways:

First, it had stricken first suspicion, and then fear into my heart. I have no pride to defend, and Tom's dark past was no secret; in fact, it had been *the* topic of conversation in the neighborhood, residents sharing snippets and rumours over fences and across driveways for at least a year after he'd moved in.

I remember the first time I crossed the man in person. I knew it was him based solely on the descriptions from friends, but it felt strange to come upon the man in a place so innocuous as a grocery store aisle. Nonetheless, there was no doubt; the stocky, black-haired sixty-something man approached, his eyes (*hard* was my only description of them when Lorna had demanded details later) resolutely straight ahead.

I recall wondering if the man had come into the aisle for any reason other than to cross me; he certainly didn't appear to be on the lookout for tomato sauce, which was my purpose.

Lorna would make lasagna if I brought her what she needed. I'm a terrible cook, but never minded shopping. It was a convenient yin to Lorna's yang – but in those days, I'd noticed her enthusiasm flagging when it came to anything physical. Age, surely. But the possibility of something else gnawed at my thoughts.

I'll admit my judgement of Tom was already pretty solid before that first encounter, and the man's stony comportment only sealed it. He was a bad man. Someone I wanted nothing to do with.

Lorna accused me of being a cynic, and I suppose she was right, but in my lifetime, I'd found a reluctance to trust people beneficial – in business, especially. Perhaps not so much since I'd retired, but you know the saying about old dogs and new tricks.

It was one of those things I'd internalized; a personal commitment to work on it. For Lorna. I'd have done anything for her, including housing and incubating the massive tumour that ate away at her, even then. But that proved to be the most devastating of failures in my life: the inability to save my wife.

By the time they found it, it was nearly the size of a full-term baby. Doctors said many tumours encroaching that size were benign, and maybe Lorna's had been, too. If only we'd checked in sooner…as it was, Lorna had only given in and gone to the doctor because I'd noticed an odd bump in her middle as she slept on her back one morning.

Seeing that bump where there should have been none, moving with Lorna's breath, so obviously part of her, made my blood run cold. I'd known in that moment.

And I'd prayed to God that I'd follow her quickly from that point onward. MARS-21 took up the task, but in the years between her death and my own illness, I'd had the chance to progress from cynical to bitter. And my view of the world – and the people left in it – was sorely unforgiving.

So, gazing upon Tom's figure at the bottom of my porch stairs fuelled a panic more intense than I'd ever known. The rifle was in my hands and aimed at him before I'd even thought to get dressed.

I couldn't see anything to redeem what I knew about him – he was a hardened criminal, having served who knows how many years for crimes as varied as you could imagine; assault and battery, petty theft, larceny, grand theft auto, tax evasion (though it was said that that was due more to laziness than malintent), breaking and entering, possession with intent to - ah, but the rumours were more explosive than what I had found in some careful sleuthing. In truth, the list was nothing if not long; none of Tom's crimes had qualified for the type of sentence that would deserve the reputation gossiping had afforded him.

But then, I was among the gossipers. Better there than at the table with the man at the club. I'd watched him throw darts with men I'd counted as friends and allies, but I was world-weary and suffering with the loss of Lorna. That suffering never eased. That's the truth. If I hadn't been so alone, maybe it would have, but we'd never had children. The promise of a simple life with the freedom to do whatever we pleased, whenever we pleased, had been more attractive to both of us. Thinking back on it, though, we'd never been the adventurous sort, and we ended up in a routine that, while simple, erred on the side of mind-numbingly boring, especially for her.

But I digress.

The second effect of Tom's appearance took longer to recognize, but was far more profound.

It shook me up.

I was sick; had been for weeks, which is rare if you're one of the sufferers who ultimately succumb. But I've told you I had been determined to die for a very long time. I'd made up my mind that MARS would kill me, even if it needed a little encouragement.

And with that decision, I'd stopped doing nearly everything. And I'd declined ever so slowly, eating very little and sleeping barely at all, just to speed things along. But by the time Tom came, I'd become angry. Because it *wasn't* progressing. It had seemed to lull, its effects waning instead of waxing. The bony protrusions I'd felt at my elbows were still safely beneath the skin, and my jaw still moved smoothly at the hinges. I feared the lockjaw the most; it seemed so cruel as a final symptom, leaving you unable to eat or drink enough to get well – which, of course, meant an IV. But I'd refused. This was *it*; this was the answer to my years of prayers!

I'd see my Lorna again, at the end of it.

But the answer to my prayers was taking its time.

And then, there was Tom, who'd been rumoured to have died himself from MARS-21, but who appeared to have had the opposite – a resurgence in his health on the whole!

That pissed me off, too.

But, by God, as the rest of the day wore on and I went over the details of his visit in my mind (including the last bit, which I felt a little ashamed of...), I supposed calling the cops had seemed the best way to get at him, but when I'd heard the siren stop on the main road and realized he'd been picked up, I'd been overcome with regret.

After all, if the man was there to loot my house, maybe he'd have sped the goal of my demise along a little, too. And that would have been a favor.

And if I'm really honest, the whole interaction had been the most human contact I'd had since the newspaper interview. And it had left me exhilarated along with frightened and pissed off.

I sat in the front room with the blinds open for the rest of the day, on alert for a return appearance, and not entirely dreading the possibility of it.

But by the time the windows had gone dark and I'd given up on the thought, something else was niggling at me. I noticed it first as I removed my dentures; an ache at the hinge of my jaw.

An odd stiffness.

And for the first time, I questioned myself. My goals. And goddamn it if it wasn't too late.

CHAPTER 13 – ROOT

Walking became both a comfort and an effective way to pass the time in the following days. I found myself falling into a routine – three meals, the first walk of the day to get the paper and jaw with young Jeremy, who I was finding to be wise beyond his years despite his seemingly unshakeable goofy temperament. I'd spend hours reading, on alert for interesting prospects, but after my blunder with old Jed, I was reticent to rush into anything.

Let it happen... right?

With that in mind, I tried to be mindful about my reaction to what seemed to be a whole lot of nothing. The only progress - besides my attitude - that I could point to was that I'd had to loosen my belt a couple notches, and my thoughts had wandered a few times to fishing. It seemed to be a home base throughout life; that happy place people talk about.

Mine was a gorgeous, flowing river with me in the middle of a shallow bend of it, wearing waders and my fishing hat and reading the water and the wind. Chasing brookies or splake or salmon – it really didn't matter which; I loved it all.

But they were only thoughts, and with no further direction and no obvious way forward, I saw no option but to attempt to live as I had before. But better, because I had the opportunity to.

I had no clue whether I was on the right track, but seeing that progress in some personal areas... well, I let it fuel me.

My knuckle continued to heal, the bruises a fascinating myriad of changing colours day to day, not to mention the occasional *crunch* if I grasped something too tight – but even then, the result felt healing, as though the joint was snapping back together rather than worsening its state.

I was getting used to not drinking, too; at first, the absence of cravings was puzzling. It was like the feeling during the first few days after school exams; you think of studying just as much as in the days (or weeks) before, and the realization that you don't have to anymore feels more strange than a relief.

Sleep was another area of interest; much like the drinking, the urge – even the ability! – to sleep half a day or more away just wasn't there. And I found I was only able to sleep at all when I'd been productive. I supposed it would come in handy once my new "work" really and truly ramped up.

The thought that that depended solely on how quickly the sick succumbed made me shudder every time.

So, with all that in mind, and with a newly clear head, I soldiered onward. I found myself walking each afternoon, too, usually to the grocery store to pick up something fresh for dinner. The cashiers and packers smiled and greeted me in those transformative days, after years of keeping their eyes down as I approached. I figured the change was the result, perhaps, of my meeting their eyes in return, with no ill-will in mind.

But maybe it was the sickness, too. Our strange apocalypse had changed us all, and many were like Jeremy; too desperate for human interaction to prioritize social distancing - or even judgement - anymore.

Then there were those like Jed, who'd shut themselves up in their houses for so long they may as well be hibernating.

The city was starting to take a sort of inventory, it was

said. A macabre exercise of knocking on doors and checking the remaining living against the census. I wondered if I'd still be around to learn the results, but didn't hope for it.

I knew I wasn't in control of that. Besides, I wasn't sure I *wanted* to know just how many of us had been taken out by MARS-21.

So, on the day that things changed, I was on the first walk of the day a little over a week after my grand epiphany, and feeling rather comfortable with my developing routine. I was even starting to enjoy it, especially with my newfound energy and revitalized foot. And that particular day, I was excited, because I'd thought to make BLTs for lunch. With cheese. It was a long-time favorite that had fallen to the wayside when grocery shopping – not to mention cooking – had become a chore.

But there was no clunky motorized cart to hinder me anymore, was there?

Reflecting on it, it seems I was ready for something to happen, because I was no longer floundering in the transition to a new sort of life. Rather, I was settling in it and feeling quite good.

I had even taken the letter out. I'd pinned it on the fridge with a magnet I'd gotten in Montreal years before, so I'd be forced to look at it every time I opened the door. And the last few times I'd fixed my gaze on it, the name "Lou-Anne" written in the top left-hand corner making my heart flutter, I could imagine just reaching for it, taking it down and tearing the seal.

Just the fact that it seemed a possibility was satisfying… but I wasn't in a place to actually do it, just yet.

I made my purchases – fresh, local tomatoes and lettuce from the *Potager Eardley* were a privilege the locals didn't miss; there were many suffering from the abandonment of local farms. And the bacon was local, too. Much of the complex supply chain between countries and even provinces had fallen into ruin with the pandemic, so the grocers that were still open stocked fewer shelves with higher quality, local goods. Yes, the variety had plummeted, but the overall shopping experience had improved, in this old man's opinion. Less aisles and more open space – essential in the beginning for social distancing, but carried on because it made sense with fewer goods and customers alike.

In any case, the store across the street was quiet that day, so I accomplished my tasks in no time, then shouldered my light, reusable bag and started back home.

I don't know what made me take a different route that day; before, I'd stuck to the fastest possible path from home to wherever I needed to go, and back again. But that day, I crossed Wilfrid-Lavigne, waving at Jeremy through the convenience store window, and then paused at the entry point to my little portion of the neighborhood. And I stood there, bag slung over my shoulder, the contents cooling my back, and pondered a change.

In the end, I shook my head and turned left to walk further up the main road, wondering why I hadn't switched things up before.

I passed the next road, too, happy to wander. As long as the bacon was cooling me, it had to have been cool itself, and fine to wait a bit longer before being fried up. The air was still balmy with lingering summer, but the breeze carried a hint of chill, and the nights had been coming on faster. *September,* I thought. Just over three weeks since I'd died.

I stopped at the next road, unable to deny an overwhelming urge to turn right. I peered down the street, named Bois-Franc, which was heavily lined with blue spruce and pine, and boasted houses with smaller yards, but more modern architecture and craftsmanship than the 1970's-era houses on my street.

I rarely ventured down Bois-Franc, despite the otherwise heavy pedestrian traffic. The draws were a community center with a thriving children's soccer program, no less than three playgrounds for local children, each aiming to satisfy a different age group, and of course the off-leash dog park behind the center itself and beyond the trees.

My darts companions spoke often of the place, many being dog owners and one being a proud grandpa to several blossoming soccer players – otherwise I wouldn't have known a thing about the goings-on of the area.

I shrugged; my stomach was starting to complain, anyway. I could either turn around, or cut down Bois-Franc and then back to the right, toward des Saules, where I'd fix myself *two* BLTs with cheese. *Sharp cheddar,* I thought as I trundled down the street, the sounds of what little traffic travelled Wilfrid-Lavigne quickly fading behind me.

I was nearing the turnoff to the community centre – I could see the squat, industrial-looking building beyond the trees ahead and to my right, when I was distracted by the distinct sound of a dog whining. I halted, listening for more but still thinking about my lunch.

It came again.

I looked down the street perpendicular that would lead me back to my own little neighborhood. *It's no surprise I can hear a dog so close to the dog park,* I reasoned.

But it sounded – urgent. It came again, and there was an undeniable quality to it that made my stomach clench. It was either hurt or scared. Maybe both, come to think of it.

I walked toward the turnoff, passing the quick route to lunchtime with a mild sense of exasperation. It was very hard work being the new me.

The whining had quieted for such a long time that, by the time I reached the parking lot outside the dog park, I turned to go back. I was even picturing sandwiches again by the time I could see Bois-Franc.

But it came again as I passed the small copse of trees dividing the most colourful of the playgrounds (*for toddlers?* I'd mused as I passed it) from the road.

I squinted into the brush, pushing some of the foliage away and recoiling when something stung my finger. I grimaced at the little dome of blood that had risen on my finger. It appeared to have been pierced. I peered into the leaves for what I assumed to be an offending insect, but found thorny burdock instead. "Fucker," I muttered. I hated that shit. I sucked at the wound absently, then remembered my task. "Hello? Uh – dog?" I voiced, feeling self-conscious despite the fact that I hadn't so much as spotted another walker since I'd turned off the main street.

There was no answer.

Increasingly irritated, I squatted and whistled in the way I'd heard people call their dogs. "You in there?"

Nothing.

Sighing, I stood, intent on being finished with hidden dogs for the time being. The metallic tang of blood still sang on my tongue, proving how I tended to be rewarded for good intentions.

But when I exited the little off-road, there was a knocking sound from the house across the street.

What now?

I shielded my eyes from the sun. A figure sat at the picture window on the second floor of the handsome sage green two-story across the street. It was impossible to make out details through reflections on the glass, but I could see that whoever it was was gesturing frantically to the trees behind me.

I muttered under my breath as I waved at my nosy onlooker, then turned back toward the trees, rolling my eyes. "Hey, puppy!" I called half-heartedly.

And, despite my seconds-earlier reluctance, my heart thudded to a canter when there was an answering whimper. I knelt, squinting into the trees again, and there was a shuffle that made me jump. I glanced over my shoulder, fully expecting to see the interfering neighbor across the street to be on the front doorstep, either laughing at me or waiting for me to do a job that should perhaps have been theirs. But there was no one. I couldn't tell if he or she was even at the window.

Fed up, I stomped toward the trees. *One more try and then I'm* done, I committed. I pressed saplings to the side and called out. There was another rustle, and I jumped again, that time growling in frustration. "Shit!" I yelled, and there was an answering whine to my left.

I don't know how I didn't see her from the start; while her brindle colouring served as effective camouflage against the leafy ground, she was a blur of movement, her tail wagging so hard and fast her entire body shook. She peered up at me, her ears laid back and her head down, clearly terrified.

I won't lie; every sharp edge of me softened at the sight of that face. As cynical as I was, I can say with full confidence that I fell in love with that dog as soon as I laid eyes on her.

I found myself in a crouch, talking softly to her before I'd registered the situation. She shook with fear and excitement.

"What's wrong?" I reached for her and she recoiled with a yelp. I pulled my hand back immediately. "I'm not gonna hurt ya," I soothed, registering the appalling simpering quality of my voice. I was suddenly overwhelmed with memories of my childhood, during the entirety of which I'd longed for a dog of my own. "Hey," I reached out again, injured finger throbbing, and she lowered her head until her chin touched the ground.

I waited, hand outstretched, using her hesitation to study her – she was obviously young; her ears and snout still had that puppy roundness to them, and her eyes were charmingly big for her face. Her ears flopped and her multicoloured fur curled in clumps and wayward tangles – and a patch of it on her right hind leg stuck together with what appeared to be dried blood.

"Aw, what happened?"

She whimpered, and her wet eyes looked so sad I had to swallow a lump in my throat.

"C'mere." I patted my thigh.

She inched forward, her entire body still wiggling as she wagged. I thought of the contents of my shopping bag with regret; there was nothing I could give her, not until the bacon was cooked up. I'd need to get her home before I could – *what? How are you even contemplating taking in an injured stray?*

Frowning, I pulled back slightly.

You're dead, *old man. Your help won't mean much.*

I tilted my head to take in the sight of her leg again. *It'd mean something right now,* I reasoned. And maybe she did have an owner; the interested party across the street could just have been too sick or old to get her on their own.

It was the pup that decided it; suddenly she was wiggling her way forward, licking her lips and crying the whole way. I reached again, letting her lick my fingers before the silly thing flopped to her back, her shaggy paws curved at her chest.

"Jesus Christ," I muttered, my fingers scratching her velvet tummy on their own. She was adorable. I gently took hold of her back leg, my eyes on her face for a reaction. She froze when I rolled her toward me but allowed me to continue. I pressed gently around the wound, which was more like a deep scrape than anything else. She peered up at me with her sad eyes. "Looks like you've been dragged over pavement," I said quietly.

She licked her lips, then let her tongue hang from a longish snout.

I couldn't help but smile. "What *are* you?" She was long, like a dachshund, but with flopping, oversized ears. "Bit of spaniel in there?" I rubbed her chest. "Will you let me pick you up?" I put the grocery bag handles over my arm, then gathered her to me gingerly, careful of her leg. She went still except for her tail, which still wagged enthusiastically. I carried her to the dirt road, wondering if she'd been hit by a car, or if she'd gotten into a fight at the dog park. Aware all the time of the warmth of the little bundle in my arms. I looked down into her face. She regarded me intensely, "Hi, pretty girl," I said. She panted quietly.

Suddenly remembering my onlooker, my eyes went to the picture window across the street. The figure was there. I pointed to the dog I cradled, then to the window, miming a *this yours?* with mixed feelings.

The figure shook its head.

At a loss, I gave the thumbs-up, which was returned, and then started for home.

CHAPTER 14 – CARE

Her name became Molly. I didn't try and think of a name for her; rather, it came to me when we reached home and I let her down. I wanted to test her leg, but also to give her a chance to take care of business before I took her inside.

She immediately sat, her left hip on the ground to favour the injured one. She looked back at me over her shoulder, and it was just there.

I tried it. "Molly?"

She tilted her head and her tail hit the ground a few times.

I backed up, then squatted. "Come here, Molly."

She turned on the spot, her hip still on the ground.

Shit, I thought, considering having to take her to a vet with a broken leg. "Come on, Molly-girl."

She lowered her head. Maybe she was just scared, still.

"I'll make you some bacon if you show me how your leg's working."

She stood, slowly, head still down.

"That's right!"

Her tail took off wagging again and she was making her way to me, just as she had in the trees. I watched her steps. All four paws were hitting the ground, but she had a pronounced limp on the right. She poked a dry nose into my hand and I gathered her up again. "Good girl."

I took her in and got to work assigning her some bowls and filling one with water. I frowned at the empty one for food when she sat in front of her dish and begun to drink. I'd have to go back out.

"Strange way to drink water," I muttered, eyeing her left-hip sit again. But I thought she'd be OK; she just needed time.

I got a pillow from the couch and set it up in the corner of the kitchen so she could watch me cook, but it proved too small and, out of options, I found myself retrieving one of the pillows off my own bed and trying that, instead.

"You must be pretty special," I mumbled as she curled up on it as if it had always been her own.

I couldn't relax as I went about the business of cooking the bacon and making the sandwiches I'd anticipated all morning; I found myself glancing toward the corner and getting lost in plans for Molly – I'd need to get her a leash and a collar as well as food. Some toys, of course, and maybe some puppy pads, just in case she'd never been trained. She looked to be past that point, though surely she wasn't a year old, but who knew?

Molly did.

The next time I looked up, I found her sitting by the door, her sweet, sad eyes on me.

"When did -?" I set the knife down and took her outside, setting her on the grass of the small side lawn, where she immediately sniffed around, this time holding her right hind leg up as she hopped around to find a spot to pee. Once done, she sat, looking up at me again.

"Smart girl, aren't you?"

She tilted her head.

I picked her up with a chuckle. I was toast.

The sandwiches were everything I'd hoped. The experience was made a bit sweeter, too, as Molly gently took bits of bacon from my outstretched fingers. I wondered why I hadn't gotten a dog earlier. There'd been no denying foster families or frequent moves for some years... and I no longer lived as though I'd be back behind bars any day.

It was as though a life of feeling denied had instilled a mindset in me to perpetuate it.

Little Molly could be the first creature on the earth that seemed to care about me without prejudice. Most of that was my fault (I know now that we teach folk how to treat us). And it may not even be true; the woman who'd grown me in her womb may have loved me. All I knew about my birth mother was that I killed her before she even laid eyes on me.

How I wished I'd been given a choice in that first damning act of violence. How would the world have been different if I'd been able to give my life for hers?

Caring for Molly, in case you haven't noticed, got me thinking a lot about things I'd spent a very long time purposefully *not* thinking about.

The pup was down and out after I washed the few dishes I'd used. I eyed her as she trembled slightly in her sleep, as little dogs do, and wondered what had happened to her. I found a towel in the hall closet and placed it over her, hoping she'd find some comfort in warmth, anyway, and then I went out again. I was feeling antsy, what with the unprecedented bout of reflection... all the thoughts that had resurfaced.

I realized I was headed back toward Bois-Franc about halfway there; I'd kept my head down trying to lose myself in the monotony of the pavement as it moved beneath my feet. Trying to *not* think. Funny what the subconscious does when you turn your back, though. I didn't stop until I was in front of the upscale two-story again, peering blankly up at the picture window.

Nobody looked back; the curtains had, in fact, been pulled shut.

But whoever lived there had to know something about Molly; not only did they have the perfect vantage point, but they'd proven they at least knew where she was hiding.

Before I could talk myself out of it, I was walking up the empty driveway, then knocking on the door. I stuffed both hands in my pockets and waited, leaning forward slightly to listen for sounds of movement within.

Many had stopped answering their doors altogether once the pandemic begun to prove its strength. But the change in people had come as a reaction to how the disease changed; it had come in waves of increasing devastation. The first had been barely worth noting. The second pressed lawmakers into action, but people complained about the new rules – the closing of non-essential business, the vast swath of layoffs and economic uncertainty, the social distancing, then the isolation. By then, people were showing results of a mutated pathogen, and they defied denial. They, in fact, were deeply disturbing, and worsened as MARS-21 gained purchase and learned how to defeat us.

Many essential workers weren't risking leaving their homes anymore, sick or not.

"Can I ask what your business is here?" a voice cut into my thoughts, startling me and I turned on the spot. My old self had my fists clenching in preparation for self-defence and my new self was searching for a simple answer before I even saw it was a government official.

The man frowned at my fists.

I unclenched them, then raised a hand to my heart.

"Fuck *me*," I muttered before I could catch the words and hold them back.

"Sir, if this is not your residence – and I'm certain it's not – I'd advise you to vacate the property immediately. Unless you can explain your business here."

I held both palms out then, smiling and shaking my head as I caught my breath. "You scared me is all; I was deep in thought," I lowered my hands and waited, but the man's face above his mask was all the right sort of angles for a frown. He looked young; late twenties, maybe. A flash of the cell I shared at age twenty-eight with a kid named Robert Bobton passed through my mind. You'd think he would've been on the losing end of inmate battles over that name, but Bobby-Bob, as I called him (and as he *allowed*, given our respectfully civil relationship) was also 6', 4" and had a temper like a smoldering volcano.

"Your business here, sir?"

I glanced over my shoulder at the door. "I – I found a pup in the trees over there this morning," I gestured across the street, causing the man to back up a step, despite the medical-grade mask and gloves he wore. Standard practice whenever one left their house, but rarely enforced.

"Please keep your distance, sir."

"Sorry."

"Go on."

"Someone was up there, in the window," I pointed toward the second-floor, "and now that I have the dog at home, I was hoping to find out if they knew what happened to her – she's hurt – and whether they know who the owner is."

"What would lead you to think they have those answers?"

"They, uh – the person was watching, sorta pointing me

in the right direction. Helping out, I guess."

He shook his head and hugged a clipboard I hadn't noticed to his chest. "Doesn't sound like essential business to me."

A familiar feeling – the one of being caught doing something I should be ashamed of – threatened to either fuel me into a confrontation or worse, start me crying like a fucking baby. I lowered my head, allowing myself a moment to gather my thoughts.

"Nice of you to try to find the dog's owner, though. Does she have tags?"

I raised my eyes to him, disbelieving. Wondering in that split second how many times people would've surprised me if I'd waited a second before launching an assault – verbal or otherwise.

"Don't get your hopes up; if she was on her own, chances are, her owner's abandoned her on purpose, or isn't around anymore," he continued, sending a long gaze up the street.

"She – she didn't have tags. No collar, even," I stuttered.

"Look – the fact that you're out without a mask withstanding – you seem healthy. If I were you, I'd get back to your place and consider myself lucky to have someone – something – to keep you company. Bet your dog is grateful for that, too. God knows there are more of them than us, nowadays, and a lot of them have made the streets their homes."

"Huh," I replied stupidly, still blown away by the guy's kindness.

He pointed to the door behind me. "There's only one resident here, and she's in the last stages. I talked to her earlier."

"You one of those government census people?"

He nodded. His eyes were sad. "Not a fun job, I'm afraid, but I've got a wife and three kids – all of them healthy, thankfully – to support."

"If I could shake your hand, I would," I surprised myself as the words came out. I gulped. It was a good surprise. "Thank you for your work."

He nodded. "Go on, now. Even if she's awake, *and* admits to being the dog's owner – or knowing who is - she's in no condition to take care of it, now."

"Will you do something for her?"

He shook his head. "These days, it's about saving those who *want* saving. The elderly usually refuse, reasoning that medical resources should be used on the young."

I frowned at the emotions that rose in my chest.

"Before you go, can I ask your name and address? It'd save me knocking on your door tomorrow." His eyes crinkled slightly at the corners.

"Thomas Wall," I answered. "I'm over on des Saules, number 1167."

"You the only person registered to that household?"

"Yes, sir."

"You the owner?"

"Technically." He looked up, a question in his eyes. "I rented the place from a guy; after his wife died, we became pals, sort of. Played darts over at the -" I sighed. "Anyway, he was in some stage of having paperwork made up to deem the house mine after so many years. A rent-to-own thing, you know?"

He nodded.

"He was about twenty years my senior. Appreciated that

I always paid on time and listened to him talk," I laughed. "He could talk!" I cleared my throat, suddenly uncomfortable. "Anyway - then *he* got sick, and last time I went to pay the rent, they were taking him out of the house on a stretcher -"

"Did he manage to let you know if the paperwork was complete?"

"Uh – he was in a *body bag* on a stretcher."

"Oh, shit," the guy seemed to frown at his own profanity. "Sorry, man. That – well, it's not surprising; I won't say that. It sucks, though."

I nodded.

"You'd be surprised how many folks have no clue if they actually own their houses right now, whether due to bank shut-downs or situations not unlike your own." He wrote something on his clipboard. "For all intents and purposes – meaning until somebody with authority tells you otherwise, assume it's your property, OK, Mr. Wall?"

"Tom."

His eyes crinkled again. "Tom. And I'm Ed – Ed LaFrance."

"Nice to meet you, Ed," I said quietly. And by God, it *was*. "I'll go, now. Good luck with your work. And if you need a break when you're in the neighborhood, stop by. You know where I live."

He pulled a card from his shirt pocket. "My contact information." He gave a short wave and was on his way, and then I was, too. Astonished. I couldn't remember if I'd *ever* invited someone to my home before.

I gazed up at the sky. "What have you done to me?"

CHAPTER 15 – BREATHE

I detoured for the dog food, then headed home. I could hear Molly's frantic yelps from the end of the driveway. She sounded every bit as frightened as she had when I found her in the trees. I found myself speeding to a run; something I couldn't remember doing for years. It felt – amazing. But the wind in my hair became a secondary concern as I approached the door and could hear scratching from inside.

I shouldn't have left her. How could I have thought I'd be good at this when I couldn't even take care of my own –

I wrenched the door open and the pup was on me in seconds, dribbling pee on the wood of the tiny deck in her excitement.

"Oh, what's wrong?" I crooned. She responded by whining. She was doing her full-body wag at the same time, though. I picked her up and brought her to the lawn, where she made quite a display of herself as she limped around, tail wagging, still crying, and finally squatting. I couldn't help but chuckle at the look of relief that transformed her face; her eyes drooped with it.

I carried her inside; she suddenly appeared exhausted. I wondered if she'd been frantic the entire time I was out. I was quickly confronted with the answer; an impressive layer of fluffy white stuff stretched from the kitchen to the living room. A shimmering heat boiled in my gut as rage, both familiar and foreign, somehow, bubbled up. I gritted my teeth and looked down at the pup in the crook of my elbow. Her ears were back and her eyes sad.

"What'd you do?"

She wriggled a bit.

"What'd you rip apart?" Conflicting emotions warred in me as I held back my immediate reaction.

She darted at my face, licking my mouth.

"That's not fair," I muttered as the urge to flip out dissolved. I sighed. Scratched her neck. "How'd you do that?"

She wriggled double-time. I placed her amidst the mess and looked around. The pup ran circles in it, bounding like a fawn with stunted legs. *I need to punish her. To let her know there are consequences* – but as I watched her frolic, bits of fuzz clinging to her ears and sticking to her mouth – I knew I couldn't.

Instead, I shuffled through the fluff in an attempt to find some remains of the decimated object. It only took a moment; I recognized my pillowcase, despite its state of disrepair, sticking out of a particularly generous pile of the stuff in the corner Molly had been sleeping in. I slid my gaze to the pup sitting happily in the fluff, eyes on me.

"That was my pillow!"

She wagged her tail, sending bits of fluff flying.

I found myself wishing I had a camera. "Oh!" I reached for my smartphone. I'd never used it as a camera, but I remembered the young salesman telling me I could. I fiddled with the thing until I managed to find the camera function, but when I looked up again, Molly had curled up and looked up at me with her long snout on her paws.

I took the shot anyway, then stared at it, my fool heart

feeling strangely full.

I was much less forgiving as I swept up the mess.

I fed her afterward, and she wagged her tail the entire time she ate.

As I readied myself for bed that night, I eyed her, perplexed. She'd destroyed one pillow already; I couldn't risk the only one I had left. I resolved to bring her to bed with me, wise or not. She approved, snuggling into my armpit and letting out a sigh of contentment.

"I'll get you a bed tomorrow," I muttered. She looked up at me, eyes at half-mast. She seemed to know, as I did deep inside, that a bed would be great for her to rest on when I was in the kitchen, but that she was where she belonged in that moment.

I need to figure out if someone's missing her.

"We'll go for a walk tomorrow."

Molly was already breathing deeper.

"We need to make sure you're mine."

The next thing I knew, I was being woken by stinky puppy kisses, and it was a lot less adorable than it sounds.

"Blah!" I pushed her away, but she bounded back, wriggling as only she could. When she whimpered, I clued in: she wasn't just waking me for the pleasure of my company.

Later in the kitchen, she sat and watched as I puttered around, fixing an omelette and toast and bacon with previous day's leftovers. It was odd to feel so – settled. No niggling thoughts of the negative sort to speak of – not even the dark insistence of a purposeless life. I felt strangely detached without it, but I recognized it as a reaction to change. *Who knew I'd evolve* after *I died?*

Molly got bits of bacon in her bowl of kibble, and by the

time I'd downed a glass of orange juice and done the dishes, we were both ready to go. But that morning, I headed toward Bois Franc instead of the gas station. I had a different purpose in mind.

And that day, there *was* an answer to my knocking.

I held Molly like a football as the door cracked open.

One eye peered up at me. Its lower lid stretched downward, as my own had in the last stage of MARS-21.

"I'm sorry to bother you," I said, "but I wanted to thank you for your help in finding Molly yesterday."

The eye widened, and the door opened so I could see the tiny old lady in her entirety – which was packaged in an exterior I dwarfed. I had to lean down a bit to hear her when she said, "Orrie?"

I nodded, aware of the hinderance of her locked jaw, which stretched beyond the bottom of her mask. "Molly, right," I replied.

Her eyes filled with tears as she regarded the pup, who was rapt at attention under my arm.

The woman eyed me warily, then pointed to her mask. "Hick."

I nodded. "It's OK. I've already had it."

She maintained her questioning gaze.

"I just wondered if she was yours -" she shook her head, "- or if you knew the owner?"

She hesitated.

"I only mean to get her home, if she still has one."

"Orrie," the woman said again.

I frowned.

She poked an arm out, gesturing to the corner and then down the street adjacent to her lot.

"Molly lives down there?"

Her arm dropped. "Co' ing," she said, then backed away and turned toward the stairs.

I stepped inside, surprised and hesitant. Molly wriggled to be let down. I observed a motorized chair attached to the wall of the staircase and hurried to help the fragile woman into it. She startled at my first touch, but relaxed and let me help her quickly. I bit back a gasp as I touched her elbow; a bony protrusion grew there, just as it had with me. And she smelled of...neglect. Of age. Of death.

I got her settled then stood back, my hand going absently to the elbow I hadn't even thought of since I'd died and been revived. Not only did I discover the knobby, but familiar elbow of before MARS-21, but the knuckle of the curious hand did not protest when I pressed harder.

A sense of gratitude filled me, especially as I watched the hunched old woman ride the chair to the second floor. A string of drool hung from her chin.

I followed at a respectable distance, then helped her out. Molly had already trundled off to some unseen place. I wondered briefly if the woman had any pillows lying around.

Apparently over her suspicion of me – or pushed beyond caring at that point – the woman clung to my arm as we walked the hall. The place was immaculate, but smelled stale. And the air was heavy, like that of my own home whenever I'd been out and returned, as if to say, *welcome back, Tom. No matter how often you leave, you always have this to come home to. This emptiness.*

I peeked sideways at the woman as an entirely new sensation tickled in my chest.

She paused before an open door at the bend in the hallway and looked up at me, silent. I peered over her shoulder, then back at her. "You need a pit stop?"

Her eyes were a combination of desperation and reluctance, but she backed into the room, still clutching my arm.

The poor thing wants my help.

"Oh."

She paused in front of the toilet, looking at me again with that combination of need and regret.

I nodded. "OK."

If anyone had told me a month earlier that I'd be helping a diseased old lady onto a toilet, I'd have laughed until I cried. And if they'd mentioned that I wouldn't even be mad about it – not a whisper of rage – well, I'd have discounted the story entirely.

But there it was.

She appeared grateful afterward, even if her eyes filled with tears again, and led me to the living room where I'd first spotted her through the picture window. I helped her sit in a well-worn recliner beside it, then stood back. I spotted Molly curled up on the couch.

"I can wake her," I ventured when I saw the woman had spotted her, too.

She shook her head, waving a bony arm to discount the idea. Then she rubbed her eyes and reached for what appeared to be a spray bottle from the little end table beside her.

I watched, my stomach rolling as she lowered her mask to spray water into her gaping mouth. I recalled how terrible it had felt to both drool uncontrollably, and yet feel like my mouth had been baked in the desert sun all day.

"That's a good idea," I muttered, and she turned self-consciously toward the window to replace her mask.

"It's OK; I had the lockjaw, too. And the elbow -" I gestured awkwardly toward hers.

She frowned deeply, then reached for a notepad and pen from the little table after replacing the water bottle. She scribbled something, then handed to pad to me.

And you didn't die?

I looked back at her, unsure of the answer.

She reached for the pad, shaking her head as she scribbled again. She turned it to face me.

Obviously not.

There was some humour in her eyes, and I smiled but said nothing.

She wrote again.

Linda.

"Hi, Linda. I'm -" I hesitated, confronted with the threat of my past. I didn't want to scare the woman before I got any information from her, but lying felt – impossible. I flashed back to the massive vomit session I'd had when I'd pushed beyond a similar feeling, and let my mouth shut. It made a small *pop!* as if to confirm my non-answer.

She wrote again.

Thomas Wall.

Astounded, I met her eyes, which appeared satisfied. Unable to deny it, I nodded. "My reputation precedes me."

Her eyes crinkled, then she wrote again. Her eyes were defiant as she held the statement out for me to read.

Not scared of anything anymore.

I glanced at a partnering recliner and motioned toward it. "OK if I sit?"

She nodded once.

"Things are different for me since – since I was sick," I looked toward the trees as I sat. "I'm no threat to you," I met her eyes again.

She rested her head back on the chair, then turned to observe the sleeping Molly.

"She's OK. Even walked a bit on the way here." I looked over at the little pup, suddenly surprised. "And she got up on your couch!"

The woman's eyes crinkled at the edges again as she pointed at an ottoman half the height of the couch.

"Ah." That made more sense. "Uh - you were pointing around the corner; is that where she's from?"

She wrote again, but lazily, leaving her head on the seat back instead of bending over the notebook.

Molly is her owner. Young girl, used to read to me. I paid her.

I frowned, something unfamiliar tugging at my heart. "Molly is her owner?" I shook my head a little before continuing. "Can you tell me her house number so I can take the pup to her?"

She turned the notebook toward me again.

101.

I nodded.

The woman seemed to doze.

Maybe she's dying! I cringed inwardly at the thought, but even more at the excitement behind it. Had I found someone to help? "It's OK," I tried.

The woman's eyes parted slightly, but she was frowning.

"I mean, you must be tired. Of all of this," I gestured to her, feeling again like it was wrong. Like I was messing it up.

She chuckled quietly, then scribbled something.

If you lived, I can, too.

I sighed. It was exactly what I hadn't intended to do, but what, then? Adrift, I glanced at Molly. "Can I do anything for you before I go?"

She hesitated, then wrote.

What did you eat? And how?

Ah, the terrible dichotomy of starving and being physically unable to take in food. I shook my head sadly, then thought twice. "OK if I check out your kitchen?"

She nodded, closing her eyes.

I took the spray bottle on a vague notion, then went downstairs. The kitchen was sadly understocked. I decided to get her some groceries on my trip later in the afternoon before considering it. It was just a sudden knowing. I found some Gatorade in the fridge and replaced the water in her bottle with it. At least she'd get some electrolytes into her. A scan of the cupboard revealed nothing hopeful. I thought of popsicles and soup, and of another spray bottle full of chicken broth, and another with water.

I frowned at the ceiling. *This isn't all me.*

I left the house feeling emptier than I had before I'd come. Molly was curled under my arm again, but how long would I have her, now? And I'd left the Gatorade for the old woman, but it wasn't enough.

And I still had no idea what I was supposed to be doing.

I eyed the corner, still intent on finding Molly's home, but reluctant, too. I looked down at her. "You OK with taking care of Linda before we get you home?"

Molly only peered up at me with wet eyes.

And because I had no idea what she'd choose, but for the first time in my life I knew I didn't want to part from something – someone - who needed me, I chose for us both.

CHAPTER 16 – TEMPEST

I took a risk that afternoon; Molly came with me to get groceries. I carried her football style the whole way, and she was good as gold, quietly fascinated by everything around her.

There were few people in the store, as usual, and most of them kept their eyes down as I loaded my own cart with food for the old woman – bouillon cubes, tomato soup, more Gatorade, more spray bottles and, in a moment of inspiration, several pouches of baby food. I wasn't used to shopping for anyone besides myself, but minimalism had served me well; my pension was more than enough, and unlike the emergency funds set up for laid off workers and students during the early days of the pandemic (which still suffered technical and procedural issues) the pension and disability programs that were already in place functioned as they'd been automated to.

My drinking habit had resulted in my only being able to break even during the final year of my life, but that had changed, too, and it felt good to do something worthwhile with the overflow.

What else was it for, anyway?

In any case, I met no protestations over Molly until I arrived at the cash. Even then, the cashier only eyed the fluffy bundle in my arm with a frown.

I had puzzled over possible responses to concerned staff,

and still vacillated between claiming she was a service pet and apologizing, then promising not to bring her into the store again.

Instead, I found myself saying, "She rips things up when I leave her alone."

Huh.

The cahier's expression softened. "She's so pretty; what breed?"

I studied Molly's coat. "Dachshund, surely, and I'm thinking maybe Spaniel?"

The woman, whose nametag said, "Jan," smiled. "Because of the ears."

I nodded.

"Well, I'll ring you through, but if the manager asks, I told you she can't come in anymore."

"Roger that," I muttered, pleased.

Molly and Jan were on a first name basis by the time we left, the grocery bag slung over my shoulder. "That went better than expected," I whispered in Molly's direction as we crossed the parking lot. She wriggled to be let down and I complied, realizing as she shook herself that I'd forgotten the leash. "Oh, well," I smiled down at her. "They probably didn't have them, anyway."

She sat, looking up at me as if to say, *what are we waiting for?*

"Same with dog beds," I added as an afterthought.

I could see the pup testing her leg as we walked a leisurely pace toward Wilfrid-Lavigne. "Good girl!" I praised her when we reached it and she showed no signs of using her freedom to run off.

I eyed Bourgeon, directly across the road. It would lead us home. My eyes went to the pup, who was pointed in the direction of Bois Franc.

"You don't want to just head home for a bit? Maybe take a nap?"

She didn't flinch.

"Watch some TV?" I remembered the varieties of static I'd discovered the last time I'd switched the thing on and sighed. She was right; I was on borrowed time. Lounging around and wasting it wasn't an option.

I felt a surge of something powerful. I'd never experienced it before. I thought at the time it was simply the fact that I had something to keep me occupied. Now, I recognize it as something more profound: *purpose.*

"OK," I said, quietly, and Molly wagged her tail.

She walked beside me until we got to the crosswalk, then sat. I frowned. Either the dog's sense of direction was uncanny, she was oddly intuitive, or we were *both* being led. "Who's giving you directions?" We'd taken the roads within the neighborhood before; how could she know the way via the main street?

I shook my head, stepping into the road, and she yipped, snapping at the hem of my cargos. I jumped back just in time to feel the *swish* of a passing truck. I stood, frozen dumb, for a moment, then looked down at Molly, who yipped again, then stepped into the empty street. I looked both ways, still in shock, then followed her.

I watched as she led the way to the head of our destination street, grateful her limp seemed to be lessening. In awe of her as she glanced back to make sure I was following.

Aware of the magic that fuelled us.

Linda didn't answer the door that time. It didn't surprise

me; the blinds had been pulled at the picture window upstairs. I looked back at Molly, who sat at the end of the driveway, watching. "Guess you're not surprised, either?" I hung the sack of groceries on the doorknob and went back to the pup. My heart sank as I did; she was looking eagerly between me and the corner.

Toward her own home.

Conflicting emotions warred within me, which had become sort of a regular thing, but still felt strange, given my previous predilection for anger. It hadn't varied much in life; there was anger and then there was repressed anger, then there was unleashed anger. Many different sorts of anger, and not much else.

"You want to go that way?"

She stood.

I gazed in the direction of home. "You sure you're not hungry? Tired?"

She wagged her tail.

A heaviness pressed on my chest. I clenched my jaw. Inwardly scolded my own behaviour. Then, started around the bend. "OK, come on!" I called over my shoulder, and suddenly she was ahead of me, skip-hopping now and then as she led the way.

I'd never been much of a follower, and now a little, lame dog was my pied piper.

"You've gone fucking *soft*," I murmured aloud, if only to gain back some semblance of control. Of footing in a world I was supposed to be of value in, but hardly recognized from behind newly-cleared eyes.

The pup halted before I could dwell so long as to fall into darkness. *Distraction is good.* I gave her head a scratch.

I straightened to regard – dubiously - the split-level house from the end of the driveway. Its windows were dark, reflecting the grey sky. Mail stuck every which way out of the metal box by the door. I eyed Molly. "Doesn't look like anyone's home."

She started toward the door. Her limp was more pronounced by then; I realized she was tired and hurting but had pushed onward to get home. She'd worked so hard. Dreaded tears gathered in my eyes, hot and hated.

Have I been that hard to live with?

I gritted my teeth and moved forward, silently clutching at the hope for a silver lining, should I lose Molly that day. *At least I didn't buy a dog bed – or even a leash!* I lamented the nearly full bag of dog food I'd left at home, but couldn't decide whether I'd bring it later if Molly stayed.

I took in the details of the place as I ruminated. The un-mowed grass was typical in those days, rather than telling. I could see that the handsome blue spruce that dominated the yard had previously been trimmed at the base, but it had been allowed to grow wild for some time, awkward branches filling the space in like stubble on a tired face.

An odd smell filled my nostrils as I approached the sidewalk, and I gagged reflexively, bringing my arm to my face and halting on the spot. A basement window was open behind some impressive hostas in the little front garden, but my gaze went toward the fenced-in yard at the end of the driveway. I headed for the gate without hesitation, but Molly barked, and I stopped. "What is it?"

She stood, then pawed at the door.

I frowned toward the back, where the smell seemed to be coming from, but went to Molly instead. It had been her idea to come. Besides, the government guy had been on that road just two days earlier; if he'd noticed anything amiss, surely he would've had it taken care of.

A knock inspired no response. Molly pawed at the door again, but whimpered, that time.

"I'm not just going to open it," I looked down at her sternly.

She stood, front paws on the door.

"Don't hurt your leg, silly!" I picked her up and she wriggled frantically until I released her again.

I knocked, loudly.

Molly yipped.

"Anyone home?" I called, really shouting. I was in no hurry to receive answer or invitation – the place felt off – but I thought I'd give it a good try, for the pup's sake, anyway.

And, to my surprise, there *was* a sound from inside.

Molly practically danced as a female voice floated to us.

I stepped off the cement step and backed onto the lawn, observing for the first time that the upstairs windows were open, too. "Hello?"

"Go away!"

I was instantly transported to my recent confrontation with Jed Baker. I looked at Molly, who appeared to be ready to blow a gasket.

I sighed. "I have your dog, I think!"

Silence answered me. Even Molly had quieted, frozen in a gaze up to the open windows with her back leg raised slightly.

"A Dachshund mix? Young? Really cute?" I called, then covered my mouth. *What the fuck is wrong with me?*

Nothing.

"Hello?" I was ready to go. I'd tried! I pictured picking

the pup up and heading home. Even thought about catching a quick nap with her curled up in my armpit.

But then, there was an answer.

"'Enny?" Higher-pitched, and noticeably strained.

The occupant's jaw was locked.

"'Enny?" came the repeated call, and Molly whined so long and loud it turned into a howl.

My heart pounded. I'd already lost her. Thoughts raced – the girl was sick; she was in no shape to take Molly.

I remembered that the old lady had said it was the girl's name; Molly. "Molly?" I called, more quietly.

"'ome in,"

Shit.

The smell was terrible, but it didn't match the one from the back yard, entirely. There was something a little less rotten and a little more *filth* inside. I wanted to go even before I closed the door behind us, but Molly was already gone; she'd scampered up the stairs before I was fully inside.

I heard a sound like high-pitched laughter and crying at the same time. A happy reunion.

I should just go.

It was so compelling, I nearly did. "I'll just leave you to it, if that's alright!" I called toward the stairs.

"No!" the woman – Molly – cried.

Molly – the pup – appeared at the top of the stairs. If a dog could look conflicted, she'd gotten it spot-on.

"She's your dog, right?"

Some garbled words, unintelligible. She was crying harder, then.

"Molly?"

"You...'ick?"

I blew out a lungful of air. "Not now," I said, finally.

A pause. "'ome ut?" A gargling sound made me grimace. Molly ran off.

"I'm just going to go -"

I wanted nothing more. The dog was back where she belonged, and by the sounds of things, her owner was overjoyed to see her. And Molly *wanted* to stay.

It had been foolish to consider her mine. I felt stupid and something else. Something familiar.

I felt betrayed.

"'lease!"

I climbed the stairs, wanting out the whole time. Angry that I had this new sense of obligation, despite the lack of direction. But everything faded when I rounded the corner and saw her.

She was slumped against the bathtub. At first glance, I would've thought she was already dead if I hadn't just been talking to her. Besides the eyes - they were riveted on me in an upward stare, the bottom curve of her eyeballs revealed by the unnatural pull of her wide-open mouth. Her locked jaw was so extreme that her chin touched her chest; her shirt was soaked with drool. And the corners of her mouth were bleeding and torn deep into her cheeks, though the blood and scabbing prevented me from knowing exactly how bad.

"Oh, God," I found myself whispering.

"'ying," she said, as if in explanation, and I heard the word as she'd intended. Dying. And oh, yes, she was.

I moved forward, simultaneously appalled and

compassionate. It occurred to me that I'd felt it before; the sick combination of the fight-or-flight response and the instinctive desire to help. To make things better. I couldn't place it within my memories, exactly, but I thought I'd been very young.

The intensity of the light after I flipped the switch caused Molly – the woman – to groan and turn her head, but her eyes would not close. She seemed unable to lift an arm against the glow, so I flicked it off again, muttering, "Sorry."

"What can I do?" I squatted. Helped her turn her head so she could look at me again when she faltered. The top lids of her eyes were drooping in obvious exhaustion, and the weight of her head in my hands was impossibly light. Her cheeks hollowed darkly on either side of her grotesquely skewed mouth, likely as much from starvation as for the fact that her cheekbones seemed to be missing entirely. *Some of her bones have dissolved*, I realized inwardly.

I could still see the tracks of her tears from earlier.

Molly put her paws on her owner.

The woman's eyes crinkled at the sides, but the smile did not reach her other features. My stomach clenched at the smell of her breath.

"Can I help you? Take you to your bed? Get you comfortable, at least?"

Her eyes rolled up, eyelids fluttering.

Then my stomach rolled again as I was overcome by another smell, this one emanating from the filthy toilet bowl beside us. *That's why she's in the bathroom.* I'd glimpsed the soiled and darkened state of her lower half, though, too. The toilet had lost its purpose some time ago.

Her eyes met mine again. She tried to say something, but her tongue moved uselessly, doing nothing but making a soft tearing sound as she lifted it from its resting place.

I thought of the old woman. Her spray bottle. And I remembered the feeling of the lockjaw again. But I'd never been as bad as this.

She tried again. I found myself clenching my fists as I waited for her to speak; an impotent wish to help her. I thought of the old woman again - rather, her notepad - and glanced around, helpless.

"'ill ee," she said, finally.

I frowned at her.

"'lease."

I shook my head, not because I didn't understand her but because I immediately realized what she wanted (I had been a kindred spirit in the wanting to die category, after all), and I knew I couldn't do it. Not ever.

She cried, eyes struggling to shut, saliva welling up behind her teeth.

I found myself suddenly panicked, which was simultaneously understandable and bizarre, considering I'd been searching for a way to realize my new purpose. Now that it was before me, I found I was woefully underprepared. Scanning the area for answers. Ideas, at least. "I could – I could get you some water. Try and get some food into you! Call an ambulance -"

She started to shake her head but blanched as her eyes rolled back again.

"You're young -" I added, but there was no conviction in the words. She was barely able to stay conscious. She was close, whether I was ready for her to succumb, or not.

"'lease," she begged again, her sad eyes on the dog. I saw the softness in the expression.

"I found her across from Linda's," I said, grateful for

the distraction, smoothing Molly's fur and noting with some anxiety that the pup was trembling.

The woman grunted, seemingly trying to move her hand, and I reached for it. Her eyes looked sideways at me. Wary, still. But desperate.

I placed her palm on Molly's fur, and my hand on top of hers.

More tears streamed down her ruined face.

And then she was trying to move her other hand. After a moment of confusion, I took that one, too, but the fingers curled around mine – so softly, just so lightly – before I could move it, too, to the pup's warmth.

She seemed to relax a bit as the three of us sat joined in a rough circle on her bathroom floor. I'm sure it was only a moment, but that time in the quiet, in the stench, and under the weight of impending death stretched unnaturally. And in that strange moment that I'm sure will remain clear in my memory until my memories are no more, the atmosphere was something close to peaceful. Her head rested against the tiled wall and she met my eyes with some effort before she spoke.

"'ank... you."

It sounded like a goodbye.

My breath caught as her eyes dulled. "No," I whispered, but it was futile. I watched as the life drained from her face. Actually felt a rush of tingling cold as it left her. I shivered absently as I gazed at her, my mouth agape. It had happened so quickly it seemed impossible.

Molly whimpered and lay her head on her owner's lap, and I folded the woman's hands over her abdomen, suddenly wanting separation, then fell back to sit awkwardly before her.

She was gone.

I looked at the pup, so obviously mourning her loss. Then I gazed at the ceiling. "What was all this for?" I shook my head in disbelief. "So I could watch her *die*?"

I'd been scared to come. Scared because I wanted the pup. I hadn't thought about my new reason to live. And now – now she'd died, and Molly was – what? Mine?

I didn't feel relieved, nor encouraged. I looked up at the ceiling again. "Is *this* what I'm supposed do?" The prospect was immediately devastating.

I shook my head, aware of my own breath. Stared at my hands, felt my blood course through my veins, then took another look at the ravaged corpse before me.

It wasn't fair. To anyone! This woman hadn't deserved to die, and yet she'd suffered a litany of horrors before I had apparently helped usher her out of her body - me! A man who'd gratefully welcomed my own death! How had the one that had brought me back imagined that I'd be equipped for this?

It was building in me, now. Everything turned red as barely-contained rage simmered in my belly. I stood. I wanted to run. Or sink into the floor. Or yell. But what actually happened was far less explosive than I felt.

"I can't do this," I muttered.

Molly hadn't moved.

"Sorry, pup," I said, and after a momentary, desperate floundering for what to do next, a spur-of-the-moment decision had me leaning to scoop the dead girl up. Molly stood and watched, bewildered.

The considerable *lightness* of the girl's frame did something to mollify the rage-fuelled adrenaline that coursed through me. The shock of having witnessed her death seemed to have a double effect: one was that dulling of anger, and the other was to bring everything else into focus. Her shoulder blades dug into my forearms. Her legs were like twigs. And the smell...

The smell had intensified when I moved her, hitting my nostrils in a sickening wave that had me gagging. But I did not slow. I carried her to the first room that housed a bed, and I lay her down. I regarded my jacket sleeve, newly doused with the dead woman's waste, with apathy. I should have been mortified, maybe, but I wasn't. I felt nothing and everything all at once.

I should put clean pants on her.

It was a natural, compassionate thought for one who was trying to help, but one I disregarded right away. I was already beyond my scope. *Far* beyond my emotional threshold.

I would call Ed. That seemed the only tolerable next move. I did remove my coat, though, draping it inside-out over my arm as I considered just stuffing it into the first trash bin I came across.

I looked at her face once more, then covered her with a sheet that had seen better days, too, I was sure. And then I scooped Molly up and headed for the stairs. She settled quickly into the crook of my arm, her chin in the palm of my hand.

We stopped at the top of the stairs. There was a painting opposite – a fresh-faced auburn-haired girl holding a short-haired, multicoloured Dachshund.

Smiling into the lens like all was right with the world.

She'd been beautiful.

"Is that your mother?" I looked down at Molly, who only sighed. I looked at the photo again. I'd meant the dog, but the term could have been applied to both subjects. "I'm sorry."

I wasn't sure who the apology was for, only that I was truly sorry.

I sat on the cement step outside, my rage completely dissolved along with my energy, watching Molly curl up on the grass as I pulled my phone out of my back pocket. Remembering Ed's card, I gingerly unfolded the ruined jacket to slip it from the inside pocket.

"Census Canada," was the answer.

I hadn't thought at all about what I'd say.

"Hello?"

"This Ed?"

"Yes; can I help you?"

"This is Tom Wall. We met the other day?" I leaned an elbow on my knee, suddenly exhausted.

"Oh! Hi, Tom. What can I do for you?"

"Linda – the sick lady on the corner of Bois-Franc?"

"You talked to her, I take it?"

"I did, and she pointed me to the pup's owner."

"Oh! A happy ending."

"Not exactly."

"Oh."

I gave him the address. The basics of what had happened. I closed my eyes, suddenly sad as well as exhausted.

"I know the place," the bounce had left Ed's voice, too. "No answer when I was there."

"I – I put her in bed," I stammered. My voice was high. I'd have made fun of someone so emotional before.

Before.

I rubbed at my temple and realized Molly was at my feet. I rubbed her temples, too. It was comforting for both of us, I think.

"You say she passed while you were inside with her?"

"Yes."

"And that she'd asked you in?"

"Yes. She was – she couldn't move, really. She was yelling from upstairs; must've taken everything out of her to do that. And I told her I had her dog."

"Right. I'm sorry you've had to go through that, Tom."

I had no idea how to respond.

"Are you there, still?"

"Uh-huh. Not feeling so great, though. I'd like to take the pup and go home."

"Was – did you see anyone else there?"

"No."

"Hm. There was a boyfriend; his family thought he'd be where you are. It was on my route to check tomorrow."

"Oh, shit," I thought of the smell I'd first encountered as I approached the house. "Check the back yard," I said, my voice quiet. Tears threatening. "I didn't, but there's a smell."

Ed made a sound. "Tell you what; you head home and take it easy. I'll come see you after everything is taken care of."

I nodded, then muttered something in the affirmative.

"I'll have an officer with me; don't be alarmed."

Suddenly I was alert. "What? Why?

"No worries, Mr. Wall; it's just procedure. We'll need your statement to close the file."

"Tom," I said blankly.

"You OK to walk home, Tom?"

I nodded again. "I called the dog Molly."

He paused. "Uh – oh! That was her owner's name."

"I found out after. Then the woman – the *person* Molly – called her "enny,' but I don't know what that meant. Because her jaw – her face is -" I sobbed, then. Something I'd never heard myself do.

"It's alright, Tom. Go home."

"Now I can't even call the dog by its *name*."

I sounded like a toddler. I sounded like a toddler trying to put everything they felt into one complaint but failing.

"It's a girl pup?"

"Uh-huh," I blubbed.

"Jenny, maybe? Penny?"

"Penny?" I asked Molly, but there was no head tilt. "Molly," I tried, and there it was.

"I think it'd be a real nice tribute to keep calling her Molly," Ed's voice was distant and I realized I'd let the phone lower from my ear.

"I can't do this," I muttered. Again.

"Tell you what, you just stay put and we'll get you taken care of, too."

And there it was, surging back: rage. It was almost a relief, cascading over me in a hot wave. I took a deep breath. "No. I'm just a stupid old man. I'll see you at my place, Ed." I bit my cheeks to stop from screaming. Gripped the phone, hard, until I heard it crack.

"OK, Tom. Take it easy. See you later."

I hung up, then flipped the phone over instead of throwing it with all the strength I had. A small crack had appeared under the case.

I picked Molly up. I was fuming. I held her gently, mindfully, and walked. I remembered my coat and I kept going. Leaving it behind. I looked up at heavy-bottomed clouds. Breathed in.

Breathed out.

And said, "Fuck this."

I looked down at Molly. "We're going to spend whatever time I have just eating bacon and being slobs. I'm not doing this anymore."

She raised her head, barked once.

I looked up again. "Hear me? I'm done. Whatever waits, it can't be as bad as *that*," I thrust a finger in the direction of Molly's former home. Molly's home. Then I breathed in the fresh air – air less polluted than it had been in over a hundred years, according to the papers – and enjoyed the walk home.

CHAPTER 17 – FLOOD

It started before I was even fully asleep; I was aware of the dog curled warmly in my armpit, and of the sound of my breath. But I could see the levels as though I was looking at a massive apartment building cleaved in half. The floors blurred at their boundaries, and there was movement there, as if those on each level could traverse the borders. Like it was mesh instead of cement and steel.

I squinted in my effort to see details, studied one level at a time because it felt important, though I couldn't have said why.

The scenes on the levels near the bottom reminded me of movies about massive ships, with workers slaving in the lower berth where the light couldn't reach over hungry coal fires, endlessly shoveling fuel into the mouths of perpetual flames. It got increasingly lighter as I focused higher, until the scene somewhere near the middle looked familiar. The level was higher and wider, with more movement, too. There were too many figures to track, too many connections to fathom. It was *solid*. It was *life.*

I inhaled sharply, the sound echoing in the blackness around me. In that moment I became aware that I was floating in a blackness more complete than I'd ever known, and yet my own thoughts seemed to echo. I scanned the lower levels again. If that middle section was life, what evil was *that?*

"Hell?" I questioned aloud, softly, but the word echoed, pulsating around me with gathering intensity until I was swatting at it around my head like a swarm of angry bees. It only subsided, fading into nothing, when I felt I could stand it no longer.

I peered at the middle section again. Tried to move closer. Wanting – something. Wanting to be in it. Wanting to belong there. But I remained stationary; invisible boundaries holding me back.

Dare I look upward? If I could get no closer to life, would I even be allowed to look upon the levels of ascension? I flinched before I tried it. Anticipating being struck, I suppose, by a bolt of lightning, either real or metaphorical, for the attempt.

But I *could* see higher, and just that much had tears flowing over my cheeks. I couldn't make out details, but there were hints. Glimpses of impossible lightness, unimaginable peace. It got brighter and brighter, more and more obscure, until the levels disappeared in a monolithic burst of light at the highest point.

I wept over the existence of the light. I remember that. But what I saw – those obscure details – were fading long before the dream was over.

It took enormous effort to tear my eyes away from the light, but I did, for there was a cold brush of air at my neck.

Suddenly, I could hear my heart.

My breath came faster.

And then I saw something else; moving balls of light on the outside of the levels, trailing glittering paths behind them as they moved between the levels effortlessly. I leaned forward, needing to see them more clearly, and without hesitation, the entire scene zoomed in. My heart thudded in my ears. But I *could* see them - beings of light. Pure. Painfully... perfect. Then one stopped.

And looked at me.

I tried to shrink back but was held fast as it approached, and soon it was behind me, warm. Comforting, at first, but turning cold as it guided me back, just a bit. Let me glimpse that living level again. Let me see her – that one person I had an undeniable connection to. Inseverable – and I'd tried.

I saw my Louise-Anne.

She was bent over someone – someone fading, barely there, and the look of empathy on her beautiful face drew a sob from my chest.

At the sound, she turned her head, and for one sweet second, our eyes met.

And the force at my back pulled me downward, swiftly.

"No!" I cried, reaching, failing.

She walked toward me – toward the edge, peering into the blackness to find me, and said, "Daddy?"

The pounding of my heart swelled in my ears at the sound of her voice saying that one, sweet word. But then the word echoed and faded, hindered by the speed at which we fell – the ball of light and I, until I was face-to-face with a level that felt familiar, too. Not because I'd lived it in the physical sense, but because my soul had dwelt there, even as I'd lived.

We'd stopped. The deafening beat of my heart had stopped, too.

"Am I dead?" My voice echoed, hollow in the blackness.

"Watch," came the answer.

I watched them working, sweating and grimacing in the steam and heat. I watched them scream as layers of shiny, raw flesh melted from their bones. I watched them contort and burn and die, grasping for finality but never finding purchase, only to be renewed and begin to work again.

Too blind to make progress.

Too lost to know they could be found.

"Look up." The words came at my right ear with a whisper of breath that made the hairs on the back of my neck stand up.

Clenched by fear, I raised my eyes up, up to that brighter, bigger level. My daughter no longer looked over the edge, but the edge itself, the lightness of it – it was sheer desire.

"Now look ahead."

I shook my head, neck at an angle, tensing all over. "Please," I begged.

There was a pressure at the back of my skull. "Look forward, Thomas." The voice had changed. It was low. It was dark.

"No," I whined, feeling the heat of the fires. Fearing the lick of the flame, the intertwining, the shimmering transformation of myself and of the fire, together, at last.

But then my head was wrenched forward with incomprehensible strength and I was seeing it all and I was crying out in fear and defeat and regret and oh, God, I belonged within it. I hung my head as tears streaked my face and simmered off in steam.

"You decide, Thomas."

I was let go.

I cried, the sounds of my sorrow echoing around me, and then I pushed back, away from my fate. I peered around myself, desperate as I floundered. "Decide?" I cried, uncaring that I sounded weak.

Knowing I was.

"There is only one chance to see her, Thomas. One

chance to do some of your work on that level rather than *here*. One chance to regain some of what is already lost."

The weight of the ultimatum pressed on me like an avalanche. "That's not fair!"

"That doesn't matter."

"What?" I was yelling, then. "How can it not matter?"

"Because you choose, Thomas. You always have. You chose it all in the beginning, and you chose to keep going, to stay the same, and now you have the chance to choose again."

"You saying I chose the life I was given?" Laughter boiled out of me and I turned my back to the levels. Looked into the blackness, feeling the satisfaction of being lost. "Why wasn't I given the choice when I was a baby and being beaten bloody?"

I gestured impotently into the darkness.

"How was *that* a choice?"

"Thomas."

I laughed until I cried. I cried and I cried, the tears of a lifetime liberated.

"Thomas." Softer, then.

I buried my face in my hands and curled into a ball. Floated like that, wishing for that to be my destiny. For weightless darkness to be my fate, and nothing else.

"You have a choice *now*. As for the rest, all will become clear... *if* you choose correctly."

I looked into the black expanse again, then turned to see it in the distance - the metaphor of existence. "Is this a game to you?"

There was laughter.

"Is it *funny?*"

"No."

"I don't know what to do," I cried.

"You decide."

"I don't know how." And then I said the thing I'd never allowed myself to say, no matter what. Because of pride or stubbornness or ignorance, I can't say, now. It isn't important, anyway. What is important is that finally, I let it come. *"I need help."*

And then everything went black, and I was cradled rather than floating in nothing. And two words were whispered before I awoke in my bed and sprang up to get the letter from Louise-Anne and open it, Molly barking, high-pitched, the whole time:

"Then, ask."

CHAPTER 18 – AFTERMATH

It started quietly.

If circumstances had been different, I wouldn't even have noticed it right away. Would have passed the stiffness in my back off as a worsening of common side effects of long hours and mounting stress.

Could have blamed a frantic schedule, with kids, ex-husband, house and work – the heaviest of my burdens – for the fatigue that weighed on me with increasing insistence. Could have ignored the niggling whisper from my subconscious.

Stop, it said. *Pay attention!*

I knew.

Stop, Lou-Anne.

I felt it in my bones and in the way my movements stiffened. I wore my mask and the full ensemble of protective equipment, changing it frequently, thanks to an overabundance of gear to make up for the shortage when it all started. I wore it to protect *them*, though, instead of the other way around.

You're sick.

Maybe it was just the flu.

I threw myself into the daily grind; Each day I went

home and checked through the kid's homeschool assignments. I made dinners and sorted mail and drank tea. I took Tylenol for the never-ending headache and Ibuprophen for the fever and inflammation.

Because there was a fever. And swelling at my joints.

Lou-Anne.

I wore my mask all the time, telling the kids I was around too much; that I needed to protect them, too.

Beck frowned when we did the exchange, eyeing my mask and reminding me of an old sepia-colored photo of his grandfather in Germany, whose temper was fabled to be as stern as his military upbringing. We named Mads for him, but true to my boy's sunny nature, he proved the name to be just that: a way to honor an ancestor whose disposition, thankfully, did not accompany the title.

"Just taking precautions," I said, before he could ask.

"Why now?"

I shrugged. "I've always been careful at work; I guess I just decided to be careful all the time, for the kids."

His frown didn't waver, but he ushered the kids into his apartment. Then he surprised me. He closed the door behind himself and stepped forward. "Are you OK?"

I instantly broke out in a sweat. Beck was nothing if not observant, especially when it came to a person's well-being. It was in his gut as well as his profession.

"You're not."

I let out a breath. Rolled my eyes. "I might have a flu or something. I'm just tired."

He immediately put a hand around my back, his fingers going for my spine. I ducked out of reach.

"Stop it, Beck!"

He frowned into my eyes.

"What?"

"Let me."

I sighed. Held back tears.

"I still care about you, you know."

Let one fall.

"And it's better to know. The kids -"

Lou-Anne.

They were teaming up on me; my ex and my inner voice.

I let him.

He went to reach around my waist again, but it was too close. Almost intimate. So, I turned. Closed my eyes as he examined me. Turned back to him when he stopped.

He looked puzzled. Shook his head.

"What?"

"I can't tell."

I let the words sink in. Let them buoy me up, just for a moment. Let myself hope. Maybe it *was* the flu.

"You know that could just mean it's early. Do you have stiffness?"

"Beck -"

"Anything else with your joints?"

"I'd tell you if -"

"You need to get tested, Lou."

The tears refused to be held any longer.

He hugged me.

I let him.

Then he held me at arm's length, meeting my eyes in that way he had; eyebrows raised. The *I mean business* look that had always made me feel like a child being scolded.

"OK," I gave in.

"You'll get it back quickly -"

"I know."

He sucked in a breath. "Of course, you do. I'm sorry."

We looked at each other.

"Do you want me to do it? I have a kit in the truck." His eyes said he knew the answer.

I shook my head. "I'll do it at work myself."

"And you'll let me know."

I nodded. "Don't tell the kids. Not yet."

"It'll be alright, Lou. We've come this far."

I chuckled. He still talked as though we were a team. I wiped at my cheeks, sniffling. "Thank you. I'm sorry."

"You don't need to say that. Just – just be OK, Lou. We need you."

Jessie was yelling inside.

He smiled, then went in, and I stood there for a minute. Part of me had known he'd bring it to a head as soon as he saw me. Part of me was relieved.

But most of me was terrified.

That little whispering voice, at least, was silenced.

CHAPTER 19 – SUN

Father? Dad? Stranger?

Thomas,

I don't know what you are to me, exactly, but I know who you are. My mother told me everything she knew about you; it was part of her recovery. And then I did my research back when I was a teenager, still curious. Still holding on to some fantasy that you were something more than what she said you were.

A criminal.

Uncaring.

Mentally ill.

Without remorse.

An adulterer.

A deadbeat dad.

I found nothing to counter the labels, however. Quite the opposite.

I'm sure you know Mom isn't the most stable person in the world – but she tries. She said nice things, too. But the fact that you abandoned us is heavier evidence than flimsy sentiments from a woman who was likely high when you met, and only in the early stages of her recovery when you left.

Regardless, a hard fact remained: in addition to all the other things I knew you to be, you were irrevocably something else.

My father.

And now, you've reached out. But it's cold. Don't reach if you don't want me to grab on, Thomas. Our genes unite us, but I owe you nothing.

If you want any sort of relationship with me, I need you to prove it. Answer my questions.

1) Why was a life of crime more attractive than being a father?

2) Where are you, now?

3) Who are you, now?

4) What do you want from me?

5) Do you care what I want from you?

Again, prove it.

If nothing else, the current state of the world proves that life is short, and time is cruel. Don't wait too long.

You have two grandchildren.

Lou-Anne

I stared at the letter for a long time. I re-read it countless times, over and over, then parts of it that stood out; *Don't wait too long... what do you want?... prove it.*

Shame crept into my heart like a dirty secret. Blood rushed to my face.

The temptation of the old, tried and true response reared up. I wanted to be angry. But the acknowledgement of it quickened my heartbeat and lunged in my stomach.

It was familiar, but that didn't mean it was right.

Molly put a paw on my thigh, making me jump. I looked down at her, confused. As though her presence was a surprise all over again. "How long have you been there?" I patted her head. I sat hard on the linoleum, still working to come back to reality, but part of me lingered in the past. In the letter from my daughter that asked so much, but not nearly enough. Not even close to what she deserved.

And...*you have two grandchildren.*

I gulped, tears springing to my eyes.

Two grandchildren. How old? How many years have they *lived without a grandfather? What do* they *know of me?*

I'd abandoned them, too.

"Shit," I cried, my face in my hands. Molly climbed into my lap and poked her long snout at my hands. I put a palm on her back, laughing a little. "Thank you, Molly."

She settled back, then curled up on my legs, seemingly happy to nap.

"Do you know I don't deserve you?" I whispered.

I shook my head. It was true, and yet, there she was.

I knew I needed to answer Lou-Anne's letter, and I needed to do it in that moment, without hesitation. But was it too late? Hadn't I already answered, by not answering at all? Not even *opening* her letter? I frowned down at the pup. The tears kept coming, but they felt like an indulgence.

What if she got sick? What if she's gone already? What if her kids -

It was too much. I covered my mouth as I sobbed. "I'm so sorry," I cried. Pathetic...but openly and acceptingly. I had been pathetic for so long but fought it. Masked it... for what? Pride? Bravado?

Sheer stubbornness?

I took Molly into my arms and she grunted a bit as I stood, then settled into our football hold as I went for a pen.

I had to smile when I opened the old whiskey cabinet, suddenly grateful. "Thank you," I said quietly. I took down my notebook and opened it to a clean page. I stared at it.

Then I took it to the table. But I didn't sit; I brewed a coffee instead, thinking. Letting the words come together in my mind before I attempted to bring them into reality.

Planning.

Molly was content in my arms. I listened to the coffee drip, my eyes on the early morning scenery. The mist that clung to the grass, the dreamy kaleidoscope of orange, pink and purple clouds, inspired by the rising sun.

Then, ask.

The two final words of my dream. I sharply inhaled, my eyes widening. Molly perked up. I looked into her eyes.

"Will you help me?"

I had to start somewhere.

She licked my mouth.

"Blech!" I chuckled. My eyes went again to the brightening sky. I thought of the visit with Ed and a young police officer the afternoon before, when I'd given my statement about the death of Molly's owner, whose full name was Molly Anne Mitchell, I'd learned. Anne like Louise-Anne.

They had found her boyfriend in the back yard, naked and splayed out, ravaged by the sun.

They said they'd seen similar circumstances; some went mad with the pain...

They had thanked me for my help. And when they left, they told me to call anytime. The young officer – Jonas – had given me his card and shook my hand. And then Ed had lingered, shaking my hand with his gloved one, too, and saying, "Was it you who left groceries for Linda Patterson?"

I thought that if the time came, they'd help me, too.

The coffee was finished. Molly was asleep again,

I thought of the levels. Of *my* level. Considered my circumstances, tears flowing yet again.

And then, my eyes still on the sky, sent out a whispered plea, "Please help me."

CHAPTER 20 – BREAKING GROUND

The phone rang as I picked up the pen.

I frowned at it as it buzzed against the countertop. Looked up at the ceiling. "Is this a test?"

Molly wriggled until I let her down, then stood on her back legs, her long body stretched comically toward the phone.

"What?"

She yipped.

"OK, OK," I grabbed it. It was a number I didn't recognize.

"Hello?"

There was a deafening clearing of the throat.

"Who is this?" I was instantly on alert; the person at the other end was surely sick. Most likely at the lockjaw stage.

"'ong Waw?"

It was a man's voice. Gravelly. Familiar.

"Jed?"

"Cang you cong o'er?"

"Jed Baker, right?"

A sound of frustration.

I laughed. "You can't blame me for making certain, Jed.

Not after last time."

There was a pause, and then a sound that could have been the result of laughter or tears.

"Jed, at the risk of staring down the barrel of your shotgun again, I'm going to assume you're asking me to come over."

"Uh-huh."

I wondered absently how a person could sound so angry with just a short utterance of confirmation.

"OK; give me an hour, though, Jed. I have something to finish, here."

A sound that was certainly crying, that time.

I sighed, my eyes on the blank page I'd turned to in my notebook. "It's urgent, huh?"

Sniffling sounds.

"OK. I'll come now."

"'ank you, 'ank you, 'ong. Horry."

I didn't know if the last was meant to be *sorry* or *hurry,* but both seemed far out of character for old Jed.

"Oh! There'll be a dog with me; is that alright?"

There was a garbled utterance that could've been anything, but I took the tone to be accommodating enough.

"See you in a few, Jed."

He hung up.

My eyes went to the notebook again, then to the letter. I touched it lightly. "I'm sorry to make you wait again, darlin'."

Molly was waiting by my shoes.

"How do you always know?"

She stood, wagging her tail.

"OK, OK," I found myself pushing the motorized cart to the side. I was sure I'd been doing it since I'd come back to my body with a new purpose, but it wasn't until that moment that I really looked at it. I slid into my shoes, frowning at the beast of a thing. "You still here?"

I toyed with the idea of leaving it where it was...a lingering obstacle, just in a different way. A reminder.

But I'd already begun to see; there were possibilities in life that couldn't be transferred to the dead. I needed my body to do the things I was meant to do, and for that reason, I'd been restored. I couldn't forget that. Couldn't forget what it meant.

Couldn't stop learning what it meant to the others I was meant to... *serve.*

I pressed my lips together, then got to work. I unlocked the wheels and steered the thing manually into the living room. I put it in the corner beside the useless television, then stood back to look at it. "Don't need you anymore," I muttered.

Molly barked from the door.

It didn't feel right. Not yet. "But... thank you?"

I nearly laughed.

"What the fuck has happened to me?" I shook my head and went back to the door, scooping Molly up and kissing her on the head. Smelling that puppy smell.

Knowing I'd made fun of myself out of habit. Knowing I'd only walked away from the cart after appreciating it... appreciating the significance of not needing it... because *that* had felt right.

The door was open at Jed's. Molly did her telltale wriggle before we went in, scampering to the grass first. I waited, peering into the gloom through the crack in the door with some hesitance. On the phone, he'd been *crying*. And it was obvious he'd worsened; his jaw hadn't been locked the last time I'd seen him.

"Hey, Jed," I called, leaning into the crack a little. "Molly's just making a pitstop on your lawn. We'll be right in."

I looked at the pup squatting comically, eyes on me, and realized I hadn't brought anything to clean up after her. I leaned into the darkness again, noting the stale quality to the air as I did. "Might need to borrow a plastic bag from you; sorry about that. This is all new to -"

"'us' get the huck ing here!" came the shout of a reply, and I recoiled. But it was a relief, too. The man was still alive. And kicking, by the sound of it.

And he'd officially invited me in.

Molly slipped into the house before I knew she was beside me. I shrugged and followed suit. The place was dark. I stood awkwardly in the doorway for several moments, wondering mundane things. Like where he was. And if I should take my shoes off. It was Molly's bark from a hallway to the left that brought me back to myself. *Fuck it,* I thought, leaving the shoes on and starting down the hallway.

"Jed?"

"Ing here!" There was some pissed-off muttering after, but I understood none of it.

I halted by the first door with a light on; my heart galloping in my chest as I tensed. It was a bathroom; even peripherally I could see that. But the increased heartrate was due to the vision of Molly – Molly Anne – that popped into my head. My pup's original owner slumped against the bathtub, dying with one hand on her pup and one curled around my own.

I exhaled loudly when I brought myself to look. It was

stark and white and empty.

"Jed?" I called out again. As though I needed to warn him I was coming again, in case he needed to make himself ready in some way. But he didn't answer that time.

I found him in a bedroom lit only by the open window, toward which his head was turned. I could see the gaping jaw and elongated features in his profile, but there was something else, too. The man's cheekbones appeared to be deformed, rising out beyond his nose like blades and intensifying the effect of hollow eye sockets.

"Hey, Jed."

He turned his head to see me. I had to stop myself from jumping back. The cheekbone on the previously-hidden side drooped down instead of out, like the other, his eyelid on that side yawning downward in an exaggerated fashion. The overall effect evoked an image of some unseen force stretching his face on the diagonal. "Oh!" was all I said.

"I 'ow," he waved my reaction away. "I'ng a hucking 'onsger!"

It was almost funny – the stubborn anger of the man refusing to fade in even the worst of situations – but landed as disturbing instead.

"I'm so sorry," I said, quietly.

He breathed laboriously, eyes peering up at me, smile stretched to grotesque proportions. It was all I could do not to run.

Finally, he raised an arm to point at a paper beside the bed.

Molly appeared again, whimpering quietly from the entrance.

"What is it?" I turned back.

She danced a bit on the spot, then took off again.

"I'll be right back," I looked back at Jed, whose eyes had closed as much as they were able. The yawning, pale lower lid of the worst side appeared dry and I grimaced, imagining the discomfort.

I jumped when he patted the paper again. Then I took it. The man was dying. Molly could wait.

It was just a sheet, marked heavily with blue ink on both sides. The one facing me bore one sentiment, repeated dozens of times: *I just want to die.*

I glanced at Jed, who appeared to be dozing, then flipped the sheet over. The writing on that side was neater – surely older, too, because it said this:

I'm starting to think I can make it. Maybe it's not too late. I've done an injustice to myself and to Lorna by spending my days between her death and now in misery. I want to show her I can do better, now that I'm faced with what I've wanted for so long.

I want to be proud of the man I've been when I see her again...

There were thoughts added at the sides and in the corners, but the writing there was in varied states of legibility. The clearest said, *I just need to get over the hump.* The others were less positive: *How does one survive the lockjaw stage? I've found a way to eat, but it nearly kills me each time I try it,* and *This thing means to take over. I don't know...*

The rest was just a mess of scribbles.

I flipped it again. *I just want to die.* Overlapping and traced over and over and making tiny rips in the paper. Wounds of repetition.

I tensed at the irony. The man had repented after years of misery. He'd intended to make things better, and instead, MARS-21 took hold and in a slow and unusually long dance, managing to twist his bones so fast in the final stage, and leave him unsuccessful in his plans.

And then there was me.

I shook my head. "I'm gonna help you, Jed."

He didn't move.

Inspired, I went into the hallway and toward the kitchen, which I'd glimpsed when I'd come in. Molly was pawing at the fridge and I opened it, expecting – what? A solution? A miracle? I wanted to help the man. I wanted to save him so he, too, could do what he'd decided, late as it was.

To do good.

But there was no miracle.

There was, however, bowl of something I couldn't identify right away. I could see through the saran wrap that the contents were brown. Against my suspicions, I reached for the bowl, then peeled the wrap off.

The sharp tang of mould hit my nostrils before I saw the film of it on the surface. But there was something else... chocolate? Yes. It was chocolate pudding.

Old chocolate pudding.

That's what he'd been eating.

Nearly frantic, I rifled through his cupboards, looking for more. By the time I was into the bottom cupboards, I was sweating. Not only were there no boxes of pudding mix, but I'd realized during my search that I hadn't seen milk, either.

The last cupboard, however, held paydirt: Dozens of chocolate pudding cups – the kind you bought in packages of four in the snack aisle – were lined up within.

"Yeah!" I punched the air. Molly wagged double-time.

The stuff was thick; too thick to try and feed him as it

was. I wondered if he'd started with the cups, then moved on to the boxes he could mix himself, so he could thin it out. "Ha!" I muttered, going back to a cabinet which contained plates and bowls.

Molly danced at my feet.

"No milk," I said, then glanced at the sink. Water would have to do. I worked the gelatinous pre-fabbed goop with a fork and water from the tap, a little at a time, encouraged as it finally came together as something Jed would be able to swallow, even with a jaw rusted open at its hinges. I would smear some at the back of his tongue…

I spilled some of it in my excitement as I carried it back to the room.

I paused outside the door, looking back at Molly, who sat at the mouth of the hallway.

"Coming?"

She curled up on the floor, resting her muzzle on her front paws.

I frowned.

I looked into the bedroom again.

Jed was still, but then he'd been sleeping. I watched for the rise and fall of his chest but saw no movement in the dim light. My eyes went to the window. It had clouded over.

I went to his bedside, the bowl of watery pudding heavy in my hand. "Jed?"

I waited. Held my breath.

I touched his shoulder and he jumped, making me jump, too. Watery pudding sloshed onto my fingers.

"Shit. I thought you were dead, old man!"

He raised his hand. Touched the spot on the bedside

table where his sheet of notes had been.

I just want to die.

"Nah," I sat on the edge of the bed. "I've figured out – actually, Molly helped me." I gazed fondly into the hallway. She helps a lot – anyway, I've made you some chocolate pudding."

The shake of his head was barely there, but I saw it.

"Come on, Jed. There's still time. Hang on, eh?"

His eyes moved slowly to meet mine.

"I read what you wrote. It's brave of you to want to survive this thing! To start something new for yourself. For the memory of your wife. Maybe for her..." I struggled, "her *soul*, too."

I thought of the levels. Of the dream that had fuelled me to open the letter from Louise-Anne, finally.

"It's not too late," I said.

To my dismay, a scant tear rolled down his better side to puddle on his protruding cheekbone as he shook his head.

"I can help, Jed. You might not believe this, but I've had an epiphany of my own recently."

He nodded calmly, eyes on mine.

"You – guess you could tell."

"'elk."

"Huh? Helk? Oh – *help*." Hope surged in my chest. "That's what I'm here for, Jed. I'm going to take care of you. Get you to a hospital -" I recalled the article I'd first read, the one that showcased Jed's animosity toward hospitals. "Oh. Wait; I'm sorry. No. I won't take you if you don't want to go."

He tried to squeeze his eyes shut in a show of frustration. I watched his epiglottis tremble as a broken wail came from his raw, exposed throat.

"No – Jed, everything is going to be OK." I spooned up some of the brown liquidy stuff from the bowl, but let it fall when he cried out again.

"'elk 'ee!" He cried, his eyes desperately on mine.

"*I'm trying!*" I heard impatience cut my words. Felt the old, but familiar heat at my temples.

"'ease," he cried, tapping on that spot on the table beside the bed again.

I want to die.

I scolded myself inwardly. *Fuck, Tom. You just can't stop messing up, can you?*

I put the bowl where his sheet of paper had been and let my shoulders slump. Let it come – the thought I'd been holding at bay in preference of hope. But it was pointless, because I knew the truth: I was there to help, but not to help him *live.*

I shook my head. *I don't know if I can do this. Not alone.* I looked toward the hallway. "Molly?"

The pup appeared in the doorway in seconds.

"*Now* you come."

She scampered to me, put her paws on my knees.

"I need help," I said, lifting her to the bed. She curled up at Jed's side instantly.

Jed made a noise of surprise, then went back to the wretched sounds of his crying.

Gently, gingerly, I placed his closest hand on Molly. And amazingly, his expression eased up a bit.

My emotions warred within me. What if he could live? What if – but no. I knew why I'd been brought back. I hated it, but I knew the necessity of it as the visage of the levels came back to me again. I needed to see Louise-Anne again, either on this, the living plane, or when we both left it. And I knew I had work to do.

I took Jed's other hand in my own. His face was a mask of relief.

"I'm sorry about before. I wasn't listening." I scanned the room as the sun came out from behind a cloud. A painting caught my eye – a boy fishing from the bank of a serene lake, its surface like glass. "You like fishing?" I looked back at Jed, who regarded me from behind half-closed lids. "I tie flies – well, I used to." I swore I could see his eyes brighten, if only a bit. "Too bad we couldn't see a way to being pals in this life, eh? I never had a good fishing partner; always thought of it more as a solitary thing, you know? But now I think – I think maybe it would have been nice to have a partner there. A friend."

It happened slowly – first, his eyes crinkled at the sides, and then he was making a choked noise and I sat up, terrified he was going in that second – that he was choking on his own spit as I reminisced about something he probably didn't give two shits about. But then, he was laughing.

"What?"

Molly raised her head and peered at him with as much confusion as I felt.

Jed was trying to say something.

"I can't hear you when you're laughing, you old fool."

"'ucking 'oftie!"

"What? Fucking...what? What's 'oftie'?" I'd heard the way the "s" sounded with the "oftie," then. "Softie?" A smile crept onto my lips. "You calling me a fucking *softie?*"

I wasn't even sure what it had meant, except that it was funny to him. And indeed, he was laughing again.

"Jesus, man. You lay here dying and you want to make

fun of something I shared with you… "

He howled as only he was able, mouth gaping in a grotesque smile, and near death.

"Weird what makes people laugh when they're dying," I muttered, and he patted the hand he held. I'd forgotten I was holding his. I watched him as he settled. "I'm glad I entertain you," I said, and I'm sure that if he'd had it in him, he would have taken off laughing again.

Molly rested her snout on his hip and his eyes drooped heavily.

"You know, Jed – I don't think you doing all the things you wrote about on that sheet of paper – I don't think the doing of them matters so much as the *desire* to, you know what I mean?"

His eyes softened.

"I think the intention itself…well, that's enough to take pride in, Jed. And enough to make your wife proud, too. I know she's there, waiting for you, old man. I've seen it."

That was it; he left his body on a rattling outbreath of air that spoke of gratitude and release. Final, beautiful release. I felt his pain go, too.

And then *I* was crying, elbows on my knees and face in my hands, just sobbing like a baby while Molly licked my arm worriedly.

I covered him like I'd covered the girl, then went to the kitchen. Saw the note I'd dropped on the counter with fresh eyes. Let myself acknowledge that, even though the type of helping I'd wanted to give was different than what had happened in the end, I *had* helped.

My eyes caught on another framed picture as I dialed Ed and waited for him to answer. That one was a photo – an old one of a boy with his father, fishing poles in hand.

"Tom?"

"Hey, Ed."

"This can't be good."

"Nope. Got another one for you."

Ed sighed. "Any reason this seems to be becoming a habit, Tom?"

"Only one I can think of is that I'm making up for bad decisions, Ed. Just trying to right some of the wrongs, you know?"

"Well, it doesn't sound fun, but I understand it. I'll call the police and we'll be there soon."

I gave him the address, then sat on the step and waited. Wondering, as Molly frolicked as though she were your everyday normal puppy in the grass, at the friendship the dead man inside and I could have had. If our good intentions hadn't come too late.

If things had been different.

CHAPTER 21 – EMERGENCE

"Let us give you a ride back?" Ed looked doubtful, even as the words came out.

I glanced warily toward the squad car. Evan Cromwell had accompanied my census officer friend, that day. It seemed serendipitous, almost, considering it had been Cromwell who'd arrested me the last time I'd come to visit Jed. But today, he'd only frowned at me before entering the place, more curiosity in his eyes than suspicion.

I shook my head. "Thanks, Ed, but I think Molly and I could use a walk." Molly looked up from the bone Cromwell had thrown her way.

"I keep some in the car; you wouldn't believe how often they come in handy," he'd muttered when Ed shot him a questioning look.

"I don't think he'll grill you," Ed glanced toward the door.

I gave a wry laugh. "You don't know him well, do you?"

Ed smiled. "Why *are* you here, Tom?"

Exhaustion rolled over my in a sickening wave. "I told you," I said as I rubbed at my eyes with my fingertips, "I want to -"

"I know; I remember what you said, but it doesn't entirely answer the question, does it? Even if you've made some sort of commitment to easing people's fears in the last moments of their lives – or something of that nature – how do you know when to... show up?"

I looked up at him. "You're interested in the semantics?"

He nodded toward the door. "He will be, too."

"Then I guess I'll wait until he's back out here. Save my breath," I grinned up at Ed, hoping for a break. He pursed his lips but said no more.

An ambulance arrived before Cromwell came out, but he met them at the door. He said a few words in a low voice to the two paramedics. I observed them curiously; I'd heard women had been heavily recruited for first responder positions due to the fact that they seemed less susceptible to the virus. As a result, the proportion of women versus men on the front lines had been significantly skewed. And here they were, proving it. Something like gratitude surged through me.

Once the paramedics had disappeared inside, fully dressed in protective garb and carrying a stretcher between them, Cromwell carried a handful of bagged items – I recognized the heavily-inked sheet of paper amongst them – to the squad car. Ed and I observed as he talked over the walkie for a few minutes.

"You two acquaintances, then?" Ed asked, quietly.

I smirked up at him. "You could say that. He knew me – knows me – from before."

Cromwell approached with heavy footfalls. He looked tired. He surprised me by taking a seat beside me on the step. He removed his hat and lowered his mask.

Ed's eyes widened over his mask. "Evan -"

Cromwell waved the concerns away before they were fully voiced. "Mr. Wall here has already had MARS-21. I'm fucking sick of masks."

I found myself asking the cop if he was alright.

He eyed me sideways. "What's gotten into you?"

Molly appeared at my feet. I reached down to pat the velvety fur of her head.

"Either you've entered a sadistic phase of your criminal activity, or you're trying to help the dying in some way."

"I assure you, I don't get any pleasure out of watching folks die."

He pressed his lips together. "I don't understand it, but I'm inclined to believe you, Tom."

My jaw dropped.

Cromwell gestured over his shoulder, toward the door. "I found the chocolate – goop – beside the bed. Saw the mess you made in the kitchen preparing it for him."

"Pudding."

"And Officer Stark -"

I raised my eyebrows. "Jonas?"

Cromwell's expression registered surprise. "Yes. Jonas. He gave me the full report on Miss Mitchell. Said they could tell you'd carried her to her bed, covered her up."

I shrugged.

"Lost a good jacket in the process," he finished.

Ed piped up. "He's been helping Linda Patterson, too. Left her some groceries the other day, and before she was taken to the hospital, she said it was Tom who'd helped her stay fed and hydrated.

"She went to the hospital?" My mind raced. I suddenly had the urge to go over to her house, see what I could do to ready it for her return.

Cromwell's frown deepened as he studied my face. "Spill, Wall."

My palms began to sweat. I'd never been good at maintaining calm during an interrogation. "What's the problem? You just said it; I haven't been doing anything wrong."

"I also mentioned the possibility of a darker purpose." Cromwell's glare didn't waver. "And don't take this the wrong way, Tom, but your rap sheet insists we ask."

I sighed. "I can't even do good for doing bad."

"It was you who did the crimes; you who built your reputation."

I shook my head. It was true. "Maybe that's why I'm trying to do some good now."

"It's late in the game for that."

I peered at him, incredulous. "You were right before; I was sick. *Really* sick. And – somehow – I came through it, better than ever."

"That's another thing; you used a cart to get around. In my experience, that type of decline doesn't usual rectify itself."

I lifted my left pantleg and pushed my sock below the ankle. The leg was still purplish, but even I was surprised at its appearance. It was mottled instead of the dark purple I'd become accustomed to. I was healing, even there.

"Holy shit," Ed murmured.

"It was twice this size, and dark purple before," I met his eyes. "Very nearly lost it. But somehow, I'm healthy." I looked to Cromwell as I let my pantleg fall. "But the virus was a bitch... look, I don't know why I'm here. It should have taken me, too. So, I decided I'm going to help folk who aren't so lucky."

"Still doesn't explain how you know who needs help, and

when to go to them," Ed voiced.

"And what you do to *help* them," Cromwell's eyes gleamed. "After all, they're dead by the time you're done."

I gritted my teeth against the familiar, hot rage that arose. He watched me, waiting. *He's testing you, Tom.* I took a deep breath. "If you think I'm helping them by speeding up their deaths, you're mistaken," I said through my teeth.

"Didn't say that, did I? There's no evidence of it."

I blew out an exhale and focused on the pup.

Ed cleared his throat. "So tell us, then. What happened today?"

I peered into the sky, hoping for some of that help I'd been promised. For *something* to get me through the sticky bits.

The paramedics had returned to the door, and we all turned to watch them maneuver the stretcher out and toward the ambulance, whose bubble lights still flashed lazily in blue and red.

Cromwell turned to me again, expectant.

"I hadn't heard from him since he called you when -" I looked at Cromwell, who nodded, a hint of a smile turning the corners of his lips upward. "Then today, he called me. I could tell he was really bad; I could barely understand him. But he asked me to come, so I did."

"Why would he do that after calling me the last time you showed up?"

I shook my head. "I told him that first time that I'd seen his story in the paper and wanted to see if I could help him in any way. Guess he remembered that. Besides, he knows I only live down the road." I gestured in the direction of my house.

"Just seems odd," Cromwell stared down at his feet, which were kicking patterns in the dirt.

"And Linda?" Ed asked.

"I told you – she helped me find the pup from her spot at the window. I went to talk to her the day I met you, to see if she knew the owner."

Ed nodded.

"She told me about Molly Mitchell; apparently the girl read to her."

Cromwell nodded, then.

"I don't know what else to tell you, guys."

One of the paramedics approached. "Please replace your mask, Evan; I need to talk to you."

Cromwell pulled his mask up over his nose and pinched it so it'd stay. "What's up, Shelby?"

The woman handed him a cell phone. "Here's his phone. Sorry, I was touching it before I knew what it was. It was underneath him."

"S'alright," Cromwell muttered, taking the phone and flipping it open. "I've got no reason to think anything criminal happened here today." His eyes flickered to mine.

The other woman approached. "Another call; this one from Luskville; we're the only unit responding in the area."

Shelby nodded, then looked at Cromwell again. "That was the worst case of facial deformity I've seen. He must've held on for as long as he could."

"Jed's always been stubborn," Cromwell answered, his eyes still on the phone. He stopped suddenly, then handed the phone to Ed as he looked up at the women. "Thanks, both of you. Keep safe."

The paramedics nodded, then were on their way.

Cromwell gestured for Ed to look at the phone. He took

it, frowning, then inhaled sharply. Cromwell gestured toward me, and Ed turned it so I could see the screen. The last call Jed had made had been to me. I took my own phone from my back pocket and opened my calls. The one from Jed matched the time on Jed's phone. I showed it to both men, who eyed each other darkly.

Cromwell nodded, handing the phone back to me. "Good."

"Yeah?" I felt as though I was getting away with something. Most likely the result of past experience.

Cromwell lowered his mask again, then folded his hands together between his knees.

"What's going on?"

The men exchanged another look, which ended with a nod from Ed.

Cromwell took a deep breath. "Tom, Ed's been telling me about – all of this – and I'm sure you know we're all short-staffed -" he rubbed his forehead, "truth is, we've got far more work than we can handle, even teaming up as we have been with the government folks," he gestured toward Ed.

I laughed out of sheer nervousness. "What are you getting at?"

"We've been authorized to deputize a few people in the neighborhoods – with limited authority and mandate, of course – to keep an eye on things."

I laughed again but stopped short. "Wait -"

Cromwell looked at me levelly. "We're desperate, Tom."

My smile faded.

"We can't keep up." He looked toward the road. "Sometimes whole families die and there's no one to notify anyone."

"Shit," I uttered.

"We don't have enough people on the ground to do check-ins," Ed added, "so we find ourselves relying on citizens to eventually call these events in. Meanwhile, mass funerals are taking place because so many people have become disconnected from each other. Out of fear or apathy or just plain ignorance – the data isn't there, yet – but nobody comes forward to claim the bodies. It's all we can do to keep the records straight."

"And here you are, already doing the work we're having to beg others to take on," Cromwell gestured helplessly with his hands.

"You want to deputize *me?*" I felt like laughing again but was too gobsmacked to allow it.

Cromwell pulled what looked to be a leather billfold from an inside pocket, and handed it to me. "If you're going to be visiting neighbors anyway – regardless of your reasons – this'll help you, and you'll be helping us. There'll be full compensation -"

I flipped the folded leather open to reveal a badge, the words "Deputized Neighborhood Officer" encircling the emblem. I peered up at Ed, then at Cromwell. Molly had sat up and was looking at me, her eyes bright. "Are you two - nobody's gonna believe this!"

Ed's expression remained sober. "You'd be surprised. People... change with this monster, and in the end, they can get desperate. It's a scary time, Tom."

I shook my head. It was surreal.

"And of course, we'll be there to help. All you have to do, really, is do a summary report each day, and full reports on events like today's. We give you all necessary contact to have things taken care of – it's straightforward."

I shook my head. "This is crazy."

"Crazy times," Cromwell agreed.

"But will you do it?" Ed asked.

Molly barked impatiently, making all three of us laugh.

I looked into the sky, sending a question out. *Does this work?* I was an ex-con with a reputation for violence that clung to me like a bad smell. Would accepting the men's offer amount to denial? A smack in the face to those I'd done wrong? That wouldn't go any distance to improving my own fate.

Or would it benefit my new cause? If nothing else, it would keep me accountable. There was no denying the badge would afford me a sense of authority – a reason to knock on doors and ask questions...

As bizarre as it was, I found myself nodding. "I'll do it. And - I appreciate the opportunity."

Cromwell nodded, but looked a bit dubious. "Someone will bring you the paperwork to review and sign ASAP. And it starts on a trial basis: three months."

I nodded, thinking it was likely all I'd need.

Thinking of Louise-Anne, and wondering how I could make her fit into what promised to be busy days coming.

Knowing I had to, lest it all be for nothing...in my own heart, at least.

CHAPTER 22 – SURGE

"Come on," Ed gestured toward the squad car again.

I shook my head.

"Come on; you look wiped out." He smiled, then. "I'll let you ride shotgun."

Huh. Never imagined that *would happen.*

I couldn't deny the exhaustion that had come over me, like the crash after a high. "Twist my arm," I muttered as I stood. Molly was already walking with Cromwell toward the car.

The ride turned out to be useful for reasons not related to my exhaustion; I figured out my next move.

"You said Linda's already been taken to the hospital?"

Ed leaned forward from the back and hooked his fingers through the metal mesh that separated us. "Yep; Gatineau."

"Why not Hull?" I craned my neck, frowning toward him.

He shook his head. "You haven't heard? The one in Hull's been transformed to act as a diagnostic and recovery center."

I nodded. "Right; I read that. I guess I couldn't believe it. Does that mean confirmed cases that need care go solely to Gatineau?"

Cromwell nodded, that time. "It works really well; the sick are funnelled to an entirely separate building from where people are tested, and then go back for rehab and recovery."

"You'd think one hospital to care for the really sick wouldn't be enough," I glanced between the men.

"At first, both were overrun, but now -" Cromwell's words hung in the air. I scratched Molly's ears as I digested his words in the ensuing silence.

"What are the rules for visitors?"

"You want to go see Linda?"

I nodded.

"Even with your shiny new badge, you need your status card; if you're confirmed tested and immune – in other words, you have antibodies to prove you've already been sick – you can visit at Gatineau between two and four every afternoon."

I'd read about the status card, too. "What about those who haven't been sick?"

"They aren't allowed in either hospital; there's no telling who's carrying the virus. Even if they're tested and prove healthy, without antibodies they could be infected at any moment."

"Shit," I muttered.

"It's controversial," Ed said quietly as he rested back in his seat. "Families are separated; the sick die without a familiar face, most of the time."

"Why not just equip people correctly?"

Cromwell shook his head. "There's still the rationing for gear; the majority goes to care centres – senior's homes, hospitals – for staff."

I shook my head. "Haven't we gotten past the shortage?"

He nodded. "But there's still the fear. While it's unlikely there'll be another wave, which is entirely due to the fact that there aren't enough of us to transmit it like before, everyone's being cautious."

I couldn't say anything. In my mind, the fear was warranted.

"Hey," Ed leaned forward again. "Gatineau is looking for volunteers – recovered victims of MARS-21 who are willing to donate blood for studies – but you'd also have the opportunity to do some work with patients."

"What sort of work?" My mind boggled at the benefits one – even one such as myself – could garner in the wake of an event that cut the population in half. But the truth was that *I* hadn't survived it, either. I wondered if I'd even test positive for the antibodies at that point, given my "restoration".

"Checking in on patients, maybe chatting a bit with them, doing simples things like wiping drool and – I don't know – just letting them know they aren't alone, I guess. In small ways."

"It matters," Cromwell added, and I looked between the men, both of whose expressions suggested they'd had experience to convince them it was true.

"Maybe I'll look into that," I muttered as we pulled into my driveway.

"They could use *anybody* at this point," Cromwell replied, but looked immediately regretful. "Sorry; I just mean -"

I laughed. "No worries. You've deputized me, Cromwell. Sorta speaks louder than your doubts about me. And I don't blame you for those."

I saw surprise light in his eyes. "Call me Evan, Tom. Alright?"

Molly put her paws on the window, her back feet dancing impatiently on my thighs. "I'll go to the Hull hospital – care centre – tomorrow; when should I be home to sign the papers for you guys?"

"We'll call you," Cromwell – Evan – answered.

"Thank you, Tom," Ed piped up as I got out, and I raised my hand in a wave as the car backed out.

Will wonders never cease?

Molly had already started sniffing around on the grass, so I sat on the step and watched her.

I thought about how the day had started – about the dream, if that was what it was, and about waking up and bolting to read Louise-Anne's letter. Finally.

And then a surge of urgency flowed through me. I needed to respond. "Come on," I called the pup and we went inside. Images of sandwiches or even better – *burgers* – danced in my head, but I sat at the table first, taking up the pen before I could get distracted again.

Dear daughter,

Thank you for answering me. You're right; you aren't obligated! Not in the least. So again, thank you.

Your questions are all fair, and if you'll meet with me, I'd be happy to answer all of them, and anything else you want to ask me, too.

These days, life is too short to put important things off anymore. I am so very sorry that I wasted so much time when it came to you: the most important person in my life, even though you weren't in my life, really.

I take responsibility for everything, Louise-Anne. It was all me – everything was, and I'm paying for it now in my old age. Wondering how I managed such a terrible thing as to throw the best things in life to the side in favour of some twisted selfish agenda that I honestly don't understand, anymore.

Please, let me try and make amends. I'll take any contact

you feel comfortable with, with thanks.

Your regretful father,

Tom

I frowned at it. I'd written it fast and without thinking; surely, I could do it better. Smoother. But no; the point was to *do* it, and I had. The only thing left was to mail it.

Frowning, I reached for the envelope to find the return address. I'd first contacted her through an online messaging system, so hadn't known her location.

How had I ignored the address?

I looked at it, then. "Huh," I said, causing Molly to look up from her little bed in the corner. "Good Hope Senior's Home." I recalled a flash I'd had of her, leaning over someone. Caring for them. But if that wasn't a shock, the next part was: *Wakefield, QC.*

A rush of emotion surged through me: guilt, disbelief, joy... but regret overshadowed it all.

Wakefield was a pleasant thirty-minute drive from my house.

CHAPTER 23 – STRETCH

I lay awake for half the night.

Molly was tucked into my armpit, softly snoring, but I was unable to let go of the crazy carousel of thoughts cycling repeatedly through my head.

She's been so close, for so long.

I'd left her mother and her in Kingston, Ontario, it was true, but Jane had voiced her desire to go back to Nova Scotia so many times I'd assumed she'd done just that. At least, that's where I'd pictured her and the baby in my mind over the years. And for all I knew, that's what had happened...

But now she was in Wakefield. For how long? Had she moved there with her husband? Was she married? Having children certainly did not necessitate a marriage bond...

And... she was taking care of the sick? I wondered if she was a nurse – or a doctor. Something in the core of me shuddered at the thought of her having contact with the virus on a regular basis.

Maybe she's had it and beat it already.

It was a comforting thought, and one that kept coming around to soothe my feverish anxieties. But regardless of its persistence, I wasn't convinced.

Finally, after I glanced at my phone for the time – 3 AM –

I refused to see anymore; psychologically batting the thoughts away in hopes of inviting sleep in, instead. I'd be signing new work papers that day, and heading to the center to try and get my – what had Cromwe - *Evan* called it? A *status card.*

I worked to release the tension from my muscles; jaw, then shoulders. Neck, eyes, abdomen. Images of fishing began to take over and I let them, because it felt so good to be there, in the river. Cool water against my waders, birds tootling in the trees.

I finished reeling my line in and scowled at the fly on the business end. It hadn't even attracted a good hit. I needed to switch it out. I gazed at the kit that hung from my vest, taking in the colours of my handmade lures with a surge of excitement. Considered the frog, then looked thoughtfully at the clouds. The day was cool; the Walleye were surely sticking to the floor. I let the case dangle without opening it and reached for my hat. I needed a sinker.

Once I'd cast again, enjoying the sharp, repetitive sound of the line and subtle *plop!* of the fly as it landed, I closed my eyes. I visualized the fly in the water, watched it sink, beams of sunlight filtering through the depths and lighting up bits of debris and miniscule, live creatures as it plunged.

And then suddenly, it was pitch dark and my hands were strangely empty.

I opened my eyes, but the darkness persisted. I cried out, hoping for an echo. Desperate to get my bearings. But there was nothing; even the sound of my cry was sucked away and swallowed up before it could travel. But there was something – I touched my chest and then my thighs. I was still in the waders. Still knee-deep in the river. I listened, holding my breath, but there were no sounds of birds, no breezes fluttering the leaves.

And the liquid that surged around my legs was very

warm.

"Thomas."

The word came to me as though from a distance, but it made me jump. I peered around blindly, trying to cry out, but my answering call was sucked up and silenced as soon as it came out.

"Over here, Thomas."

I knew that voice. The hairs on the back of my neck stood on end.

"Where are you?" The words were grabbed and stolen again. I tried to face in the direction of the voice.

"Come," it echoed back, closer.

The flow around my legs was intensifying. I buckled my knees in an effort to keep my balance against it. And then it was increasing in temperature, too. I could feel sweat beading on my upper lip and dripping down my back.

"Hurry."

I turned to the right. It had come from there. I tried to set off at a run, but the first step was a lesson; the viscous fluid that assaulted my lower legs was thick. It sucked at my wading boots with a strength water could never muster.

The heat was becoming more than uncomfortable; I could feel the material of my waders pressing against my jeans as I was pummelled. If it gave out – if it *melted* – I'd be done for.

"Where are you?" I cried, but again the words were clipped and then gone.

I focused on my steps, but progress was slow; I had to pause to regain my balance with each step, and the heat was engulfing me, then. A menacing sizzling sound filled my ears.

"Oh, God," I cried, and the sizzling escalated to a roar. I

felt my heart pound in my chest and suddenly I was doubled over as pain flared at my sternum. *A heart attack!*

Pressure mounted on my chest until bolts of lightning shot to my shoulders and down both arms. My left hand curled into a claw as it intensified.

Another sound – beneath the roaring of what had to be flames – pricked in my ears. Screaming.

Suffering.

"No," I grunted.

"Thomas," the voice was like a cool breeze.

Another bolt of pain ripped down my left arm and I squeezed it to my chest.

"I'm dying," I breathed, then managed the beginnings of a laugh as the voice came again.

"You're already dead."

And it all stopped.

I was floating, ensconced in velvet blackness and free of pain. No weight, no pressure, no failing heart.

I began to sob.

And then, in the distance, there was something.

A flash. A light.

"Come, Thomas."

I went, and that time it was effortless. I travelled forward and the brightness intensified; I was squinting, arms over my face, by the time I reached the tower. And it was displayed before me as it had been the first time – a dissection of levels stacked on one another, from the depths of all-encompassing darkness to reaching high toward unimaginable, infinite light.

"What – what are you trying to tell me?" my voice was weak, but clear. The words echoed pleasantly around me. I longed to curl up again, just release everything into the blackness and feel no more.

But then I was flying again, and the speed evoked a breathless feeling, despite the lack of lungs or air. And my destination was that middle level – the living level. But I saw as I approached that the levels on either side of it held physical life, too. Those below acted trapped and suffered; those above glowed and sought enlightenment.

It was too much; my thoughts jumbled until I felt I might explode.

But then, I saw her.

Louise-Anne.

"Baby," I whispered and sobbed at the sound of the word. *My baby.*

"Watch," said the voice.

Nothing could have stopped me.

She looked like her mother; dark hair that appeared somehow unkempt and stylish all at once. I wondered if her eyes were the watery grey-blue of her mother's too. Those eyes had captivated me in the early days of our relationship, but I remembered little else, besides the shouting.

My daughter was moving fast, doing too much to fathom. Her arms blurred between tasks, her face a mask of pained concentration. It hurt a bit to look at her, as though witnessing her suffering lent some of it to the watcher. I don't know how to explain it to you, even now, but in that chaos, I saw her life. And I knew at once that she was sick.

And things went sideways.

"No!" I growled the word, like an animal.

She stopped. Looked up.

"Louise-Anne!"

She straightened and faced me, and suddenly she was doing one thing only: walking a long hallway toward me, uncertainty clouding her expression.

I cried. I cried so hard I felt it might drag me under and I'd find myself in the flow of fire again, with no motivation to resurface.

She was nearing the edge, her eyes resolutely on mine.

She said something, but no sound reached me.

"I can't hear you!" I panicked, needing to know her voice. "Please, try again!"

She frowned. Looked at her watch, then glanced over her shoulder.

A hospital bed had appeared in the hallway, and it was travelling toward her, unassisted. And fast.

She cast sad eyes my way. She looked how I felt. Disappointed. Afraid.

Defeated.

I struggled to go to her, but once again was held back entirely by invisible restraints. I felt the presence behind me. Encircling me. I hated it in that moment.

The bed reached her and slowed, then knocked into the back of her knees hard enough to make her fall backward, backward, until she was lying under the covers, newly attached to lines and machines. Her head lay sideways on her pillow. Her face serene as she slept.

But then it started to change.

I watched in horror as her jaw yawned open. It stretched her mouth and then her entire face as she slept on, seemingly unaware. Thank God.

But I was unable to turn from the sight. "Stop," I cried, but it was too quiet. I hadn't the strength to demand it. It was already done.

"You choose, Thomas."

I was in my bed. And before I could think to open my eyes, the voice said something else, mowing over the flaring heat of my rage before I was lost in it completely:

There is only one way for you to know her, now.

CHAPTER 24 – REACH

I spent half the day at work putting off the inevitable; the MARS testing kits were kept under lock and key, and inventory was closely monitored. Regardless, it shouldn't have been a consideration. The kits were available for staff testing - of course they were.

My hesitation was more related to the fact that access and usage of the kits required *two* staff, even if one was the recipient.

I wasn't ready to give in; to give up. My denial had been resolute. Purposeful. I had justified it in my own mind until it was the only option.

But by lunchtime, with the day halfway done and having changed my protective garb three times already, a sense of urgency overcame my procrastination. It didn't help that Beck had texted me twice, both times asking if I'd "done it" yet.

The pressure mounting, I made up my mind, finally, to get it over with. The only question was who to go to for help.

Ella was on desk duty that day, so I volunteered to watch it while she took a break. The hallways were quiet; residents ate at eleven-thirty and were encouraged to nap or have quiet time after their meals. I knew I'd be afforded some quiet moments to think if I manned the desk during lunch, whereas my office tended to be a hotbed of activity and discussion.

I'd gone over it again and again in my head. I knew all the remaining carers well, but the idea of coming clean to any of them meant I'd been hiding, or worse, lying. The only other qualified staff member was the owner's son, which at first blush presented as ridiculous. But as I absently went through the files and sorted them, Carroll pulled ahead in the running.

He was kind, and something told me that despite his position, he could be discreet, at least until the results were in, which, after various versions of the procedure had been tried, had been whittled down to less than twenty-four hours.

Besides, the only other option was to go to the testing center in Hull, and I couldn't accept the prospect of sitting in a waiting room with countless others, everyone scanning everyone else, wondering who had a death sentence and who had risked exposure needlessly.

And Dr. Jack – he was busy enough on his visits, and there'd be no seeing him for days.

"Carroll," I muttered, and brought the edges of the files down hard on the desk to punctuate the decision.

"What about him?" I jumped at the unexpected reply and was mortified to look up and meet the eyes of the man himself.

"Shit," I muttered, then giggled self-consciously. *This is not going well.*

He leaned on the desk stiffly, seemingly going for casual, and frowned down at me. I noted the uncompromised handsome set of his features, even in a frown and half-hidden by his mask. "You said my name. I'm pretty sure of it." His eyes smiled.

"I – uh – was thinking I'd come find you in the kitchen after Ella comes back," I stammered, inwardly cursing my clumsiness. I *had* decided on Carroll but had been counting on a bit of time to mentally prepare.

"Guess I've saved you a trip, then. Figured I'd walk a bit

before starting the dishes. What can I do for you?"

My stomach flipped.

"Are you alright?"

I drew in a breath, paused, then plunged. "I haven't been feeling well, actually."

His frown was back.

"I've been thinking -" I met his eyes, "*hoping* is probably a better word - that it's the flu, but -"

"Have you told anyone else?"

I sucked in a breath and shook my head.

"That's why you've been wearing the full ensemble at all times." He nodded toward my gown.

I was surprised he'd noticed. "I wanted to take precautions -"

His eyes looked sad. I noted darker flecks of green and spots of gold in the hazel. He gave a short nod. "Let's do the test now."

I gulped. "I have to wait for Ella."

He sighed, then leaned on the counter again. "Why me?"

"Huh?"

"Why'd you choose me to go into the kit storage with you?"

I gulped, completely unprepared for the question.

Ella appeared behind him. "You want to take over the desk for a while, next?" She smiled up at Carroll, her eyes twinkling from behind her transparent face shield.

While Carroll's obvious shyness caused the staff to whisper behind their hands, his attractiveness was an easy second choice where gossip was concerned.

"I'm afraid you're back on duty...unless you want to take care of the lunch dishes?" Carroll backed away so Ella could resume her position. "Lou-Anne and I have something to take care of."

I manoeuvred around the desk, catching Ella's wide-eyed look as I passed her and ignoring it.

We were quiet as we went through kit procedure. We unlocked the cabinet, recorded the removal of one as well as its intended potential victim, counted – me first, then Carroll – then recorded the remaining inventory. Then signed, both of us.

He could have begged off then, leaving me to test myself in private, but he followed close behind, then slipped into my office behind me and locked the door.

I eyed the doorknob critically. "That'll just guarantee more gossip," I tried to smile.

He blushed – I eyed his darkening cheeks with fascination – then nodded and reopened the door.

We found an empty examination room – no difficult feat in those days – and I removed my hood and face shield while Carroll suited up.

"You don't have to stay," I muttered.

"It's OK," he replied, distracted as he tied his gown. When I said nothing more, he met my eyes soberly and added, "I insist." He moved toward the kit.

"You're not testing me."

He pulled one of his gloves and let it snap, then eyed me sideways through his face shield. "I'm sure you know that accurate results can only be depended on when the test is administrated by an independent party."

I stifled a giggle. He was unexpectedly current on

procedure, despite not having to perform it on a day-to-day basis. "They just came out with that data." I struggled to untangle a stray bobby-pin from my newly-freed hair.

He nodded. "I plan to be more than a cook in the long-term."

I bit my tongue. Carroll was so quiet; it was easy to forget his position. But, quiet or not, he worked to forge connections with both staff and residents. And while his father was infamous for his strict stance on protocol, Carroll seemed happy to do as he was told. Maybe I'd underestimated him.

"I know it doesn't seem like it, but I really am preparing to take over one day. It's just easier to let it happen in a way that works for – everyone," he added, tapping a finger absently on the kit. "Should we get started?"

I crossed nervously to the table and sat while he prepared the test. It was rather simple: a very long cotton swab for what we called a "sinus sweep", and an odd-looking but simple mask-like contraption developed for the retrieval and examination of lung droplets. Basically, you had to hock up a juicy nugget of goop. Yep, it was as gross as it sounds. Finally, I'd offer up a vial of blood, which would indicate my level of inflammation, among other clues.

He raised his eyebrows as he positioned himself in front of me. Even with the protective garb, he smelled subtly fresh and clean, with a hint of something earthy.

"Ready?"

I nodded, lifting my chin for the part of the testing that seemed to attract the most complaints: the sinus sweep. Nervous, I voiced my curiosity aloud. "What is that scent?"

He paused, cotton swab in midair, and frowned down at me.

"I – sorry; I've seen this part more times than I can count

– I administer it! I just – it always seems to bother people – and I can smell your cologne. It seems familiar. Like – something natural…" I sighed, hearing how I sounded, and finally letting my chin drop.

He touched my chin with gloved, but warm fingers, tilting my head back again. His eyes twinkled a bit. "It's probably my deodorant; I'm trying one of those natural ones, you know? Less packaging, less waste and all that?" He paused and made a face, fully visible now through the face shield, pulling his upper lip down over his teeth and stretching his nostrils. I followed suit, mirroring him automatically. "I figure every little effort matters, you know?" He inserted the swab, his face still stretched empathetically, and I was wincing in seconds, finally experiencing the feeling the residents had been so vocal about. It felt like my eyeball was being poked from behind.

"Holy *God!*" I choked, but then he was reversing the swab and relief swept over me.

He popped the swab into a plastic sheath and stood, grinning at me. "OK?"

I realized I still had an eye closed and peeked through it, squinting. "Are both eyeballs still in my head?"

He chuckled.

"That *sucked.*"

He laughed enthusiastically that time, then went back to the kit to prepare what had been universally dubbed the "cough catcher," for obvious reasons. "I know," he glanced over his shoulder.

"You've been tested?"

He nodded. "Dad – er – *Marvin* insisted we get our status cards as soon as he knew they existed. It facilitates things for the business: travel, admission, etcetera," he gestured absently.

"Makes sense." I knew it had been mandatory for Beck to do as a paramedic, as well. Medical staff were usually required to test, too, but that mandate hadn't been extended to senior's homes, yet. The staff joked darkly that we'd been forgotten, but the message was clear to all of us: older folk weren't the priority.

"Yeah, except that my sisters and I are well into our late twenties and thirties and we're *still* being managed like business assets," he came to stand in front of me again.

I was stunned. I hadn't heard Carroll say a negative word about *anyone*, much less his father. Respect was all I'd witnessed between the two.

He caught my blank expression and shook his head regretfully. "Sorry. I'm... a little... " he shook his head.

"It's OK! I wondered sometimes what it was like, you know? To have your father ordering you around... "

He placed the mask on the lower half of my face and I sucked in my breath. The sudden prospect of purposefully coughing up phlegm in front of my attractive future boss got the best of me.

He looked thoughtful. "Well, being funnelled into the kitchen in *addition* to keeping the books balanced – and all that goes along with that – is a good indication of how Marvin takes advantage of our relationship." He smiled wryly, then gave a nod to the mask. "Let 'er rip."

I froze, then dissolved into a fit of giggles.

"What?" he let the hand holding the mask drop. Then he was laughing, too, and shrugging. "Just trying to keep this light; I'm sorry."

I reached for the mask. "You say that a lot."

He handed it over, then put his palms out in apparent defeat.

I cleared my throat. "Turn around."

He complied, to my great relief, and I coughed, hard. If I had to do it, I was determined to do it right the first time. "OK," I sealed it and held the thing out and he turned, looking impressed.

"That was efficient."

I nervously glanced at my watch. "They'll be wondering where we are by now."

"One more test," he murmured, already stretching an elastic tube around my bicep and pressing a finger into my inner elbow.

"Don't tell me you trained in blood collection, too?"

He met my eyes. "Of course. Did the whole nursing program, but stopped short of the qualification for Registered Nurse."

"*What?*"

He masterfully pierced my skin with a butterfly needle, then attached it to the tube through which dark red blood whizzed, then landed in the vial.

"And you're *good!*" I exclaimed, but my eyes were on the crimson liquid that held the answer to my questions. A bolt of adrenaline shot through me. I'd know soon.

"Hey," his voice was low, pulling me back to the present. "It's going to be OK. No matter what." He smiled into my eyes for one moment... but it was a moment that changed everything. I hadn't been looking for details; had never had the opportunity to know his face so intimately, even if it was through the transparent plastic of his face shield. But there he was, inches away, his eyes meeting mine, and details were all I saw: a light smattering of freckles over his nose and cheekbones, ridiculously thick, dark eyelashes, and a mouth that was perhaps a little overlarge for his otherwise defined features.

Which made it look nearly overwhelmingly delicious.

All-in-all, I realized he wasn't just passively handsome; up close, Carroll Krull was *gorgeous.*

"Why so surprised?"

I came back to myself with a shudder. "What? Surprised?" *How did he know I was having an epiphany over his looks?* "I – uh – I guess I've never seen you up close like that before -"

His eyes registered confusion, and then he was focused on my arm, replacing the butterfly with a cotton ball and pressing gently on it. He was blushing furiously.

"I mean – oh, my God – you meant about the fact that you're good at taking blood..."

"Here," he gestured for me to take over with the cotton ball.

"I am *really* nervous about this test," I tried backpedaling, but I'd already said too much. My own cheeks blazed.

His back to me, he arranged the completed tests back into the kit, and grabbed a Sharpie to complete the label. "It's no problem," he said over his shoulder.

Mortified, I started replacing my protective gear.

"You really should go home until the results are back," he turned, kit in hand.

"Oh," I sank back down on the table at the formal tone of his voice. Had I alienated the one person at work I trusted to help me without judgement? "You're right; I didn't think past the testing..."

"I'll get the results sent directly to my office," he nodded, then tried a grin. "Which, these days, is the kitchen."

I laughed, but it was forced.

He started out and I floundered, feeling adrift in uncertainty and embarrassed, to boot. But he turned back and the mirror of his expression went a long way to comfort me. But his words were even better.

"It was nice to see your face, too, after so much time behind all that gear. I think we all forget what it's like to be close to someone."

It was so kind, so unexpected, that all I could do was nod stupidly.

"I'll tell the staff you've had to leave early, and we'll talk tomorrow," he finished, jiggling the kit a little.

I managed a "Thank you, Carroll," before he went out.

And then I sat for some time, trying to be OK with the fact that I'd be going home to an empty house, with no idea when I'd see my kids again. Or return to work.

And I couldn't deny the persistent suspicion that the "when" was more accurately an "if."

CHAPTER 25 – DRINK IN THE SUN

Rage.

It was hot and red and as potent as it had ever been, and as I transitioned from dream to consciousness, I barrelled out of bed and to the kitchen in a haze.

Yelling.

Hearing Molly yelp behind me but not letting her fear fully register.

I wasn't done, yet.

I was reaching for the whisky cabinet before I was lucid; going for the medicine that would take it all away before my forced (but otherwise appreciated) sobriety popped up as a cold fact.

"Rrrahh!" I growled, slamming the cabinet with such force that Molly, who was by then cowering by the front door, yelped again.

"What?" I screamed and saw the shocked bewilderment in her liquid eyes. Nearly let it deflate me – but the freight train of my outburst had a momentum that felt *good* in an old, familiar way. I opened the door. "You want out?" The pup bolted.

Watching her tear down the driveway, then into the street, fuelled the fire in me even more. *Wouldn't it just be typical of my fucking life to have to watch her get mowed down by one of the few drivers on the road?*

I watched her until I couldn't see her anymore, then backed into the house and slammed the door, but stumbled over something soft and fell. A shot of pain coursed up my back as I landed hard on my pelvic bones. I shouted out, pissed that I'd fallen, yes, but worse, reminded, too, that I was an ungrateful shit.

The pain was shocking, even when so much of the last years of my life had been filled with it. And once again, I was acting as though I was determined to fuck it all up. I punched the linoleum floor with a frustrated yell. And then I dissolved.

Which means I cried like a baby.

Hated myself. Missed the goddamned dog already.

I thought about my book of suicide notes and grocery lists; how I'd have reached for it such a short time ago. Got lost in feeling lost. Lost in being *scared*.

I pressed myself up off the floor, noting Molly's bed as the culprit of my fall. She liked to drag it over to the middle of the kitchen when I cooked so she could see me. I picked it up and replaced it in its corner, wondering absently if she'd ever lie there again.

Serves you right if she doesn't.

I sat at the table. Picked up my pen as I shook my head, then looked at the ceiling. "You know, I never noticed it before, but my inner voice sounds a lot like you."

A tear rolled down my cheek and I laughed. "My inner voice is mean, though. You're just honest."

I stared at an empty page in my notebook. I'd always loved the prospect of a clean, neat page, divided evenly into lines on which to empty myself out in the form of words. But that morning, I was determined to do something different.

Something drastic.

To whomever finds this,

I've wanted to die for as long as I can remember, and now that I have, I understand that death doesn't solve shit.

It's life that lets us work for something better.

Problem is, I've never been very good at life - or work, for that matter. But here and now, on a fresh page after countless explanations of the death I'd always accepted would come at my own hands, I declare this for anyone who cares to know it: I want to live.

And I want to use every ounce of my energy – my better body, my determined mind (and oh, God, my mind is trying so hard to deal with change and be better, too!) to do whatever I can to save my daughter.

Signed,

The second iteration of Thomas Wall

I put the pen down – perhaps a little harder than was necessary, but I was still running on the fuel of a rage that was quickly fizzling out – and got my shoes on.

Then I set out to find Molly. Again.

CHAPTER 26 – ROOT DEEP

By the time I reached Bois-Franc, I had reviewed and re-reviewed the morning's dream until it all jumbled together in a big mess. All of it was fresh in my mind, as though I'd scripted and directed it myself, but the only part that meant anything was that I'd been shown that my daughter was sick, and told in no uncertain terms that if I wanted to see her (and anyone who had the power to reanimate my body after I'd run it into the ground and then had it ravaged by MARS-21 would know I did), that there was only one way.

And I knew I'd been brought back for one purpose.

But those two facts refused to gel in my mind.

And that's where the *real* confusing shit started.

Was Louise-Anne's illness a punishment to me? Just the *idea* of her suffering drove me mad, so kudos to whatever it was that was intent on torturing me, if that was indeed the case.

Or did she need me? Did she *need* my help? And was I meant to give it to her, for the first time in her life?

And what would I do if that was the case, when I knew the only way I could "help" would mean her death?

I must've muttered *"fuck"* a hundred times by the time I found myself on Bois-Franc, but I was no closer to a resolution.

And Molly remained out of sight.

"Molly?" I called.

The neighborhood was almost eerily quiet.

I headed toward the park. Tried to remember if I'd seen another soul since I'd left my house. I didn't think I had. A moderate sense of relief rolled over me at the sudden sound of birdsong.

I rustled the bushes by the access road to the dog park, hoping she'd be where I found her first, but there was nothing. By the time I'd made my way back to Bois-Franc, I was feeling a bit desperate and a lot anxious. I'd scared away my Molly. My *friend.*

I eyed Linda's house across the road, from where I'd first seen her. When I'd first found the pup. Her blinds were drawn - of course they were. But there was something else; something out of place. I crossed the road, my eyes on the door. I had to get right up close to it to see that the paper taped to her door was a note.

And it was for me.

"Tom" was written on the front of it, and it was folded neatly and then taped to the door. I was touched before I even lifted the flap. The woman had been dying of an apocalyptic-force virus, and she'd taken the time to write to *me?*

Why?

I lifted the flap to find out, and once I'd read it, I carefully pulled the tape from the door and folded the note, intent on placing it in my wallet right beside my own note for Louise-Anne. The one I couldn't decide whether to mail or to deliver in person.

And then I was walking toward Molly's first home; where I'd eased the passing (I hoped) of a girl that used to be beautiful, and young, with her whole life ahead of her. A girl who had loved her puppy, but lost her, too.

I didn't think I'd ever go back there, but I had to, if it meant getting Molly back.

"I'm sorry," I whispered, and my fool eyes were filling with tears again.

I know it's true when I say that I felt sorrier in that last, bizarre part of my life on earth than I ever had in my first go around, combined. It's funny what we realize when things become simple. When even the little things are as critical as life and death.

Molly wasn't at her old home; not in the front yard or on the step, where yellow police tape still fluttered over the door, and not in the back yard, which somehow still smelled rank to me. But it may have been just a memory that assaulted my nostrils, for there was no sign of the human Molly's deceased boyfriend anymore.

Everything felt heavy as I started back – my feet, my heart, my head – so I took Linda's note out and read it again.

Thank you for making the difference for me.

Thank you for helping me decide to live. I know now that the world still has some good in it.

Please, let's be friends when I am well again.

Linda.

I stared at the words, frowning, as I walked, then folded the paper and replaced it, pausing for a moment to rub my thumb along the letter I had for Louise-Anne.

I didn't know whether to trust the guilt I felt over Linda's revelations – or the odd euphoria that lurked just beneath it.

And then I heard a bark. I snapped my head up to scan the trees at the bend, sure it was Molly, then broke into a run without missing a beat. I cried her name as I approached the little dirt road, noted my heart as it raced in my chest, fluttering like a stunned bird – first in double-beats that stumbled over each other, patternless, and then tripping and landing hard, pausing, and landing again before settling into something like its regular thudding when I slowed.

"Molly!" I cried breathlessly, and there was an answering *yip!* but no corresponding appearance of her funny little wiener body and curly-haired ears.

But I found her easily enough. I laughed as soon as I did, too; she'd found a tennis ball and was alternately throwing it into the air with a toss of her head and then chasing it in the toddler park. A one-sided game of fetch executed with such enthusiasm she could have been performing in a ring.

Funny dog, I thought, and in that moment, she saw me and stopped.

"Come here, sweet girl," I squatted, heart in hand, waiting for rejection but allowing myself to hope for different. "Forgive me?"

She jumped into action, darting around until she found her ball, and then bringing it to me in a streak of flopping ears and wagging tail. She jumped into me, bowling me over, then licking my face until I managed to sit up. Her ball had rolled a few feet away and she retrieved it, then dropped it into my lap.

I picked it up, crying again. I said it before: I'm not proud. I was learning to be vulnerable. I know that now, and it was a good thing. It was a good thing, too, that Molly was a kind soul. Who better to tolerate a reluctantly healing man than a creature bred to be man's companion?

We played for a long time. I can't tell you how long, because we were immersed in it so completely, but I can tell you it was getting hot when we walked back home, Molly taking turns walking and resting in my arms. Her leg was very nearly done hurting by then, but I think her short legs needed a break now and then – and I didn't mind carrying her. Not at all.

I can tell you, too, that Ed himself was waiting for me at home, with the papers for my new job and some news about the house, too. And that when I saw him sitting on my step, I was happy.

Happy to see the clean-cut census man with his glasses and a button-up short-sleeved shirt and an odd way of looking at me like he was trying to figure me out. And a way of being kind when I expected the usual, which was something else entirely.

Despite my apparent determination to fuck things up, I *was* changing. And by then, I was ready to admit that I wanted to.

CHAPTER 27 – PHOTOSYNTHESIZE

When Ed left, it was with a fresh coffee inside him and the signed paperwork in his hand. It was official: I could carry and use the deputy badge. Was required to, in fact.

It was a feeling incomparable to any other I'd experienced. After a lifetime of despising authority, I *had* it. With no clue how to handle it. That said, I'd been at the mercy of circumstance and agendas not my own of late. I figured I'd adapt.

"Don't forget to call Meiser," Ed called over his shoulder.

I touched the phone in my pocket absently, puzzling over when I'd fit in the call to the lawyer that – apparently - only needed to hear from me to make my little house – mine.

"You OK?"

I nodded distractedly. "Just not used to having so much to do, I guess."

Ed stopped beside the driver's side door, assuming a familiar stance – clipboard held to his chest and a pensive look on his face.

"I'll be alright; don't worry."

"Time management can be challenging when you've taken on something new. You just need to prioritize."

I raised my eyebrows. "You don't say."

He laughed. "Sorry; I was just trying to work some stuff out in my head...you wanted to get your status card, and I think that's the right move," he frowned at Molly, who was laying on the step, "I'm just wondering what you'll do with her."

I eyed her over my shoulder, bewildered. I'd resolved to keep her with me wherever I went, but she'd be turned away at the testing center's doors and it'd be a wasted trip. "Hadn't thought of that," I murmured.

Ed approached again. "I could take her."

I eyed him, dubious.

"Hear me out! I've got three kids who would love to take care of her for the afternoon. It'd give my wife a much-needed break, too. She's – the kids are a lot, you know? She's been amazing – giving up her government job to homeschool them once schools were shut down – but she'd still be working if things were different..."

"Some folk are taking their little ones to the 'safe schools'," I nodded, remembering the articles. "Small classes, all the precautions."

He shook his head, his eyes going to some point in the distance. "Jackie can't do it." He met my eyes again. "I told you none of us have gotten sick – statistically, in a family my size and with an essential worker in contact with the public, that's sort of a miracle. But what you don't know is that in the beginning, Jackie's mom got sick. She was living with us at the time; had been since my father in-law passed, and we had no idea just what the new mystery virus could do. We took care of her, took her to the hospital and brought her out again. Jackie helped her do everything; dress, eat, bathe and use the bathroom before we were even wearing masks!"

"Wow. Maybe she's immune, somehow?"

He shrugged. "That's another question entirely. Sure, she – all of us! – were lucky not to get sick, but the experience of watching her mother succumb was more than enough to make Jackie decide we'd err on the side of caution, especially with the kids. And that if she had to, she'd devote her entire life – everything she has – to making sure we all stayed healthy."

I shook my head, uncomprehending.

"It's frustrating sometimes, but I've come to admire her for it. She's sacrificed everything in her own life for the one thing that matters most."

I shook my head. That sort of selflessness was foreign to me – in practice, at least.

"Anyway," Ed shrugged awkwardly, "if you need someone to watch the pup, for whatever reason, we won't mind."

"That's kind of you," I said, quietly. "I think your wife's probably someone pretty – unique." It wasn't exactly right, but Ed smiled.

"She is."

I looked at Molly. "Want to play with some folks your own age for a while?" She jumped up and bounded toward Ed. "I swear she reads my mind," I laughed as I watched her.

Ed scooped her up, then looked at me again as he fumbled with his clipboard. "There is something about her," he nodded, then opened the passenger side door and put Molly inside. "There's something about you, too, Tom," he said lightly as he rounded the hood.

"You have no idea how many times I've been told that."

"In an entirely different context, I'm sure," the man gazed at me over his open door. "I've heard things; small-town people talk, but I like to judge people based on the actions I see, rather than gossip. And so far, you've impressed me in the opposite way to how you left your impression on Evan Cromwell all those years ago!"

I tried to smile, but it trembled at my lips, refusing to form fully as conflicting emotions warred within me.

"And even *he's* seeing you in a different light now. Be careful; people are going to start thinking you're an all-around good guy, Tom."

"Amazing what death can do," I muttered, completely flummoxed, then realized my mistake. Ed was nodding, though.

"Even when you're watching it take others and skipping you entirely." He paused, and the unspoken words hung heavily between us. "Call me when you're done?"

I nodded. "I could, but I could also just drop by afterward to get her."

"I'll still be at work, no doubt. I'll bring her back tonight."

It was decided. A hollow feeling came over me as I gave him a wave, then smiled wistfully at Molly's profile as they drove off.

"Distraction," I nodded toward my own car. The old Santa Fe wasn't used often – in fact, I'd been meaning to sell it since I was relegated to the cart where transportation was concerned - but I'd never had a problem with it, and that day it started with the remote on the first try, despite sitting for many months.

My driving skills, however, had suffered a bit. Things moved so much faster than I'd become used to. And I'd discovered that I'd become a meanderer, enjoying stops here and there to fill up my time. But the car went from point A to point B before I'd even had the chance to consider my scenery. Except for the realization that the diminished population had changed the feel of the roads completely, that is. Thoroughly un-crowded, the wide lanes of pavement, with their traffic lights and roundabouts felt suddenly unnecessary.

The unsettled feeling persisted when I parked in what would have been considered a prime spot at the hospital without having to take a ticket. "Free parking, can you imagine?" I looked forlornly toward the empty passenger seat and sighed. "Guess it makes sense now that half of us are gone."

I cooperated with the well-meaning guard that met me at the main entrance and accepted a mask, then donned it clumsily.

She eyed me sternly above her own mask. "Shouldn't be walking around bare-faced these days, especially when you come *here*," she gestured to the door.

I fumbled with the elastics, working to quell the frustration that had risen as soon as she'd started talking. "Sorry," I muttered gruffly. "I just – I've already been sick."

Her eyebrows arched higher. "One of the rare lucky ones."

"Guess so," I sidestepped her and continued toward the automatic door. No touching necessary.

"You know, the people in there don't know you've had it and recovered. People are still scared; wearing a mask goes beyond protection in these times."

I nodded back at her.

"Still, it's a courtesy!" she called, and I turned, weighed down by the apparent obligation. "A *kindness*," she finished, and her eyes beseeched me to hear her. Months of frustration showed in the lines around those eyes.

But it did make me pause. The mask was more to ease others' anxieties than for me. Why hadn't I seen it like that before? Was I so bereft of common social courtesy that I still needed to be taught all the bits I'd missed when I was a kid?

It was a wonder I'd made it to adulthood, considering all that I'd been lacking. And I saw it in that moment; a vast "Being Human" checklist, its checkboxes unmarked - vacant and without hope of progress unless I allowed myself to be taught.

"You're right," I said, finally.

Her expression softened and something like surprise lit behind her eyes.

At first, no one had taught me. Even the most basic of tasks seemed a nuisance to the long line of fosters, and it hurt more if I tried. Hurt more if I expected and was disappointed. So, I'd stopped expecting to learn... and then I forgot to look for opportunities. Forgot the possibilities to the point that interested teachers came off as nosy busybodies.

"Thank you," the woman's voice brought me back to myself. I raised a hand before patting my mask with a smile.

I was still lost in my thoughts when I reached registration. *Maybe I have to start looking at everybody as a teacher,* I thought, but a part of me balked. It was understandable; I'd already reached the end of my life on earth, after all. The little blip of my return wasn't guaranteed beyond one moment to the next, and thanks to my nightmarish visits, I had an idea what waited for me when life ebbed away again.

"Sir?"

"Huh?" I was standing at the front of a neat line, each person diligently behind the lines marked on the floor. We'd all learned the safe distance; the lines probably weren't necessary anymore –

"Can I help you, sir?"

I shook myself out of my thoughts, then approached the plexiglass. "I need my status card."

The young man at the desk turned to his screen and began shooting questions at me, which I answered dutifully, then was shuffled into the first of a series of rooms. I travelled between them – waiting, then submitting to a needle prick and a scant draining of blood, then waiting again – with a shuffling group of fellow seekers. I watched them eye each other suspiciously, wondering what answers the blood of each would hold, and how it could affect them. The group got quieter at each stop, tumbling finally into silence as we waited for our names to be called.

I watched as each was summoned and then consulted with briefly behind a wall of plexiglass. Some responded with tears, one with outright panic, and many took their cards with looks of resignation.

None smiled, regardless of whether they were funnelled into the hallway – I assumed another waiting room was their destination until they could be further examined – or whether they headed resolutely for the exit.

And then it was my turn. People gazed at me as though I'd just materialized before them as I rose and walked to the plexiglass room. Then they watched as I went in my direction: the door.

Restoration or no, MARS-21 had left its mark.

It was a good thing; it meant I had my status card and consequently, more freedom. But I felt oddly remorseful as I headed out of the building through the carousel doors and past the security guard, who afforded me a quick nod as I passed.

It was my name being called that shook me back to the present.

"Hey, *Wall!*"

I knew the voice but couldn't match it with a face. Moderately annoyed at the distraction when I had so much more to do, I turned. And on a bench beneath a tree sat a long-time darts buddy and fellow ex-con. Sunglasses shaded his eyes and he gripped a cane beneath his chin.

"Pax?" I started toward him without hesitation, buoyed by a familiar face after being tossed so chaotically by the new river of my life. The second go at it, anyway.

But I saw my friend had changed as I approached him; the wiry silver curls that always sprung out from under his dirty tweed fedora were all but wisps, and the hollows of his cheeks had deepened as though he was being eaten from the inside. His mask stretched like a bridge from nose to ear. A cold sweat broke out all over me. He was sick, but it wasn't MARS-21 that ravaged him.

"I knew it was you, Tom!" His eyes crinkled deeply as he smiled.

"My God, Pax! I'd say it was nice to see you, too, but you don't look so good!"

He laughed until he was bent over double, then patted the bench. "Ah," he sighed, gripping the handle of his cane again, "remember that bout of prostate cancer I had almost fifteen years ago?"

My jaw dropped as I sat. In fact, I had entirely forgotten. "It's been ages since then!"

He shrugged. "Guess it was just biding its time before heading into my lungs to keep doing it's damage."

I sat back, frowning. "I'm sorry."

"Not *your* fault!" his eyes crinkled again. "'sides, the timing isn't terrible; not much to hang around here for, anyways."

I shook my head. "Seems unfair, though. You never get MARS, but your cancer comes back to bite you." Anger threatened in my gut, but I paid it no mind.

"Guess it's just my fate – but I lost a lot of family to that bastard of a disease, and at this point, it don't matter much to me which way my life ends."

It was shocking to hear a sentiment I'd repeated in my little notebook more times than I'd kept track of, and see the sorrow in it from the outside. The *waste*. "You never know; you could still have things to do."

He eyed me suspiciously. "That what you're doing? You say I've changed, but I barely recognized *you*!"

I looked down at myself guiltily. I was slimmer, fitter, and altogether more capable than I had been since our days in the Kingston Pen together.

"Who's *your* doctor? Mine just told me I have just days to live; maybe yours'd have a different opinion," he chuckled, but quickly doubled over again, this time going breathless from coughing.

I hesitated, then patted his back gently. Realized it had been many months since I'd thought to touch someone. Besides Molly. It was a privilege taken for granted in the past, but all-but forbidden with the advent of the apocalypse.

Pax finally straightened, gasping. "Shit. Thanks, buddy."

"Are you admitted here?"

He laughed weakly. "You think I'm spending my last days *here*?"

"Guess it'd be the Gatineau hospital, now."

He chuckled again and I tensed, waiting for the coughing to take him again.

But he only shook his head. "I'm going home. Figure I'll do what I've always done: drink some rye, watch UFC and fall asleep in my chair. Only this time, I won't wake up desperate to take a piss!" he laughed again but stopped abruptly and cleared his throat at the look on my face. "What?"

Pax had always been rough around the edges; born to ex-cons and raised on a yo-yo between his folks when they were sober and the foster care system when they weren't, he came by a life of crime honestly. In recent years he'd mellowed, growing quieter and more settled as his children grew up and had children of their own. Some of them even seemed to be on the straight and narrow, despite the fact that his own children had been born and raised by the same brand of folk he had. "Pax," I said, fumbling, but needing to help, "what can I do for you?"

His eyes went blank for a long moment.

"Maybe you want to spend some time at my place?"

There was a beat of silence, and then he was laughing and hacking all over again. I felt stupid; he'd want to be with his family. I folded my hands, conflicted, and waited for him to regain himself.

"What's gotten into you?" he gasped, finally.

I shrugged. "I feel like I wasted most of my life now that it's coming to an -" I looked at him, worked to rephrase. "Now that I'm old and the world's gone crazy."

He studied me carefully until I squirmed uncomfortably.

"You're one of the good ones, Wall."

I thought about Louise-Anne and shook my head. "I'm not. I just – I want to do the right thing for once in my life."

"I'm jealous, Tom. I don't think there'd ever be enough days in this lifetime for me to come to that conclusion." He looked over the parking lot toward the trees. "Both my daughters have died, leaving my grandkids with no mothers, and one of my sons will die in jail, if he hasn't already." A tear trailed from his eye to his mask.

"I'm sorry, Pax."

"My other son may as well be dead; he's *depressed*. So much like his mother, that one. She went ahead and died, too, when everything started going to shit.

"Oh, God."

He waved it away. "I'm a bit mad at her, actually. She threw in the towel and left me to deal with everything alone."

"Suicide?"

He nodded.

I frowned. "Wait. Hadn't you two divorced years ago?"

He shook his head. "We were never married, actually. But yes, we'd separated. Were just trying to find a way to come back together when everything...changed."

Once again, I was speechless.

"Anyway, that's the worst about my youngest – he's healthy, but done in by all the death. All the change. He's scared, like so many, but he's been frozen by it." He met my eyes. "The way I figure it, whatever waits after this body gives out has to be better than this."

I saw Louise-Anne in my mind's eyes as I'd seen her in my dream, and a sense of urgency surged through me. The note still sat in my wallet, which was a lump between myself and the bench. I suddenly knew I had to deliver it in person, whatever the consequences. I fixed a hard gaze on Pax. "Why are you here, if you're not staying?"

"Waitin' for a cab," he gestured at the curved drive between us and the parking lot.

"Let me drive you home," I stood.

"Well now, you can do *that*!" He allowed me to help him stand and walk him to the car, which took considerably more time than my sense of urgency was happy with. But I rested inside myself; forced myself to be patient on that: the last walk I'd have with an old friend.

And then I drove him home. Listened to him ramble about his grandchildren or sat quietly when words failed him. Then I got him settled in his chair, placing two full bottles on the end table, along with a paper I'd found in the kitchen, and a pen.

Because more likely than not, he'd have something to say before the cancer took its final bite.

And then I got back into the car, intent on driving to Wakefield.

CHAPTER 28 – GROW

I lost my nerve.

I can't explain it, even now, but I left Pax in his chair fully intending to drive into Wakefield, then sat in the car in his driveway for a long time, frozen.

My mind went blank, and then my options started to filter through.

I could drive to Wakefield as I intended, to her workplace, hoping to find her there. Also surprising her in a way that was sure to be unwelcome.

Or, I could go get Molly and throw the ball for her until dinner.

I shook my head.

Pax was dying inside. I could sit with him. Ease the passage in whatever way he needed...it was my *job*, right? But he *wanted* to be alone.

I could go to the Gatineau Hospital, fresh new status card in hand and donate blood for testing. And maybe I could find Linda, too. That was what Ed and Cromwell expected me to do; what I'd led them to believe.

I backed out of the driveway and called Ed on the hands-free system, feeling settled in my decision.

"LaFrance, Neighborhood Census."

I cleared my throat. "Ed?"

"Oh! Hi, Tom. Everything OK?"

"Yep. Got the status card and now I'm heading over to the Gatineau Hospital; just wanted to ask your opinion on something."

Huh? My own words surprised me.

"Sure; shoot."

"I, uh -" I cleared my throat again. "I have a daughter; haven't seen her in years."

There was a pause, then a puzzled sounding, "OK?"

"But I'd like to."

"Ah," Ed sighed, "I'd love to help, Tom, but I can't go into the records. Literally! There are very few of us who have the authority to -."

"No," I gritted my teeth. "Forget it."

"Any other way I could help?"

"I – I've heard from her, actually, and she put the address of her workplace on the envelope. It's in Wakefield! She probably didn't want me to know the address of her home. I don't blame her, but -"

"So close...that's wonderful, Tom! A positive first step!"

"Yeah, and I've written her back, but I sort of feel like waiting for the mail service would be stupid, given the circumstances..."

"Are you asking me if you should drive up there?"

I chuckled. "Yes, I guess so. Sorry; I don't really have anyone I can ask about this sort of thing." I scratched my head even as the words came out. I could've asked Pax; I could even have waited and spoken to Linda that afternoon. Somehow, though, talking to Ed felt right.

"No," he said.

"Huh. You sound sure."

"Look, Tom – I know you've got good intentions, but popping up suddenly might scare her off. I don't know her or any of the circumstances around your relationship, but I know from experience that people appreciate a heads-up for surprises like these."

I bit my lip, considering.

"That doesn't mean you have to be a slave to snail mail, though. My advice would be to call the place, first. Leave her a message... let her make the decision."

I nodded. "Yeah. That sounds more... fair."

"Tom, I can't tell you how many doors I've had to knock on with hard questions or bad news. Hell, even *good* news is a shock to most! If they're expecting you, though, it tends to go over better."

"I should just mail the letter."

"You *should* mail the letter, maybe. In good faith. But call the place, too."

"Yeah?"

"Sounds like the two of you haven't seen or spoken to each other in a long time."

"Her whole life, I'm sorry to say."

"Well, if there was ever a time to show her you're willing to do *more,* this is it."

My eyes welled with tears, blurring the thin traffic ahead of me. I blinked hard. "You don't mince words, Ed, but you do have a nice way of saying them."

He laughed. "Thanks. Hey, and by the way, the kids adore Molly, and Jackie said she's made herself at home. They're all having a good day."

"Good. Thanks again for that."

"Oh!" There was a brief muffled sound. "Gotta go, Tom, but I'll see you tonight."

We hung up. Gatineau it was, but I questioned it, still.

"Weird day," I muttered to myself. Nothing felt certain anymore.

The hospital had an eerie quiet to it. I needed to check the new sign that'd been hung near the entrance; they'd reorganized the place. A separate sign, in French and then English, was posted beside it, like an afterthought:

All testing and rehabilitation for MARS-21 is conducted at the former Hull Hospital, now called Center for MARS-21 Diagnostic and Recovery. Please visit the information desk with questions.

I found the lab on the map – it hadn't changed locations – and went there, as per the advice of the doctor who'd handed me my status card that morning. There were two places to check in: one for first-time donors, and one for returning donors. I wondered why they'd be different but found out soon enough when an orderly sat me down to draw blood and explain the procedure.

"It's a much simpler process after today; we just like to explain procedures and have to get a few forms filled the first time around."

"I see." I watched my blood travel to a bag pinned to the chair with interest. It had tested positive for the antibodies, but what else could it reveal, if the lab techs had known what to look for? "Hey, uh-" I puzzled over a thought that had occurred to me, "do antibodies build up in people who eventually die from the virus, too?"

He finished writing on a clip board, then turned to me with a sigh. "Yes, but our interest is in people who've beaten it; we're looking for differences between their blood composition and those that failed to recover." The orderly's eyes were heavy-lidded.

"OK," I nodded, hoping he'd go back to his sheet. Wondering if I was harming their studies with my blood.

"I have some questions for you; if you're feeling up to it, you could fill this out now, or -"

I reached for a second clip board, which he'd retrieved from the desk behind him. "No problem."

"This won't take long," he gestured toward the bag, "but you might feel woozy afterward. We ask that donors stay on the premises for at least twenty minutes afterward. There are two different recovery rooms; one is dimly lit and quiet for those who want to rest, and the other has a movie playing. We give you a snack either way," he finished a speech that had undoubtedly been given hundreds – even thousands – of times.

I looked up from my questionnaire. "I was told donors could spend some time with patients?"

He folded his arms and studied me. "We usually reserve that for people who've gone through an application process, but I happen to know there've been precious few to apply, lately." He shook his head, making a clicking noise with his tongue. "Seems like, after people got used to being disconnected with one another, they forgot it was an option."

Uninterested in making small talk, but wanting to have a positive outcome, I offered to apply then and there, and he handed me another set of sheets.

"Do you have any sort of training – medical, social work, caregiving – that could make you a good candidate?" he asked with a level gaze as I bent over the sheets.

I had to restrain a laugh. I'd been the *recipient* of those things – whether it had been a short checkup before being slapped with a drunk and disorderly, or through rehab and/or probation – but it was safe to say I hadn't *provided* those things, nor had I had the authority - I gasped, holding up a finger, then pulled my new badge out. "I've been deputized to keep tabs on the neighborhood; check on folks and whatnot," I said, my voice lacking conviction as I flipped the case open clumsily.

He nodded, accepting what I myself felt to be a difficult-to-believe story, automatically. "That's a good program; I'm glad they're doing it. And there's a spot on there to check it off," he pointed toward the bottom of the first sheet. "You'll be accepted, for sure."

I fought the urge to laugh; to shout, "But it's *me!* Tom Wall! Has anyone thought this through?" *If my probation officers could see me now...*

Still doesn't solve the questions of next steps with your daughter.

Damned if the inner voice wasn't right again.

I was surprisingly woozy as I stood; the orderly watched closely as I wobbled a bit.

"Here," he pressed a banana into one hand, and a juice box into the other. "Sit down; I'll get you a wheelchair."

I held a hand up. "No." But the room was spinning and a wave of hot nausea rolled over me.

"You're sweating. Have you eaten today?"

I sat without choosing to, and frowned. "No, I don't think I have."

He made a disapproving noise but paused before speaking. "I should've made sure you had. I'm sorry; I've been working so much -"

I pointed to the garbage bin beside him with some urgency, but he produced an emesis basin instead. I dry-heaved painfully for several minutes, gasping between tear-inducing stomach convulsions. When I finally looked up, my repentant orderly was gone.

The next thing I knew, a pretty young woman with a stethoscope around her neck was shaking my shoulder gently. "Mr. Wall?"

"What happened?

"You fainted, Mr. Wall. John feels terrible; he's been working too many hours. He wanted me to pass along his apologies."

I waved the sentiments away. "Send him back in; I want him to know I appreciate his work."

She opened her mouth demonstratively, thermometer poised, and I mirrored her expression, waiting. "I sent him home after he came back with the wheelchair and found you passed out; it's really good he went. Poor guy."

The thermometer beeped and she withdrew it, then frowned at the reading. "You're a bit cold. How do you feel?"

I sat up, despite the pressure of her small hand on my chest. "I feel good."

She raised her eyebrows.

I picked up the banana to demonstrate, ignoring the lingering nausea that gripped me. The first bite nearly elicited a gag, but I chewed on, then swallowed. And surprisingly, my stomach lurched for more. I took a second bite. "I'd like to visit the patients today."

She glanced at the clipboard on the side table. "Your application will be approved, I'm sure, but why not wait until you're stronger?"

"I promise I'm feeling much better, now."

She sucked in a breath, then pursed her lips. "You have a loved one up on one of the floors?"

I gave a gruff laugh. "You caught me."

Another uniformed woman poked her head into the room. "Janie, they need you on six."

Janie stood, nodding. A look of determination fixed itself on her face.

"What's six?"

"It's the critical care floor." She puffed up her cheeks, blowing her breath out slowly. "You've been deputized?"

I fumbled for the badge and flipped it open. It flopped heavily to the floor. "Sorry; I'm still new to this."

She laughed. "You want third and fourth. If you know where your friend is, go on up." She rifled through her hip pack for a moment before handing a laminated card to me.

"Thank you," I mumbled.

She took a brochure from a cardboard stand on the desk and handed it over, next. "This explains procedure. I can't guarantee there'll be staff to speak with you today."

"I'll get by."

"I have to go; take a few minutes to recover first, alright, Mr. Wall?"

I gave her a thumbs up, and she scooped up the clipboard and left.

I did not take a few minutes to recover. I was exhausted and overwhelmed, and wanted to go home, so I wanted to finish my list of things to do quickly. Somehow, holding off didn't feel like an option.

I finished the juice box and banana in the elevator. I'd chosen the fourth floor for no reason in particular; I was going by my gut at that point. But I was wrong, and it took a disorienting trip around the floor to confirm it, as I couldn't find a staff member to save my soul.

Patients in varying stages of the sickness slept or gazed blankly out the window. It was rare to meet their eyes; they seemed as unwilling to connect as I'd been for most of my life. But the ones that looked toward the hallway – whose eyes lit with hope when they caught sight of me – their loneliness was clear in the cast of their gaze. I felt pulled to each one of them, but resolutely walked on, determined to find Linda. I smiled at each one, though, hoping they felt reassured.

I'll come back.

Unsuccessful, I resolved to try the third floor. The dizzying movement of elevator had me holding my breath; I felt better, but not completely recovered. I yearned for my bed.

Thankfully, I found Linda quickly; a nurse at the front desk smiled as she greeted me, and after barely a glance at my laminated card, directed me to room three-twelve.

"Thanks; I couldn't even find anyone on fourth."

Her eyes grew sad. "Staff is overstretched all over the hospital." She paused, then perked up. "But this floor is a little different; patients here are making improvements and need less care."

Something inside me brightened. Linda – an elderly woman whose jaw had been at least as bad as my own had been – was improving?

"To be honest, though, we need volunteers such as yourself as much as we need staff; Studies are showing that the support of peers, no matter the connection or lack of, greatly improves the rate of recovery."

"That's – interesting," I frowned, remembering Linda's large, but quiet home.

"We're having patients share rooms; almost always, we see vast improvements when they have someone just to share a space with, whether they chat or remain quiet, or completely ignore each other." She shook her head. "It's fascinating."

I puzzled at my nervousness as I approached three-twelve. What if the old lady didn't want to see me? She'd said she wanted to be friends, for God's sake – but visiting her at the hospital? Maybe it was too much.

I muttered a curse under my breath. I'd never worried about such things. And then I was in the open doorway of Linda's room, my eyes fixed on the sleeping woman whose back was turned to me. I nearly turned around right there. That underconfident, nervous, newly revealed part of me was already resolving to heed the doctor's advice and come another day. But then the curtain around the bed opposite Linda's was pulled back and I was faced with someone even more intimidating than Linda: a stranger.

It was a young woman, perhaps only a teenager, and she was smiling.

"Are you a volunteer?"

I cleared my throat. "Uh, yes, but -"

"Did you bring anything?"

"Huh?"

She rolled her eyes. "Books? Music? Anything?"

I held my palms out dumbly. "I didn't think. It's my first time -"

"Ugh," she pulled the curtain closed with a huff and, contrary to my first instinct where such rudeness was concerned, I found myself to be entertained rather than annoyed.

"Tom?"

Linda had awoken and was smiling at me over her shoulder.

Smiling. Teeth touching.

"Oh, my God!" I exclaimed as I entered the room.

She worked to sit up, and I could see by her wavering arms that she was still weak. An IV line ran from her left forearm to a bag labelled "TPN," so I knew she was still getting her nutrients intravenously, but the absence of the lockjaw was undeniable progress.

I halted at the end of her bed. "Wow, you look wonderful!"

She smiled again, but it ended in a grimace, that time. "Still hurts," she touched the hinge of her jaw gingerly. I could see where the stretch of the lockjaw had done its damage at the corners of her lips.

"Don't smile!" I laughed, but tensed, overcome by the conflicting anxiety that she'd reinjure herself and the joy I felt over the woman's improvement.

She reached a hand out as she rested against the elevated head of the bed. "I'm so glad you've come."

I sat on the side of her bed, taking her hand and not feeling awkward at all. No, really. It felt... nice.

"I'm a volunteer here, now; I'll come every day, if I can."

Her eyes lit up. "Mr. Wall, you've changed."

My smile faltered. "You'll never meet the man I was. Thank you for being part of that."

"Oh," she said as her eyes filled with tears.

My cheeks burned and I cleared my throat, uncomfortable at the show of emotion.

"How are you, Tom? You look a bit worn down."

"It's been a strange day," I admitted. "I crossed paths with a friend I haven't seen in a long while."

"Oh, but that's good, isn't it?" she patted my hand.

I shook my head. "Only in the sense that I got to say goodbye."

Her features fell. "He's sick?"

I nodded. "Cancer."

She grimaced. "That doesn't seem fair at all, does it?"

I smiled. "No, except that he's lost a lot of his family – his kids -" I hiccoughed and wiped a surprise tear from my cheek. "Sorry. I guess it's affecting me more than I realized."

"Of course, it is. And that's alright; you're allowed to feel exactly how you feel. You know that, right, Thomas?"

I couldn't answer; the words seemed strange to me.

She patted my hand again. "You'll come see me when I get to go home, won't you?"

I nodded before I could think of a way to say no. Then I realized I didn't want to say no, anyway.

She squeezed my hand. "So much of my family is gone, just like your friend," her eyes had a faraway look to them as she gazed toward the window. "I think people need to see family in every person they're lucky enough to have in their lives, these days."

I wondered who she'd lost. Who she had left. Felt privileged to be one of them. I gestured over my shoulder, toward the teenager's bed. *"Everyone?"*

She laughed, but it was weak.

"You're tired; I'll go."

She squeezed my hand again. "Only if you meant it; you'll come back tomorrow?"

I paused. "I need to make an important phone call tomorrow – I might need to drive to Wakefield, too, but if not tomorrow, then the day after."

She frowned but nodded.

"I promise," I said, and I patted her hand, that time.

She leaned forward, just a little. "She likes to read; anything and everything will do," she gestured toward the younger girl's bed, then winked at me.

I shook my head. Never had I catered to a person's whims to get on their good side, much less a snotty teenager. It had never mattered if people liked me, before. I pulled Linda's covers up around her and said goodbye, then walked toward the elevator feeling off, still, but moderately recharged. It occurred to me that anger had been the only emotion I'd allowed to flourish in myself...before. What I felt that day, about the dream I'd had, about lending Molly out so I could get things done, about the advice Ed had offered me, and about Pax sitting alone in his worn-out easy chair, dying alone...it was all foreign. It was almost too much – but instead, it was just strange and confusing. I'd been returned to an old man's body, but there was something in me that had reverted to that of a toddler. I was learning the things I'd missed the first time around, and I'm pretty confident in saying it's harder the second time around.

I neared the elevator, starting to think about the comforts of home, when I heard something like my name again, from one of the rooms. Surprised, I whirled, and found myself looking into another familiar face. But it took me a moment to place it, disfigured as it was by a severely locked jaw and odd, horn-like protrusions on his forehead.

Oh, no.

My stomach dropped as I went in to greet a young man I'd grown fond of, even thinking about him on the days I hadn't had time to buy the morning papers off him. Which had been a lot, recently.

"Jeremy?"

CHAPTER 29 – WILT

Pascal (known to his friends only as "Pax") Sebastien Lafontaine died at eleven twenty-five PM. He was pleasantly drunk on rye and ginger ale, spent of emotion and relieved of loose ends after phone calls with both sons and conversations with the grandchildren who'd lost their mothers, and emptied of secrets and confessions, thanks to the listening ear of an old friend.

He'd made a last, long trip to the bathroom, during which he showered, shaved and applied Mennen Speed Stick as well as aftershave, and combed the remnants of his hair into a careful, uncharacteristically neat style. And then he dawned his fedora.

He dressed in the only suit he'd ever owned – he'd worn it to two of his children's weddings as well as his own, and thanks to the hungry monster that had ravished him from the inside, it still fit, if not appearing a little loose.

He laughed and talked, then watched an old DVD of a Clint Eastwood western, growing quiet as the night stole in and he sunk, content, into his final decline. There was some pain. There were distressing final minutes of rattling breaths, the space between them elongating until the final exhale left him and he was gone.

He let go of life with a warm, friendly dachshund-spaniel mix puppy curled up on his lap and with me – the old friend – beside him.

I hadn't planned to go back to Pax's; he'd been clear that his plans to die alone should be respected.

But then I got home after a draining day and discovered that the comforts of being there were unsatisfying. The banished pleasures of TV and a few tumblerfuls of whiskey to end my day weren't missed, necessarily, but their upgraded replacements – Molly, a *purpose*, and other surprising friends and allies – were absent, too.

It was with great relief that I met Ed at the door. Ed, that was, and Molly, whose full-body wiggle was easily as enthusiastic as it had been on the day I'd found her. And I asked Ed to come in and he did, though he glanced at his car in the drive with not-quite-masked wistfulness.

"It'll just take a sec," I pleaded, surprised at myself. All I'd thought I'd wanted all day was home and rest, but there I was, begging for a friendly ear.

"Sure," he smiled, but there was concern in his eyes, too.

It was strange to see him in jeans and a t-shirt, topped with a flannel shirt which remained unbuttoned on a night that was typical of the transitioning of seasons from hot to chilly. Life to quick decline.

Canadian seasons were nothing if not individual in their extremes.

I made coffee while Molly got reacquainted with the place, sniffing each corner and every alcove. She finally settled into eating her dinner as Ed told stories of her day with his family, and by the time I sat opposite Ed, both of us with steaming mugs before us, she was curled up in her little corner bed.

"How was your day?"

That was all it took. I spilled the events of the day to my new, if not unlikely, friend without hesitation. His eyes grew wider as I spoke, and at the end of it, he sat back in his chair and folded his arms. I could almost see the clipboard he liked to hold against his chest.

"So yeah, it's been a day," I chuckled, already unburdened enough of be thankful for warm coffee as I put my mug to my lips.

"No kidding! Are you – I mean, how are you handling everything?"

I shook my head. Everything was jumbled together as though the days' events had all become one thing. "I don't think I've ever had to handle so much – so many things at once before."

"You were surprised; you expected your status card and some blood tests, and found yourself confronted with a friend who is getting well when you'd been sure she'd be dying, another long-time buddy who, in opposition to the first, is dying of cancer, and then a recently-acquired pal who appears to be in the last stages of MARS-21!"

My conversation with Jeremy had been short, and even then, fraught with discomfort on my part. The kid's unfailing enthusiasm still sparked behind his eyes, but his frustration at the inability to speak was evident in the way he sighed and pulled absently at his sheets. His fever was so high I could feel it off of him.

"Just seems so unfair," I shook my head.

Ed nodded, his eyes sad.

"I shouldn't keep you from your family," I smiled. "Thank you for listening, Ed."

"I'm sorry you had a rough first day," he smiled in return, but didn't rise.

"Holy God," I laughed. "I hadn't thought of it that way, but you're right: this is my *job* now."

Ed stood, then. "It's not an easy one," he lamented.

"Thanks for hanging out for a minute."

Molly was up and shaking the sleep off, making both of us laugh.

"She had a big day, too," Ed said, then looked at me again. "You didn't mention the fact that contacting your daughter has been on your mind, in addition to everything else."

"Still is. I'm hoping to call the home in Wakefield tomorrow; leave her a message, at least -" I slapped a thigh, making Molly jump. "Shit! I was going to drop that letter in the mail!"

"It's no wonder you forgot."

I shook my head. "No; I have to get it out or I'll be up all night thinking about it." A familiar weight resumed its position on my shoulders. It was guilt. It was the acknowledgement that I'd failed her again. I went for my wallet on the island, determined to walk to the mailbox at the entrance to the subdivision right then and there, but my phone rang before I could get to it.

Ed and I locked eyes.

"It's OK to take a night off, Tom."

The desire to do just that clashed painfully with the knowledge that time was no longer on my side. "It's alright, Ed. Go home; I'll call you tomorrow."

"I could drop the letter into the box -?"

The man was unfailingly kind. I didn't understand it. "No, but thank you, Ed. I feel like I need to do this for Louise-Anne. To show her, you know, that I can do more? Like you said."

He pressed his lips together and nodded, then disappeared into the night with a short wave and an "I'll talk to you tomorrow."

"Hello?" I focused on Molly in an effort to ground myself.

"Hey, uh, Tom?"

Pax's gravelly tone was so similar to how Jed's had been that my heart took off at a gallop. I was transported to the day the old man had died, then gripped by something like fear as I considered that Jed, too, had been restored. Only maybe *his* job was to retrieve wayward souls whose second chance had run out. But then Pax spoke again. Laughed, actually, and the resulting coughing fit clued me in.

"Oh... Pax?"

"None other," he managed between coughs.

"What's up? You OK?"

"I'm *dying*, you idiot," he laughed again, and I held the phone away from my ear as he hacked and gasped. It was several moments before he spoke again. "Look, before I kick the bucket on the phone, I'd better spit out what I called you for."

I gritted my teeth, unsure if I could handle any more that day.

"I know I said I wanted to be alone, but -"

He wanted company. *I'll drop the letter in the post box on the way,* I thought. But something in me balked. My whole body ached. I needed sleep.

"- but to tell you the truth, the normal routine feels a little different tonight. A little scary, if I'm honest, and you can go ahead and laugh, Wall -"

I didn't feel like laughing. A grizzled old guy like Pax admitting he was scared to be alone wasn't funny. It was straight-up *sad.* "Do you mind if I bring my dog?"

He hesitated, and when he spoke again, he sounded

grateful. "Don't mind 't'all."

I'd hung up, resigned. "Want to sit with an old friend of mine for a while?" I asked Molly, who ran to the door and looked expectantly up at me, tail wagging.

And I did mail the letter.

And I did sit with my friend, and so did Molly.

And I helped him make his calls and get to the bathroom. I refilled his glass and listened to his last confession – which was lengthy. And more than a little entertaining, if I'm honest.

And then I watched him breathe his last, tears streaming down my face. And I didn't even care anymore that I was crying all the time. I just regretted.

And I wondered which of the levels my friend would find himself on, and whether I would meet him there. And for the first time in my life – at least the life I lived in that body – I purposefully asked something of that *other* being. Maybe not the one that had ushered me into death and out of it again, and brought me back in my dreams, but the one that *that one* asked for things, too. And thanked. I asked that Pax be judged more on those last phone calls to his children and grandchildren than the contents of his lengthy confession.

And then I curled up on the couch, where Molly soon joined me, and faded into sleep with the strange knowledge that I had *prayed.* I had prayed and felt like it was *right.*

And then in the morning, I called Evan Cromwell about my dead friend in hopes that Ed was sleeping in.

CHAPTER 30 – WITHER

I heard the message from Ella as she left it. In the past, I'd have dropped whatever I was doing to race for the phone; I'd always imagined the worst at the sound of a phone call, and that only worsened with the divorce and then the pandemic.

What if it's Beck and there's something wrong with the kids?

What if it's work and another carer tested positive?

But things had changed.

I'd only been home a few days, but in that space of time I'd only seen my kids through online chats and I'd only heard from work to make sure my home wellness visit went as planned – I needed to comply with the care guide in order to be kept on as staff and receive sickness benefits.

I'd already applied for sick leave, though; sick pay from work would last two weeks, max, so practicality had ruled in my first few hours of isolation at home. I'd booked my wellness visit, applied for sick leave, prepared two large suitcases and left them on the step for Beck and the kids to pick up – which they did, the following day, but by then I was feeling panicky and stir-crazy and a little desperate, and I spent the whole visit apologizing.

And they spent the entire time encouraging me. Beck had quick-tested all three, and they'd be getting the intensive testing later that day. So far, so good. Considering the amount of time I'd spent beating myself up for waiting too long to get tested, the hopeful quick-test results were well-received.

But they wouldn't visit again until the weekend, and with immediate practicalities taken care of, I plummeted into depression like a fast-descending roller-coaster car.

The home visit by a city nurse was cold, uncomfortable, and ultimately useful only in that it confirmed I was sick, and that I was worse than even a couple of days earlier. Don't get me wrong; I wasn't in terrible pain, but I ached, and I had a fever that wouldn't be quelled by any pill or prescription. But it *really* hit home when the nurse examined my skeletal system; where Beck had been unable to palpate noticeable signs of bony deformities, the nurse instantly found them.

"But my back doesn't hurt any more than usual!"

She looked at me with sad, tired eyes. "If you have back pain in regular day to day life, the effects on your spine will be less obvious, at first," she replied with a heavy French accent.

My stomach had dropped; *at first…* it was such an ominous portent. "How long will it… take…?" I left the words hanging because I knew the answer. It could take days or weeks before I even knew if I'd decline into the worst of the symptoms. The question of life or death was even more difficult, for there wasn't enough data to show reliable trends. It seemed haphazard to me; some with lockjaw survived and some who were asymptomatic died!

The nurse patted my hand with her gloved one. "You are young, otherwise healthy, and have a family. The worst thing you can do right now is imagine the worst."

Easy words for one who had her freedom, who could walk out the door and go on to the next job. But I was stuck inside. Alone, like I'd wished for so many times when the chaos of family life and work and the uncertain state of the world was too much.

And I had no idea whether I'd come out of it.

So, by the time Ella called, I was well-ensconced in a windows-shut, TV binge-watching, near-catatonic funk. It didn't even occur to me to pick it up. I barely heard her words.

Hi, sweetheart. I just wanted to check in and see how you're surviving. My cousin Sandra did puzzles when she was in isolation, did I tell you that?

(She had).

Anyway, there is one more thing –

I perked up at the change in her tone.

A call came in for you today – I spoke to the man first, and then I transferred him over to Carroll, because I wasn't sure what to do. Sorry about that; you might not have wanted everyone in on it – ugh, I'm messing this up.

My stomach clenched. I knew it was my father – or *about* my father – before she continued.

The guy said he was your Dad, Lou. *I didn't know what to do... anyway, I just wanted to let you know. I don't know exactly what Carroll worked out with him; the guy wanted to leave you a message, at least. I didn't tell him you were sick...*

I sank back into my chair. He was *alive.*

He was alive. *I* was sick. It felt... unfair, at best.

Ella's voice faded into the background, but she was onto other things; sounded like personal updates and work gossip before ending her message.

Absently, I ran my fingers through my hair. My thoughts raced. My fingers went back to a spot at the center-front of my hairline, examining something a little more carefully.

What had Carroll said? What had they spoken about? *There's some comfort in knowing it's Carroll who ended up taking care of the call,* I mused, frowning.

Frowning at the unexpected turn of events. My estranged father couldn't have picked a worse time.

And frowning because the knot on my head was too big to be any of the things my subconscious had been listing – a bug bite, a swelling from a forgotten collision, a cyst – and it was harder, too. Like rock.

Like *bone*.

Grimacing, I left the sanctuary of my couch and made my way to the bathroom.

Still wondering at the news about Thomas Wall. *Why now?*

I could see it before I parted my hair, a small bony protrusion about an inch back from my hairline, smack-dab in the part.

"And now I'm a fucking *unicorn*," I muttered to myself. Tears welled as a lump formed in my throat.

And just when I thought I couldn't be more overwhelmed, there was a knock at the door.

CHAPTER 31 – DRINK
IN THE RAIN

I spent the following days at the hospital. More accurately, I spent the following *afternoons* at the hospital. In the morning, I took a walk with Molly, ran errands, and knocked on doors, as was mandatory for the job. Those mornings were quiet. Routine. Comfortable. Even the cold calls to check in on folks I'd lived near for years but hadn't even thought to connect with – were uneventful.

Most were unanswered, for various reasons, I'm sure. Some were sick, some were dead, some were gone – many had moved to summer homes or with family, leaving their old lives behind without bothering to secure a real estate agent or talk to their bank. In their defence, there were less of agents and banks alike. Few cared about mortgage payments anymore, so even best efforts were unsuccessful.

But sometimes I'd walk away from an unanswered door only to spot a scowling face in the window. Whether it was my reputation or fear of the virus, I can't speculate, but maybe both.

People had changed.

Those who answered had either given up on fear - as young Jeremy had – in favor of human connection, or to confront me, wary of my purpose. *Most* were surprised to see my badge. *All* were thrilled to welcome the pup.

Once the rounds were over, I'd cook up a lunch for myself and feed Molly, then head to the hospital.

Would you believe it was something I looked forward to? I could spend hours visiting patients, never once looking at the time. And Molly either stayed home or went to Ed's, depending on the day. Either way, she was happy.

I'd made more friends. Lyla, Linda's eye-rolling roommate, was the first. I brought her a stack of my own books and the Ottawa and Gatineau papers for both of them every day. She'd softened immediately, and I learned that a chocolate bar was good for bonus points. But the girl was quiet, losing herself in reading as soon as it was in front of her.

Linda and I had long talks – I'd never have figured an elderly, well-off woman for such a comfortable companion, but she was. Maybe it was because she'd decided I was a friend already; she never questioned that status, so I didn't, either. Both she and Lyla were on watch for release to Hull. Jerna – the same day nurse I'd spoken to on the first day I'd come – said they might just send Lyla home; she was doing that well.

Jeremy and I played games – Yahtzee, cribbage, Scrabble, checkers – you name it. He even coerced me to try the racing games he was so fond of on the game system he'd brought in. The latter were not my favorites.

The kid, contrary to Lyla and Linda, was not improving. His frustration over the lockjaw continued, but I'd brought a medicinal balm in to treat his dry, cracked lips. Especially the corners. The hospital provided spray bottles, which Linda swore was her idea long before it was theirs, but Jeremy suffered on. Loneliness, I think, was at the heart of his melancholy. He never wanted me to go, and that's saying something, considering I've never thought of myself the world's most pleasant companion.

By far.

You may be wondering why he didn't spend time with other patients, if he was hurting so much for human contact. But you mustn't forget that he was a teenager. When I talked about introducing him to Linda, and especially Lyla, his eyes had widened and he shook his head. Jeremy was far too self-conscious, especially considering the despised lockjaw.

I agonized over what I could do to ease his pain – physical or otherwise – but playing games with him seemed the best I could do.

And I hoped for his recovery. Desperately.

There were so many others; the fourth-floor patients were in critical condition; unable to spray their own mouths anymore. I would read to them, spread cream around their bony deformities and just chat – a skill I had resolved to have been bestowed upon me in addition to the restoration, given I'd never possessed it during the first go around.

I'd return home with Molly (or *to* her, depending) feeling a mixture of satisfaction and apprehension. My work had become more than my purpose; it had taken on the critical role of distracting me from thoughts of Louise-Anne, and the call that had stymied my progress in finding her.

Or helped – if the young man I'd spoken to had fulfilled his promise on his end, he would talk to my daughter; tell her I was hoping to contact her. But he'd asked for some time, said circumstances were difficult. Asked me for patience.

And Oh, God, I was trying. If you haven't picked up on it yet, though, patience has never been a virtue of mine.

So, the apprehension that came along with returning home was due to the typically quieter evenings and nights ahead.

But that night I was tired. I'd been present for two deaths on fourth floor that day. I knew it was more than coincidence that had me in the right place at the right time – and though it seemed odd, perhaps, that a volunteer would be allowed to stay during those last moments, the staff asked for nothing different. They watched as I held the hands of the failing sufferers and eyed me perhaps a little curiously afterward, but it had all gone without a hitch.

Which was why the first phone call that evening came as a shock.

Molly was already curled up in my lap and snoring softly when my phone vibrated, forgotten, in my back pocket. I squirmed a little until I could get it. Molly didn't notice.

"Tom Wall."

"Uh, yes, hello, Mr. Wall. This is Charisse; I'm at the Hull Center?"

Something's wrong. A spark of anxiety awakened in my chest and it was suddenly harder to breathe.

"Mr. Wall?"

I shook my head. "Yeah – I'm here."

"We've been getting the reports from your volunteer work at Gatineau. Looks like you've become quite popular."

I frowned, sinking back into the chair. "I – thank you?"

The woman laughed. "You're right; there's another reason for the call. Did you get the chance to read through your procedures pamphlet?"

Shit. "Um – not really; I sort of jumped in, I guess."

"No problem, Mr. Wall. The staff at Gatineau are very pleased with your work. But when a volunteer is present during patient deaths, it's procedure to have you come in for a post-event evaluation."

"A post – what? There were doctors and nurses; all I did

was hold their hands -" the old defensiveness was fighting to surface.

"Don't worry, Tom – can I call you Tom?"

"Sure."

"You're not in trouble; nothing like it – but volunteers are rarely present during the last moments of patients; I'm sure you understand. And without the training of official hospital staff, we need to do our due diligence to ensure you're handling the events well."

I frowned down at Molly as I ran my fingers through her silky fur.

"We just want to make sure you're OK," the woman added.

I nearly laughed. If she only knew what I'd seen...

"Tom?"

"I'm here. I just – if this is for my benefit only, it's not necessary. Is it – do I have to?"

She laughed again. "Not at all! But if you don't, you'll be prevented from attending the bedside of severely ill and declining patients, I'm afraid."

I laughed that time. "Oh, the irony," I muttered. I wondered if the being that had given me my assignment was laughing, too.

"Sir?"

"I just – the only reason I'm here is *because* the only person I've ever thought of is me, and now I can't do what I'm supposed to do because someone *else* is worried about *me*..."

"The – only reason you're here?"

I chuckled again. "Sorry; I'm babbling," I rubbed my forehead, a wave of exhaustion rolling over me. Realized my sleep had evolved again since I'd been brought back – I'd gone from not being able to sleep to needing an almost immediate recharge when events of the day caught up with me.

"Dr. Edna from Gatineau said there were *two* deaths with you present today."

I nodded. Closed my eyes, all traces of humour draining quickly. "They were peaceful," I said, wanting nothing more than to get off the phone.

"Why don't you take a day off?"

I had to smile again. A day off seemed an unimaginable waste, given I hadn't a clue if it would be my last. "I can't do that."

"Well, let me check the schedule; we might not even have a spot tomorrow, and I know the head of the blood study wants to see you, too -"

"What?" The spark of anxiety was back.

"Oh! That's the second reason I'm calling; apparently they'd like to take more blood; there were some interesting anomalies in your results."

"What does that mean?"

Another laugh. "I'm not sure, but it's not enough to take you off volunteer duty, so it can't be bad!"

I sighed. "Can you try very hard to get me in tomorrow? I'll do whatever time; early is fine."

She made a ticking noise. "Let me see…"

Molly looked up at me, stretched, then hopped down and went to the door.

"Well, you might regret saying you'd come in early; both the psychologist – her name is Bhupinder - and the study head – Dr. Pendleton – are in at the crack of sunrise. Could you do six?"

"Yep."

"Oh! Alright; let's schedule the bloodwork for six and give Dr. Raja – she likes everyone to call her by her first name – a chance to settle in. There; six forty-five at the psych department on second. Sound doable?"

I would have said yes to three AM if it would've gotten me off the phone. "Absolutely." I got up and opened the door for Molly.

"Great. It's booked. I won't be in until nine tomorrow, but I'm usually in appointments and scheduling on first, OK? And it's Charisse."

"Lucky you; it's probably rare to get to sleep in, these days."

There was an awkward hesitation before she answered. "I'm actually getting my blood drawn, too. We'll both be up early, I'm afraid."

She was sick. "Oh. I'm sorry."

"No worries; drop by the office anytime, Mr. Wall."

"Tom."

"Tom. Have a good night, Tom."

"Thank you," I muttered, and hung up. I looked at the phone, transported from overwhelmed and exhausted to exhausted and sad.

I put the phone on the island and went to the porch. I flicked on the light and Molly was bounding toward me right away. I bent to scratch her ears and she licked my face enthusiastically.

"Blech," I laughed, but it was a weak protest. "Let's go in."

But there'd been another call when we were outside,

and I recognized the name immediately: Carroll Krull. Heart hammering in my chest, I dialed the number. Voicemail picked up after five rings and I crumbled, my forehead on the cool countertop.

He hadn't left a message for me, but I left one. I couldn't *not.*

Carroll? I saw you called – just missed you, actually. Feel free to call me back if you get this tonight; don't worry about the time.

I closed my eyes, breathing deeply and trying to steel myself; the desperation at the edges of my words was verging on pathetic.

If not, call me anytime tomorrow; I'll have my phone all day.

I paused, evaluating the many other things that wanted to come out of my mouth, then dismissing them.

Thanks, Mr. Krull, I said instead, and hung up.

I'd never felt so – *deflated.*

Molly gave a high-pitched yip that made me jump.

"What's wrong with you?" She was sitting at the entrance to the hallway. She turned and padded down it, as though there was no option but for me to follow. And the thought of a soft pillow and peaceful darkness proved too tempting to ignore, so I did.

CHAPTER 32 – REVIVE

The heavy-lidded nurse that took my blood had little to say; when I asked why we were repeating the tests, she sighed and said the doctor would be in to speak with me after the blood draw. I swallowed my frustration – I was up early, too, and uncomfortably full. I may have overcompensated where I'd lacked the first time around, only to discover that *overeating* didn't help, either.

Nonetheless, the quiet nurse was efficient, and I quickly found myself alone in the exam room, waiting, with nothing to occupy my mind but my own thoughts.

Never a good thing.

I focused on the day so far. Perhaps unwise, given it was a mere six-fifteen in the AM, but it seemed safe, at least. I'd slept deep and heavy, which was a welcome relief. I even awoke a few minutes before my alarm would've sounded; I'd pondered the many such events as I switched it off. Wondered whether my newly-acquired internal clock, not to mention the sense of tact – even outright *compassion* – I'd gained was the work of forces beyond the earthly realm. I dropped the musings quickly, though; I'd never considered such things, and existential theorizing seemed an insurmountable force to navigate when added to the already challenging current of my second go at life.

Molly had slept on, only moving to burrow into the covers with a comical groan when I rose. I went about the business of eating bacon, eggs and toast while checking the news online. I hadn't thought about what to do with the pup until the last second, then realized I'd waited too long to ask Ed's family to take her. I was considering taking her along and keeping her in the car with the windows cracked when I went back to the bedroom to get dressed, but the sleepy pup wouldn't be roused.

"You don't want to come?"

She grunted and tucked her long snout into the blankets.

"I'll be a few hours." I'd settled on an expanded route for neighborhood knock rounds that morning; by then I knew where people were and who was sick, as well as where the "empties" sat. Ed and Evan had both been impressed by the makeshift maps I'd sketched; they'd even hired a student to transfer the data into a spreadsheet so we could track stats.

I checked on the living that were healthy once a week; most wouldn't welcome even that. The sick were looked in on daily, and I would contact resources for them – meal delivery, grocery delivery, medication delivery, and the home-visit staff of the local "CLSC," which was the organization of medical clinics in Quebec. Ambulances were a rare, but vital call, and – thank God – I rarely had to call in the post-mortem resources. As long as I kept tabs on their well-being, my duties where death was concerned seemed concentrated at the hospital, which was fine by me.

And apparently, my work was helping. Even Cromwell had muttered a wish that every community had one or two of me, and I'd let it sink in good. That was another new trick; praise had bounced off the wall I'd built around myself all my life, but now, it felt good. So good, I clamoured for more.

"OK," I whispered. "But you're not allowed to eat anything but your food while I'm gone, and if you have to go outside, you're going to have to hold it."

To my astonishment, the pup appeared from under the

blankets and jumped down from the bed without a backward glance.

She trotted to the door and sat, head down and eyes still heavy, until I let her out, where she did her business, then demanded entry. I couldn't help but laugh as she returned to the bedroom; I couldn't blame her. I followed, jaw agape, and watched her dive under the covers again.

"You're no ordinary pup, are you?" I had asked quietly. And I almost expected her to answer. When she didn't, I went back to my business and prepared to go.

Actively shoving down the realization that I wouldn't have years to enjoy her. Or long at all, likely.

I'm not saying I didn't think of Carroll Krull's call the night before as I got ready that morning. It was barely held at bay. Nor had I been able to stop considering *why* he'd called. Surely, he'd had something new to say. He must've talked to Louise-Anne, or else why call me back? But then, it was him calling, *not* Louise-Anne, which may have meant that she wasn't ready to talk to me at all...the possibilities circled endlessly as I tried to keep busy.

And I checked my phone obsessively, just to make sure the ringer was on.

It was entirely new to ruminate on something that wouldn't bring me personal gain in the form of physical pleasure, money or control. Contrarily, the effort to contact my daughter had brought more inner turmoil to my life than any of my past brushes with the law – and promised to bring more! But rather than feeling bad, it conjured something else: *hope*.

And I wasn't willing to let go of it.

I won't tell you I spent long hours considering my actions or drowning in regret; I'd done that already, with a notebook full of "goodbye, everything" letters to show for it.

What I was doing during that time was different, I think. It was growth in ways I'd never known existed.

I shook my head and stood, pacing the small examination room with mounting anxiety. I was done wallowing in the past – even if it was the events of that morning! Time was uncertain.

But likely short.

I poked my head into the hallway, but found it empty. Not willing to sit again in the quiet of the in-between, and aware I was minutes away from meeting with the psychologist one floor up, I opened the door on the opposite side of the room labelled "Staff." And nearly ran smack-dab into the doctor as she reached for the handle.

"Oh!" Her hand fluttered to her heart.

I stepped back quickly. "Sorry."

"Mr. Wall?" She gestured to the table with its wrinkled paper covering.

I sat. "Yes. I – uh – I have another appointment…"

She regarded me from her newly-gained height advantage. "Yes, I know. No worries, we'll have you on your way in no time." Her smile was tight. "I'm Eva Pendleton; I head the study you're a part of. I want to thank you for participating."

I nodded, unable to speak, lest the words *get on with it* come out.

"We've asked you to do the tests again today because there were some anomalies in your blood. I'll address the least interesting first: have you ever been diagnosed with hypertension, Mr. Wall?"

I made a face. Surely, they'd gotten my records from my family doctor -? "Borderline; I haven't seen my doc in a while, though. I filled out the information in my intake forms last time..."

She scanned her chart. "Right; Dr. Barnes was your family doctor, which explains why we don't have your records."

I frowned. "How so?"

She raised her eyes to mine. "When's the last time you saw your doctor?"

I pondered. "Huh. Probably the day he prescribed the cart."

She raised her eyebrows.

"Oh," I smiled and gestured around the room at the lack of a cart. "I don't -" I cleared my throat, suddenly awkward. *I should've thought this through.*

"Why did you have a motorized cart, Mr. Wall?"

"I – uh – I had some circulation issues and needed help getting around, but -"

"Do you have diabetes?"

I gestured to her chart. "That I *know* is in there."

She scanned it again, lips pressed into a tight line. "Right." She frowned at me. "It's very rare to reverse circulation problems related to diabetes – especially to the point you no longer need equipment you've been prescribed."

I nodded.

"What's happened?"

It should've been easy. My first instinct was to lie; the truth would have me out of the volunteer appointments at the hospital, at the very least. But the words wouldn't come. All I could do was clear my throat again. My greasy breakfast was a rock in my stomach.

"Mr. Wall?"

"I – uh – I lost a lot of weight, started moving around more. I walk a lot. I have a dog, now; we – oh! I'm deputized, so I spend a lot of time checking in on folks. And volunteering!" I found myself validating my good health rather than explaining my recovery.

"You're saying that you've overcome your diabetes-related issues due to being more active and losing weight?"

It was my turn to press my lips together.

"And you've also come through the MARS virus.'

I nodded.

"That's extraordinary, Mr. Wall."

"Tom."

She nodded. Her dark eyes remained fixed on mine.

I squirmed. "I'm better, so I wanted to help people." *Huh.* Those words had come easily enough.

She nodded slowly, considering, then waved a hand. "Let's get you to your next appointment, shall we?"

I frowned. "Wait – aren't you going to tell me what else you found? You said the hypertension thing was the least interesting!"

She smiled tightly. "Why don't we wait until these results come back, so we have something to compare the last ones with?"

"But – can I go back to the hospital?"

"Yes – despite what we've found, we're sure you're not putting anyone at risk – quite the contrary," she laughed, and I moved forward on the table.

"I'd really appreciate knowing what that means."

She tapped a finger on her clipboard. "Preliminary findings were confusing, which is why I'd like to wait, but I can say that we're excited to see if we can replicate the results."

Unsatisfied, I reversed her trick and stared her down. Amazingly, it worked.

"We can see you've had the virus, and that you've recovered -"

"Go on."

"But there's something else; you still have virus cells!"

"Wha' – you mean I have MARS still, but have the antibodies as well?"

Her eyes lit up as she nodded. "Yes, but the MARS cells are – different. Mutated so that they appear to be dormant. And -" she hesitated, "- we found what looks to be an antigen – which is something that induces the production of antibodies – *attached* to the dormant cells."

"I don't understand."

She shook her head, but the light in her eyes remained. "We don't, either. And that's why we needed more from you. If we can't replicate the findings, we know something went wrong the first time around. But if we can – we may have found the answer we've been looking for."

"What? Like, a cure?"

She lowered her eyes. "I won't say that. Yet."

The room spun.

"Mr. Wall?"

"Tom." My own voice echoed as I blacked out.

"Tom!" there was the sound of a clipboard clattering to the floor and then small but strong hands gripped my biceps. "Tom, stay with me."

I blinked rapidly. I wouldn't waste a day on a faint. Stars burst in front of me, and then I could see the doctor. "I'm alright." I took an effort to straighten myself, as the room seemed oddly tilted.

"Mr. Wall – Tom – I'm also a little concerned with your blood pressure; it's been high on both visits. We usually chalk it up to nerves, but -"

I rubbed my eyes, breathing deeply.

"Have you been having a lot of dizzy spells? Any chest pain?"

Yes, and yes. "Some," I muttered into my palm. The strange episodes of irregular heartbeats came to minds, too. The crippling pain of my dream came back to me and a sense of foreboding threatened to darken my vision again.

"I'd like you to have a workup," she regarded me sternly. "This may sound selfish, Mr. Wall, but if your body contains *any* answers to MARS-21, we need you healthy. We need you *alive.*"

I shook my head. "This is too much," I mumbled. I pressed my palms against the table, crinkling the paper. "What am I supposed to *do* with this?" *I wasn't supposed to save the world!* was what I was thinking. *Or, maybe I'll die again before they can use whatever it is I'm carrying!* That *would make more sense, where I'm concerned. An epic failure as the last straw on the haystack of an existence that I'm largely ashamed of, according to my newly-enlightened standards.*

"You're not alone, Tom. I have a whole team of people who will make sure you're well taken care of; look, why don't you go to your appointment and then come back to the nursing station to let me know you're finished? I'll get you into the lab right away and we can at least check you over and figure out what we're working with."

I stood. "I can't."

She looked perplexed. "Why not?"

"I have important things to do," I said, flustered. "My pup is at home alone and I need to do my rounds; I'm doing a new route today. Houses I've not been to at all, yet. And I'm expecting an important call..." to my horror, my eyes filled with tears as a sense of overwhelm threatened to ruin any hold I had on my focus.

She patted my bicep, her hand gentle rather than the vise-like grip she'd demonstrated moments earlier. "OK, Tom. It's alright! I don't think you're going to fall over on us suddenly," she chuckled reassuringly, despite the hint of desperation in her eyes, "but I *would* like to get you back in for a workup – it might even make sense to wait until we've looked at your blood, so we can do all the tests we need to do at once." She looked up at me, her eyes wide and sincere behind the obvious plea.

I nodded. "But if things - I can't -" I fought to voice the thing that ate at me, "I can't get – stuck – here. I have too much to do."

She nodded firmly. "Then I'll do everything in my power to ensure we work with you on an outpatient basis. Sound fair?"

"If this is true," I shook my head again, disbelieving, "if you need more from me – what will that mean?"

"You don't have to worry for now, Tom. We'll work together, OK?"

It was so comforting, I let it placate me.

She smiled. "Off to Bhupinder, now. Don't worry; she's fantastic."

CHAPTER 33 – REPAIR

"So, you've been incarcerated at least five times, with your longest consecutive time spent inside being three years?"

I nodded. Yawned.

She smiled. "I know this is all old news to you, but if I'm to understand who the man in front of me is today, it is helpful to learn his past."

Her Indian accent was pleasant, as was her gentle, quiet manner, but I was beyond my tolerance limit. "What exactly do we need to accomplish here to get me back to the hospital?"

She leaned back in her chair, looking oddly satisfied. "You're an intelligent man, Thomas."

I frowned.

"The fact that your criminal activity never escalated to the point where it would alter your entire life speaks to that, and so does the fact that you've made so many changes of late."

I smirked. "You should know that most of the changes I've made are due to obligation rather than some grand epiphany." It sounded right, but didn't feel it.

"You still have a *choice*, Thomas, even if your sense of obligation is running on overdrive."

Do I? I supposed I could choose to be deaf to the spirit that had interrupted my demise, or blind to the opportunity I had to change things beyond the earthly plane. I could go to that dark, sweltering place and exist in a way quite similar – at least metaphorically – to the way I'd lived my life on earth.

Then again, the common theme throughout my contact with the one who'd brought me back had indeed been *choice*, hadn't it?

"Thomas?"

I looked up at her instinctively, but my thoughts whirled on.

"Sometimes circumstances and events, especially if they occur in formative years – childhood, in other words – change us in such a way that we aren't even able to see other possibilities."

"I'm not going to blame my actions on my rotten childhood," I muttered. My arms crossed in front of my chest, seemingly of their own accord. I wondered how many of my actions had been so automatic. How many had been changeable, if I'd only known to hesitate?

"I'm not suggesting you use your past as a crutch or an excuse; I'm only suggesting a different perspective. That you acknowledge that, while you have made the choices in your life, they have been heavily influenced by circumstances beyond your control."

I thought of the dreams I'd been having. About the orders given by a presence far more powerful than I'd ever known one could be, and nodded. "You might be right about that."

She nodded, but said nothing.

"But what if – what if the choices I've made to change for the better have been at least as heavily influenced by outside sources as the ones I made throughout my life?"

She shook her head, chuckling. "It doesn't matter, Thomas. *All* choices matter, and based on the very little you've shared with me, I am impressed by you."

I clenched my jaw. It was an uncomfortable compliment.

"It's alright; it may take some time for you to accept that, despite the reputation your past has earned you, you are a good person."

She regarded me as I silently digested her words.

"Let's try something."

"Huh?"

"Will you humour me for a few moments?"

I shrugged. I was thinking of the pup and of Linda and Jeremy. And I was tired.

"I'm going to ask you a series of questions and I want you to give me short, *fast* answers, OK?"

The word "fast" perked me up. "Sure."

She grabbed a pen and notebook off the table beside her, making me realize she hadn't written anything, yet. Odd for one in such a position. She flipped to a clean page, then looked up at me, eyes hard. "You said your mother died giving birth to you; how?"

"What?"

"What exactly caused her death?"

I clapped my mouth shut. The knowing that *I* had caused her death had always seemed complete. "I – don't know."

"And your father?"

I shook my head, dizzy at the sudden transition.

"Quickly, Thomas."

"Unknown."

She raised her eyebrows. "Have you tried to figure it out?"

I frowned. "I guess I never had the opportunity."

"Why not?"

I thought back, reluctantly. "I guess whenever I asked about it, I got shut down."

"Who did you ask?"

I shrugged again. "Fosters. Social workers. Later on, I talked to a lawyer -"

"Oh?"

"A court-appointed one, but they weren't mandated to delve into that kind of thing -"

She made some notes, I watched her breathe through her nose, wondering if I should say more.

"You had one foster family?"

I laughed. "No."

She looked up. "Two?"

I shook my head. "To be honest, I lost count, but I don't think you could count them on both hands."

Her brows furrowed. "That's unfortunate." She wrote some more.

I squirmed in my seat.

"Did you keep in touch with – any of them?"

I only laughed.

She wrote some more. "What about personal relationships?"

"Huh?"

"Friends? A family of your own?"

"I have buddies," I replied with a noticeable defensive edge to my voice.

"Are all of your friends – like you?"

There it was – the spark of anger I thought would come much earlier in the session. But they'd been right; Bhupinder was good.

"I ask because ex-convicts tend to feel comfortable with other ex-convicts," she smiled, no judgement apparent.

I nodded, thinking of the guys I'd played darts with. "For the most part. Not now, though."

"And a family? Did you ever marry?"

I cleared my throat. "Technically, I'm still married." My voice was quieter than I'd expected, even with an admission I hadn't spoken aloud since my last court appearance, which had been over a decade earlier.

"Oh!"

"I haven't seen her in years," I added quickly.

"Is she still alive, then?"

I shrugged, my cheeks burning. "I don't know." I perked up. "There've been others; my most recent girlfriend left - er, she's passed since then, actually - she had issues," I chuckled, "- issues like mine, I guess," I finished, uncomfortable.

"Any children?"

I heard my own sharp intake of breath. Nodded.

"Do you have a relationship with them?"

"Her," I corrected. "And, no."

Her eyes softened. Her pen froze in midair. "But you want to."

"I do, now." Her soft eyes remained on mine. I noted the darkness of them. The shining depths. Her eyes held a sort of peace. "Maybe I always have."

She smiled.

"Is that it?"

She looked down at her notes, then stood and crossed to a whiteboard, which took up a good portion of the wall opposite. Then, she drew what looked to be a small boy. She smiled over her shoulder, then said, "If *I* had a son named Thomas, I'd call him 'Tommy,'" she said, writing the name above the figure. Then she wrote the number nine in brackets. Looked back at me again. "He's nine years old," she explained.

I was reminded of the torturous, never-ending days of elementary school, with teachers at the blackboard, expectant. I remembered how their eyes would pass over me as though they hadn't seen me at all, and how their faces hardened when I spoke. How they looked to be teetering on the edge of disappointment before I said a thing.

Next, she switched her black marker for red, then looked at her notes, scribbling bullet points around the figure: "orphan," "no known family history," "bounced around foster care," and then, "abused," before looking back at me again. "Is that fair?"

My heart was hammering in my chest. "I never said that."

She tilted her head slightly to the left, eyes soft.

"Guess it was implied," I muttered. Then, "It's fair."

She kept going, each word solidifying parts of my life I'd never considered from an outside point of view. My eyes widened. She'd brought us back around to perspective. She *was* good.

She kept going, adding, "little to no support system, trouble with the law as a minor, at the mercy of his reputation, estranged from loved ones," and more, but I stopped trying to keep up when she wrote the last one.

Loved ones.

Even if they didn't love me, they were loved. By others, surely, but most relevantly, by me. I found myself swearing under my breath.

She turned, breathing a little harder, and regarded me expectantly. "It's a lot for little Tommy here, isn't it?" she gestured to the small figure, who'd become surrounded by the words. A tangled cage. And then she kept going, but the words started to cross the figure completely – "conditioned" over his face, "traumatized" across his chest, "abandoned repeatedly" obscuring his legs.

By the time she turned back around and gestured backward to the ruined figure, I was fighting to swallow a lump in my throat. "This little boy believes the words that cover him because it's all he's ever known. What's worse, every time he reached out for help, he was disappointed. She turned, writing, "helpless" over the other words, and "hopeless" on top of that.

"Stop," I cried, my voice cracking.

She turned. "He only had a choice much later in life, when he had the chance to realize he could affect people's perception of him. He *still* hasn't learned to change his own!"

I shook my head. "Isn't this intense for a first session, doc?"

She sighed, then crossed to her chair. "You've only come to see me today because you *have* to if you want to continue the full schope of your volunteering. And that's important to you, right?"

I nodded.

"I might not see you again. But I'd like to."

I glanced at the board.

"It's easy to see why that little boy found himself on a path less desirable than the average kid when you can see him from the outside, isn't it?"

I nodded. The truth insisted on it.

"Good. Then today has been useful. But I'm going to say some more things, just in case I don't see you again."

I laughed nervously, then held my breath, the smile fading rapidly as she continued to peer seriously at me.

"In the past, I've – *we have,* as doctors – liked to steer clear of diagnoses until we've investigated thoroughly. But now, time is of the essence, wouldn't you agree?"

"Absolutely."

"Then I'll tell you that I think you have Post-Traumatic Stress Disorder, and that you've probably had it since your mother died."

"Is that possible?"

"Yes."

Since she'd died. Died giving birth to me.

"And I wouldn't be surprised if you have panic, anxiety, and depressive issues, as well."

I pressed my lips together.

"At *least.*"

The other possibilities abounded in her eyes, but she was silent for a few moments. My gaze was locked on hers, though, seeing that there was so much more, if I was only willing to explore it. *Able* to explore it. But I knew I wasn't. It was an opportunity missed in a past life.

"Would you take medication if I prescribed it to you?"

I shook my head.

"Didn't think so. Have you self-medicated in the past? Alcohol? Drugs?"

I nodded.

"But not anymore?"

I shook my head, again.

"At least there's that."

We stared at each other comfortably, that time.

"I'm going to clear you. Will you come see me again?"

I paused. "I don't know." The woman had earned my honesty, at the very least.

She smiled. "I think you're probably in the most hopeful time of your life, Thomas. I think you're going to be OK. And I think you're a good person."

My tongue refused to reply, but the lump in my throat grew.

"I like you."

It was so simple, but what it meant was enormous.

I laughed. "I think you might be the smartest doctor I've met."

"The pandemic has taught me much," she replied, her eyes sad.

"Can I go to the hospital today?"

She nodded. "Yes."

CHAPTER 34
– BLOOM

The days started to run together. Without a schedule or deadlines, I became lost in the hours and minutes and seconds, only thinking of the passage of time as the bars of sunlight made their way across the living room floor.

The kids called every night. It was what I lived for. They'd update me on their day, we'd talk about the first few days of school – being back in the classroom had brought a new brightness to their eyes. I could see it and was happy for it.

Beck would always appear briefly to flash a wave or ask how I was doing.

I wasn't doing well.

Besides the weight of depression, I was most definitely dealing with the degenerative effects of MARS-21. I tried not to dwell on it. After discovering the lone horn-like protrusion at the front of my head, I avoided the mirror... but it was hard to deny the way new angles of me poked into my recliner. Or into the mattress at night.

I was changing; becoming something new. Something *worse* than I had been. And I was alone.

But I dared not dwell on that fact, either, because It was my own fault I was alone. Hadn't I ordered Carroll away the other day? I'd seen the confusion in his eyes when the forced smiles wore thin.

He'd come to talk to me about my father, though. The idea was doomed from conception.

He'd been smiling behind his face shield when I finally opened the door and struck a comical pose in his full protective getup. I'd forced a laugh, but tears had sprung to my eyes, too. Why had he come?

Nothing seemed hopeful, anymore. I could barely believe we'd shared a moment not so long before, that had made my heart gallop excitedly in my chest. Carroll Krull could never think of me – differently. I was a single mother of two teenaged kids. And I was dying.

"I want to tell you about my conversation with your father," he'd said, adding, "I know the message from Ella was probably surprising."

A tear had dropped to my cheek. "I'm sorry, Carroll, but I can't do this right now," I'd mumbled. Every inch of me felt defeated.

He'd frowned. "I'm sorry. I should've called -"

I could see that he wanted me to refute the sentiment. And I could see something fade in his eyes when he realized I wouldn't.

This man who had revealed a wish I'd been unaware of with a moment of closeness alone. This man who'd spoken to my father on the phone effortlessly, when I'd been painfully denied the opportunity my entire life. The contradicting profundities tasted bad, somehow.

"Just leave me alone," I'd sighed, each word heavy in my throat.

"Are you – do you think it's getting worse?"

I'd rolled my eyes. "Who cares? Just go."

The hurt in his eyes was reflected in my heart.

"I'm going to send another nurse," he said.

"Whatever." I'd closed the door, my energy draining so quickly that I found myself on the floor, my forehead pressed against the ceramic. Everything hurt.

His retreating footsteps were a relief.

But he'd made good on his promise; it was two days later when another knock came. I didn't hope for Carroll, that time. Just opened it.

"Lou-Anne Wall?" Bright blue eyes sparkled from behind her face shield.

I nodded. "You're the nurse?"

She smiled enthusiastically. I suddenly wanted to kick her, but immediately felt guilty. "I'm just here to give you a checkup!"

I stepped away from the door and ushered her in.

"Oh! Your mailbox was overflowing; I hope you don't mind," she tittered as she pulled a stack of mail from her satchel with gloved hands.

I reached absently for it, muttering something along the lines of a thank you, but froze as I spotted the letter on top of the stack.

It was from my father.

"Holy shit," I breathed.

The nurse giggled as she brought out her equipment. "Told you it was overflowing."

And I can tell you now that bringing that letter in to me was the most useful thing she did. I didn't need her to tell me I was declining – to check my spine, her features darkening with each discovery of mutation. To puzzle over the growing protrusion just behind my hairline or note the stiffening hinges of my jaw. I was a nurse, too.

But she'd put the letter in my hands.

And when she left, I opened it with trembling fingers and read it quickly, holding my breath just to feel it burning in my lungs because it was better to feel that than to feel hope. To feel disappointment.

And then I exhaled and burst into tears, because his words were good. He'd said everything right, and suddenly my need for something - *anything* – from him was slaked. For the first time in my life, he'd loved me as a father should, and let me know about it.

I could've been satisfied then and there; I could've gone on to die of the disease that had demolished life as we knew it with some comfort. I'd been a good mother, a dedicated nurse. A wife who'd tried her best before she failed. And finally, a daughter loved by both of her parents.

But then I refolded the paper and saw there was something on the back of it, and my resolve – my sense of closure – changed.

I'm not going to do it this time, either, it said.

I've written so many notes of goodbye, but I never go on to do the deed. I'm a chicken, I guess. Or maybe...maybe I'm holding on to that thin thread of a possibility that someday I'll see her again.

And that's worth living for.

I was crying, knowing it wasn't written *for* me, but that *I* was who he'd meant.

The word *FUCK* was scrawled beneath the lines in all-caps and a fervor revealed through the dents it made in the paper, and near the bottom, two words, each on a line of their own:

Tomatoes

Bacon

I went to the living room for my phone and held it against my chest for a moment, eyes closed, breathing.

And then I dialled Carroll.

CHAPTER 35 – BLOSSOM

It was as though when Lou-Anne left, she took any spark of joy that had been re-establishing itself at the home with her. The residents asked after her with a twinkle in their eyes and my whole chest would fill up like it always did when I thought of her. And I'd hide the truth from them because I knew how it felt to want to be in her presence.

And to have lost the chance.

To have waited too long.

Before the pandemic, it seemed as though time was all we had; I was working to establish myself as a fixture at the home, but non-intrusively. I wanted to learn both from the staff and the residents. I wanted to see it all differently than my father. A business, yes, but an important moral endeavor, too. I'd always wanted to care for people; the business side of things was circumstantial.

Lou-Anne was this captivating presence – and not just for me! Everyone gravitated to her, and none was ever turned away. I guess that part of it intimidated me a bit. I'd always been labelled "shy," but in reality, it was near-paralysing social anxiety. My parents had insisted on years of therapy, but being at the home was better than any of that. The residents were hungry for contact, even if it was awkward or quiet. Often, they just needed a listener. And suddenly, I was trying harder just to be there with people... and I was thriving. Making connections. I'd never been so excited for anything in my life.

I complained, but in retrospect I can see how valuable it was for me to be forced into the cook position; suddenly I was in contact with everyone! I was the receiver of compliments and complaints alike, at the mercy of a rigid menu and a staff of two. I managed the two ends of the spectrum for the home – the finances and the food. Odd, perhaps, and completely overwhelming, but who knows what would have happened if I'd still been hidden away in my musty office most of the day. Or what wouldn't have happened, as the case may be.

But the change in roles had me all over the home, and offered a gift beyond the socialization I so sorely needed but struggled to attain – it meant my path would inevitably cross Lou-Anne's, and she'd smile that bright-eyed smile that made everything else disappear. And everything would feel… right.

How did she do that? I didn't know, but it gripped me with promise.

So, like I was saying, after the virus hit and things changed so much, it seemed selfish to ask for more from her, even if it was just a moment to learn my feelings.

That was why, when I was testing her and there was that moment – I saw something there that fuelled me like nothing ever had. I saw the reflection of my admiration in her eyes.

And though I tried to remain practical and cool, it blinded me.

When her father called and revealed things about her *nobody* knew, my hopes were bolstered even more. So, when I went to her house, in full garb because I knew she'd have it no other way, my mind was perhaps on the wrong things. I was thinking about that moment. I was thinking about her past – her life without a father – and that in a small way, I had a connection to her that few had, if only because I *knew*.

I was thinking all of that when I should only have been thinking that she was *sick*. And she was something else, too, when she opened the door.

She was defeated. *Beaten* by a disease that had brutally proven itself to be apocalyptic in nature. It was taking her.

It scared me out of my boyish fantasies of a future where we'd be something more than work acquaintances. In her expression – in the way she sighed and moved her limbs as though they were weighted as much with sadness as they were by illness. In the way she told me to go, her words heavy with apathy. There it was: whether Lou-Anne *had* a future at all was what I needed to be thinking about.

And since she had closed that door, it had been. It was my sole focus, much to the dismay of my father and the state of the books. I arranged for the health nurse to visit and tried to talk to Tom, her father, again. And then, I waited.

When her name flashed on my phone, though, a sense of foreboding came over me. I should've been glad, but that old feeling of impending doom was back again. Only that time, I was right.

"Lou-Anne?"

"Oh, Carroll," she cried, then sniffed loudly.

"What's wrong?"

"I just wanted to tell you I'm so sorry for the way I treated you the other day."

My stomach fell. "What's wrong?"

"The nurse I just saw is going to tell you that things are getting worse. I don't know how long it will be until I can't speak – my jaw is aching terribly – so I wanted to apologize, and to say thank you for everything you've done."

I was lightheaded. I sat hard on the cement barrier in the

parking lot of the home. She was worse. She was talking like she was dying.

"Carroll?"

I shook my head. "I'm sorry, Lou-Anne. I was being selfish the other day; I was thinking about seeing you when I should only have been concerned about your health -"

She laughed. "Don't do that, Carroll. I was *glad* you came to see me."

"You were?"

"Carroll, you have to know I – I admire you."

It should have made me feel better, but the dread that had filled me at the sight of her name only intensified. "What can I do? What do you need?"

She cleared her throat. "I need you to contact Thomas Wall again. You can give him my address. I – I just can't seem to call him myself."

"Of course."

"Oh. I thought you might need more of an explanation -"

"I just want to do whatever I can to help." I tried and failed to swallow the aching lump in my throat.

"Oh, Carroll," she sighed.

I pressed on my eyes with my free hand. "Please let me help you. I – I *admire* you, too."

There were sounds of her crying again. I waited.

"I'm so sorry, Carroll."

"For what?"

"I feel like – I've missed out on something, and now it's too late to - to -"

The emotion in my chest rose like a heatwave and

pushed tears from my eyes. "I know," was all I could say.

"I – I wondered if you could do something else for me?"

"Anything."

"I want to make videos for my children."

I squeezed my eyes shut against the pain and more tears spilled. I felt anger like I'd never experienced in that moment, though I can't say exactly why. For loss, I guess. And for the unfairness of it all. "Of course."

"OK. Can you come later today?"

I nodded.

"Carroll?"

"Yes," I said, my voice gruff.

"Are you crying?"

"Yes," I said again.

She said nothing for a long moment.

"Can I bring you anything?"

"Some popsicles, maybe?"

I thought of the freezer stuffed to the brim with them; the residents had wanted nothing more when they were sick, especially those with lockjaw. "Alright," I forced. "See you soon."

CHAPTER 36 – FRUIT

With Molly happily installed at Ed's house, I determined to spend the afternoon at the hospital. The sense of purpose I'd first hated had fully evolved into something like a healthy addiction. I wondered at how I'd never discovered it during my lifetime – the pure satisfaction of being a positive force in someone's life.

The old me would have laughed his hole off at the admission. But then, I didn't much care what the old me thought anymore.

I'd been managing the deputy duties and hospital work smoothly, and Molly and I had a nice routine at home. Snatches of time with Ed and his family – even at a distance – felt *good* rather than... well, rather than what the old me would have felt.

The only thing I'm not on top of in this strange, new life, I thought as I approached the hospital entrance, *is my own health.* And it wasn't for lack of effort on the Center's part; Dr. Pendleton's name had appeared on my phone every day since my last visit. I knew avoiding her wouldn't be possible for long, but I'd sort of convinced myself it was OK for just a little longer.

I had things to do, and something about the prospect of talking to Eva Pendleton made me feel like it was a sure-fire way into having far less freedom than I needed to do them.

It wasn't just the blood tests. *That* I wasn't even thinking about; it was too much. It was the stuff about the hypertension

– the workup. In my mind, it would have been wasteful. But how could I convey that without sounding - at the very least - fatalistic? Maybe even unstable. Certainly, negative enough to have them concerned about my mental health all over again.

The scratchy sound of paws on pavement had me turning as I opened the door. *Another stray,* I mused as I watched an emaciated German Shepherd sniff around a garbage can. I'd seen a group of strays on the way in, too. They'd been an issue since the second wave; people tended to wait too long to figure out what to do with their pets, and then found themselves unable to think about it at all. And the city had struggled to control it, even losing staff to emergency care positions by mandate. Apparently, the struggle continued.

I went to fourth first. Visiting the more stable patients on third had proven to be a balm on the wounds the fourth inflicted. I wondered, sometimes, about that first day when I was told the critical care patients were on sixth. From what I could see, people died on *fourth*. I'd rationalized it over and over – maybe sixth had more staff? Or the more complicated cases, if not the most critical? But as I gained experience, it became harder to explain away.

When I was met with Jenna's smile as I got off on fourth, though, I thought maybe it was time to ask. Jenna had been floating between floors; by then it was mandatory for what they called "desk staff" to manage more. Luckily there were still enough doctors to keep up with need, but they seemed spread precariously thin.

"You up here for a bit?" I greeted her, making sure the smile behind my mask reached my eyes.

She sighed and pointed me in the direction of the face shields and other protective gear. "Only until I'm needed on third. We've got a new guy coming tomorrow; I can't wait."

I scanned the hall. "Seems quiet."

She knocked on the desk. "Don't jinx it." She sighed again. "We've already lost one today, anyway; it's that *after* sort of quiet, you know?"

I finished suiting up and nodded. "I know."

She went back to her files.

"Hey, can I ask you something?"

She looked up. "Sure."

"What's on sixth?"

A tiny smile played at her lips. "Isn't it, 'who's on second?'"

I laughed but waited before saying anything else.

Her smile faded. "Oh."

"Should I not ask that, or -"

She waved the words away. "No, it's not that. Just – well, with all the changes in staff and stuff, and having moved the diagnostics and recovery to Hull, it sort of morphed into this," she gestured around us. "Critical care is mostly here, now."

"That's why I asked; I was originally told sixth was critical care, and -"

She smirked. "And you've seen different for yourself."

I nodded, considering my tactics for the next question.

"What?"

"Well, that was only a few weeks ago; have things changed that fast?"

The color that moved to her cheeks set me on edge. "Sort of. There *are* still some patients on sixth, but it's only a small percentage of -" her eyes flicked to the hallway and the hairs on the back of my neck stood up. "I'm not supposed to talk about it, really."

I shook my head. "It's OK."

"The truth is, there are very few of us who actually know exactly what's going on up there. It's very hush-hush."

I frowned. "Oh. But it's related to MARS-21?"

She nodded almost imperceptibly. "Please don't say anything; I actually signed a paper – a confidentiality thing – oh, God." Her cheeks burned a deeper shade than I'd thought possible.

"Hey, don't sweat it; I was just curious," I smiled. Made sure I caught her eye. And made a mental note to get up to the sixth-floor *tout suite...* if possible. I had a sneaking suspicion it wasn't as simple as pushing the right elevator button.

"The residents are right; you're easy to talk to."

I scoffed. "If so, it's a newly-acquired gift. I've spent most of my life scaring people off, or worse."

Her brow furrowed.

"But that was a different me," I said quietly, then cleared my throat. "I – my past is sort of a dark one. Nothing to worry about!" I added the last at the look of alarm that stole across her features. "That's all long behind me, now. But now, we both owe each other the courtesy of keeping secrets."

A look of gratitude replaced the alarm. "Thank you, Tom."

"I'm going to do the rounds," I backed into the hallway.

"It was Mr. Morrison," she whispered after me. "Who died this morning."

I stopped. "Oh, no." The old guy had taken my hand on my last visit; he'd never opened his eyes during my visits, but that time, I realized he knew me.

My rounds took little time; the residents were sleeping

or had little to say after the day's events. Jenna was nowhere to be seen as I headed for the elevator, though.

I found her soon enough; she'd migrated to third and was speaking with a patient, halfway in the hallway and half in the room. I paused as I changed my gloves. That was Jeremy's room. I fought the immediate stab of panic at the realization, but beelined for her as soon as I was ready.

She smiled over her shoulder at me. "Ah, there he is. You starting here, today?"

Her smile somewhat assuaged my nerves, but I looked into the room before replying, just to be sure everything was OK. Jeremy sat up in his bed and seemed well enough. I looked at her. "Thought I'd say hi to Linda and Lyla, then check in on the newbies first. This guy wants to beat me at chess, I'm sure, and that'll take a while." I tipped a wink at Jeremy, then carried on toward three-twelve.

"Tom!"

I turned. Jenna was looking incredulously after me.

"You might want to start here!" she pointed into the room.

"Why?"

"First of all," Jeremy's voice came into the hallway, "you won't find Linda or Lyla in their room."

My heart thudded, skipped, and thudded again. "What's happened?" I eyed Jenna.

She shook her head. "Just come here, Tom!"

I did the opposite, turning and rushing to three-twelve, only to find one empty bed – Lyla's – and a sleeping elderly man with lockjaw in Linda's. I whipped around to look at the door again. Three-twelve. Then I stared at the old man, my terror-filled mind playing a reel of scenarios for me to ponder and shudder at.

Then I was running back to Jeremy's room. Jenna's smile at my approach seemed odd. I went past her; Jeremy was the only one who'd given me anything close to an answer so far. And I stopped short when I went into the room, realizing how clear his words had been when they'd reached me in the hallway and simultaneously seeing what I'd failed to see the first time: his lockjaw was better. "Oh, my God!"

He smiled, and it was beautiful, despite the chapped lips and sores at the corners of his mouth. Then he grimaced, his fingers going to his jaw. "Ow. It's still not all the way better."

"But it's *better.*" The urge to go to him – to embrace him! – was nearly overwhelming. "I want to hug you!"

Jenna put a gentle hand on my shoulder. "Not yet," she said quietly, and I nodded. I knew we still had no idea how long the immunity to the virus lasted, and if somehow I'd picked up a mutated version – well, I'd ruin Jeremy's recovery with one hug.

Jeremy was shaking his head. "I don't know if it would've happened without you, Tom. And – you won't believe this, but I actually met Linda and Lyla before they were released -"

I'm ashamed to say I cut him off, but I did, turning to Jenna as I remembered them gone. "Tell me they were released to Hull."

She smiled. "Linda left you a note, of course. At the nursing station. It was just this morning, and it happened fast. A bed opened up in rehab and -"

"*A* bed?"

"Oh! Right; Linda went to Hull, but Lyla wanted to go home. She'd have had to stay, anyway; there isn't room for both of them right now, but she's been doing so well they decided to let her go home."

I let out a breath I hadn't been aware of holding. "Thank God," I muttered, then turned back to Jeremy, "and you met them, finally!"

He nodded. "Linda came in and introduced herself. We got to talking and – well, she asked if I'd like to come stay with her after all this! Said you'd told her about me and that she didn't have anyone, either..." He wiped a tear off his cheek, unashamed and innocent in his apparent joy. "She's really nice," he laughed and cried at the same time.

You ever get that feeling where your heart feels so full it might explode? Well, before that day the closest I'd ever come to that feeling was when I'd held my baby daughter in my arms. But even then, I was too messed up and selfish to let it touch me. When it happened that day, watching Jeremy cry at the prospect of not being so lonely anymore, it felt like it might knock me over.

And like my heart exploding right then might be OK.

You'd think the day was an unusually happy one for me, and that it would have come crashing down right there, wouldn't you? That's what I thought, anyway. When I got into the elevator again and pushed the sixth-floor button and a little light started flashing – one I hadn't noticed before, which had a key icon on it – I thought that was the beginning of the balancing act of my day. But as I left, the puzzle of what was on sixth grating at me, things kept looking up.

I got a call after I got into the car. One that startled me, vibrating uncomfortably between my ass cheek and the seat. One I expected to be from Eva Pendleton but anticipated with a strange rush of adrenaline. It was an appropriate intuition, because it was a call from Carroll Krull. And that time, I answered on the first ring.

CHAPTER 37 – PROVIDE

I was preoccupied as Molly and I did our rounds the next morning. Carroll Krull had given me two bits of news of opposing extremes: yes, Louise-Anne was sick – a devastating confirmation – and also she had asked him to give me her address.

Apparently, she'd received my letter.

And though that should have bolstered me, I found myself stuck on the fact that finally I had my chance, but it came with a reality that was far less desirable than I had dreamed. In any case, Carroll had talked me out of going straight there the day before; advised me to give her the night, at least, to wrap her head around seeing me.

It was logical, but *very* difficult.

I'd called Ed on the way over to pick up Molly and updated him. In an unusual bout of indecision, he couldn't say what the best move should be. We managed to end on me heading over to see her the following afternoon: not too soon, but, importantly, not too late, either.

Hence the haze during rounds. I took in my surroundings only peripherally; found myself being led by the pup. Which was a good thing that day, because she took me on a different route, and if she hadn't, I wouldn't have seen the two things that would bend our days into something less calm, less structured.

And much less free.

It was a quiet community behind one of the French elementary schools, one I'd covered early in my new career but felt little need to revisit often. It had been quiet then, too. But something felt different that morning, and I found myself roused out of my thoughts, though I couldn't say why, at first.

The distant sound of dogs barking wasn't unusual, but the fact that it was so clear was. I stopped and Molly sat dutifully, regarding me. "*Too* quiet, isn't it, girl?" She panted as she looked up at me. Not one leaf rustled in the maples that lined the street. No bird sung, no car started or backed out of a driveway. The lack of children was expected; they'd learned to play indoors long before. But God, what I wouldn't have given to hear laughter from a backyard that morning.

Molly stood and gave an anxious bark.

"OK," I muttered, letting her take me further into the little community. There was something sweet in the air, which intensified as we walked, and I saw that one of the towering apple trees was shedding its fruit, which gathered in groups on the road and sat in various stages of rot. It was rare to find such a bounty untouched; home gardens and fruit trees had enjoyed a surge of popularity early in the pandemic, and continued to be popular more than two years on. Gardening wasn't a hobby anymore; it was something people *relied* on for fresh produce when the stores were intimidating public spaces.

I felt the hairs on my arms stand on end as I stared up at the crooked branches and was reaching to help myself to a particularly shiny piece of fruit when Molly growled for the first time since I'd known her. My arm froze in midair as I followed the pup's gaze and saw why.

There was a dog at the end of the street. Again, not at all unusual, but that particular dog was unusual in itself. At first,

I couldn't reconcile what I was seeing with my expectations of any stray. Its fur was matted and it was painfully skinny, true, but that's where the similarities stopped. It was acting oddly. From our angle, I could see his back end: bony haunches and knobby spine, and that its head was near the ground, but hanging rather than snuffling through the mess of garbage that had been spilled onto the street from a long-abandoned bin. In those days, you had to take care of your own trash by taking it in city-approved bags to city-installed dumpsters placed throughout each town.

The stray was not steady on his feet, either. He stumbled drunkenly rather than walked, and seemed preoccupied with his face, clumsily bringing a front paw up to his ear, then sweeping it downward repeatedly.

Rabies? I wondered, my fingers tingling painfully as adrenaline rushed my blood through my extremities. But then the dog stumbled and fell onto his side, and I was able to see that it wasn't rabies, but something more shocking. Its jaw was open at the hinges. *Locked.*

I gasped at the sight. The dog – his dirty, curly golden fur and round, dark eyes identifying him as a doodle of some sort – appeared to have rubbed much of the fur off his own face in his confusion and pain. He must have scratched a lot, too, because blood crusted every section that was not matted with fur.

"Holy shit," I muttered as he caught sight of us and tried to right himself with another strangled cry. I struggled with opposing feelings of pity and fear. But then Molly started pulling at her leash, hard, and I followed, my eyes glued to those of the sick stray. "Dogs don't *get* MARS-21," I voiced dumbly, perhaps only to make solid my scrambled thoughts. But we were turning right; Molly had led us to the end of the street and then veered hard to avoid the stray, who'd given up on standing and was trying hard to bark but wheezed instead.

My heart hurt for the pitiful creature, but Molly

continued to lead us away, breathing hard and seemingly focused on her task alone. But my eyes stayed on the other dog's, because it was trying again to get up, trying to get to us, jaw dragging along the pavement and maybe less pitiful than I'd first perceived and a little more sinister, instead. I watched as drool flew from its cavernous open maw. As it lurched toward us with an unmistakeable growl only to crash its lower teeth into the pavement and fall back. I watched as one tooth flew and another dangled from bleeding gums. I watched him try again and succeed at righting the front half of himself and then drag his back half forward, eyes on me - always on me.

At that point, I stopped staring, turned, and ran with Molly, who seemed overjoyed that I'd finally joined her. She led confidently, still, and I let her, my mind whirling with the new reality I'd just witnessed. *Dogs can get it. What does this mean?* Visions of the strays I'd come across, even in the preceding few days, flashed in the chaos of my mind. *How many? Can they transmit it? If they can catch it, surely they can give it, too. Right? Fuck. Fuck!*

My heart was racing when Molly slowed, and that odd pressure was creeping over my chest again when she turned into a driveway. A glance over my shoulder told me the stray had either given up or failed, and I stopped on the gravel, bending over at the waist and focusing on breathing deeply. Opening my mouth wide to take air in, then holding it, eyes closed but still seeing the bursts of light that were everywhere just before I bent over. Then blowing it out. Steadying wobbly legs. Holding on to consciousness.

It may have taken seconds or minutes; I can't tell you which. But it was Molly who pulled me back to myself with a tug of her leash. Gentler, that time. I straightened and blinked until I could see again. "Thanks, sweetheart," I smiled down at the dog, then looked up at the brown duplex she'd brought us to. "Where have you brought us?"

I recognized the house from our first visit to the area, if only because there was a lopsided, rainbow-colored lawn ornament in what used to be the front garden. The first time we'd come, though, it had been spinning listlessly in the breeze.

There'd been no answer, last time. I frowned down at Molly. "Are you sure?"

She answered by pulling again. At a loss, I followed. And when we got to the door, I knocked. Then shrugged at the expected lack of response, looking down at my little dog. But she wasn't so quick to give up; she stood on her hind legs and pushed the door, which, to my surprise, inched open.

The pup sniffed urgently at the dark gap, but I didn't have to; the unmistakeable smell of death had already reached my nose. "Uh-oh," I mumbled, and Molly barked. I tried pushing the door, but it wasn't budging any further, despite a modicum of give. My guess was that whatever or whomever had died had done it just as they were leaving. Or coming home. I gagged as a new waft of decay hit me and closed the door quickly. Molly looked up at me as though I was stupid, but I sat, dejected, on the step. I was determined to catch my breath before I had no choice but to vomit.

Molly sat beside me after a few moments, and I pulled out my phone. "Sorry, girl. We need reinforcements for this one." The pup sat and put a small paw on my thigh, followed by her little snout. I scratched at the silky fur behind her ears with one hand and dialled Evan Cromwell with the other. Without knowledge of what was on the other side of that door, I couldn't simply call the morgue. And finding a way in to investigate wasn't in my job description.

When we hung up and I dialled Ed with shaking hands, I was grateful for that. I hadn't shied away from a little sleuthing in my position, but that day, I knew I needed support. It wasn't just the apparent presence of a body that had me shaken; it was the state of the stray we'd crossed paths with. So, I made sure both calls ended with a warning: *I don't know if you're aware of this, yet, but I want to tell you there's a dog on the way in; a stray, and it looks like it's got lockjaw.*

Both replies had contained elements of gratitude and curiosity (Ed in particular had demanded to know every detail of the encounter, especially regarding the dog's "apparent symptoms"), but, to my great disappointment, neither of their responses had held any element of surprise.

So, I had a lot of questions for the men when they showed up, starting with why I'd thought to warn them, but they hadn't afforded me the same courtesy, given the obvious fact that I hadn't told them anything they didn't already know.

CHAPTER 38 – MULTIPLY

Ed arrived first, and he walked toward me with his palms out, pre-emptively urging me to be calm down before I'd said a word. "I know," he raised his eyebrows as I stood, "but it's not what you think."

"I think you knew something about the dog that has MARS-21 and you neglected to warn me about it."

His hands dropped.

"It was trying to get to us, Ed. To *me.*"

He looked back over his shoulder. "Evan's got the canine patrol looking for it now."

"That's nice. Now, about the fact that I should've been warned..."

He rubbed his forehead. "We only found out this morning, Tom."

I frowned. "Really?"

He nodded. "Before today, it was just rumours, but nobody could substantiate anything. I don't think anybody looked too hard, though. Nobody *wants* to believe it."

"Holy *fuck,* Ed. This puts the virus at an all-time high in the 'this is it; I'm gonna die' category!"

He pinched his mask over the bridge of his nose, sighing.

He didn't meet my eyes.

"What does this mean?"

He shook his head. "That's still being worked out. But the canine patrol has doubled in staff overnight. It's a unit that was only an *idea* two days ago. Oh -" he reached into his shirt pocket and pulled out a card, "this is the number, just in case you come across any animals with symptoms during your rounds."

I took it, noting Ed had double gloved it, that day.

"And that's something Evan will talk to you about – the deputized folks will all be given the official debrief over Briefmedia tonight. Did you get set up?"

It was something I'd done immediately after receiving my mandate but hadn't ever used. I was sure it was a group videoconference service like any other. I nodded.

"Good, good." Ed's eyes went to the door. "I'm surprised you're not inside." He managed a wry grin.

I shook my head. "This one's different."

"I've never seen you shy away from going a bit above and beyond, Tom, especially if it means you get to bend the rules a bit," he winked.

But I didn't return his efforts at banter. "It feels weird. Molly brought us here; I was preoccupied when we came into the neighborhood and then distracted by the sick dog. And – I dunno – but why would someone die by their door? I mean – the decline's not that swift. Just strikes me as being off, Ed."

He'd been watching me, his face unreadable. He cleared his throat.

"What?"

"Do you remember how we found Molly's boyfriend?" He glanced at the pup. "Molly Mitchell?"

My eyes rolled of their own accord before I could catch the action.

Ed chuckled. "Sorry; of course, you do."

"What's up, Ed? You're acting different. Squirrelly."

He cleared his throat again. "The dogs aren't the only change, Tom," he started, his eyes sad. Maybe a bit scared, too. But then a cruiser was pulling up and Ed's features were awash with relief. "Ah! There's Evan."

I sat, feeling frustrated. Molly leaned against me but glanced backward at the door more often than I liked. "We'll get to him, Mols. Don't worry."

"What's wrong with you?" Evan's authoritative tone was as gruff as it had been in the old days, when there was reason to suspect mischief.

"I've told him about the dogs."

Evan studied my face for a moment. "Well then, you found out almost as soon as we did." He shook his head. "Higher-ups thought it better to confirm the hypothesis before letting us know we should be on the lookout." His face was dark.

"Did you find the dog?"

Cromwell nodded, then peered my way. "I'm sorry you had to find out that way, Tom."

My anger fizzled. Knowing it had been aimed in the wrong direction seemed to satisfy it. Not something I'd experienced in life until that point, but then, everything was different, wasn't it?

"What've we got here?" Cromwell gestured toward the door and Molly was on her feet in seconds, looking eagerly between the door and the cop.

I stood. "I don't know, really, except that maybe this case

is similar to that of Molly Mitchell's boyfriend."

Ed blanched as Cromwell tossed a confused look his way.

"I only just started to tell him about the, uh – more severe cases."

The cop's eyes cleared. "We can't share much at this point, except that a small percentage -"

"Growing," Ed interrupted.

"Yes, it's growing," Cromwell sighed, "anyway – a *growing* number of MARS-21 sufferers are phasing into a final stage that is more... *extreme* than is typical."

"What's the percentage?"

Ed stepped forward. "Back when you found Molly Mitchell, and her boyfriend was in the back yard, it was as little as two percent. Now, it's closer to six."

"Eight," Evan muttered, and Ed turned to him, the look of surprise I'd been watching for finally apparent.

"What?"

"Canine patrol just heard."

"Wait," I cut in, unable to simply listen any longer, "you're telling me sufferers don't just go a little bonkers sometimes because of the pain, but that it – what? Makes them lose it completely?"

Ed nodded.

"Twists their body beyond what we'd consider 'normal,' even for the disease, and their minds, too," Evan finished.

"OK; that's good to know!" I tossed my hands in the air.

"This is news to us too, Tom," Ed looked regretful.

"Uh-huh. And Crom – Evan. You say you heard from the *canine* unit about the rising rate? Why them? Do the two things

– the dogs and the more frequent craziness – have something to do with each other?"

Neither man moved to answer.

"Come *on,* guys! I'm out here risking my ass every day -"

"Speaking of which, you don't look so good, Wall." It was Evan who'd commented, but Ed nodded.

"Just high blood pressure," I waved it away. "And don't change the subject."

Ed pressed his lips together.

"Tom, we understand if you don't want to continue the work."

I stared at Evan, incredulous. "I'll do the work until I can't anymore. But I want to know whatever you know."

"And now you do," Ed said, shrugging.

"Not quite," Evan raised a finger. "New directives state that all deputies are to complete rounds in their cars, leaving it no more than a block behind while knocking on doors."

"Makes sense," I chuckled.

Ed added, "And you aren't to approach bodies; what you did today was right, Tom. Call us first."

"What about the dogs?"

"I gave you the card; add it to your contacts and if you see *any* dog that appears abnormal, get yourself in your car and call the patrol," Ed looked to Evan. "Anything else?"

Evan shook his head. "Not now, but there will be. Rest assured, we'll keep you informed, Tom, but remember, we can only tell you what we know."

I scanned the quiet street, absorbing. Trying to, anyway. Molly yipped impatiently, her paws on the door again. "So, what next?" I gestured toward the door.

Evan approached. "You said the body seems to be just on the other side?"

I nodded. "You won't get in that way if you want it intact."

His hand hovered above the knob. "Let's try the back."

We rounded the place into an unfenced back yard. Ed noted the dog house and a coiled tether beside it and we moved on.

The back door was locked, but Cromwell made quick work of it and we were inside in seconds.

"Oh, man," Ed gasped when the smell hit him.

I breathed through my mouth.

"You two search for others," Evan muttered as he headed for the stairs to the front door.

I intended on following orders. I really did – but the scene at the bottom of the stairs stopped me in my tracks. Ed froze beside me.

The body was there, alright, but that was as far as my expectations matched up with what I saw.

It was torn up. Just – shredded! The flesh hung from the man's bones in jagged sheets. And the blood – I couldn't see the floor beneath him, for the massive, dried pool of blood he lay in. But it wasn't just there; it was on the door, around the doorknob especially, and if one were so inclined to look, they'd see it was on the walls, the ceiling, and the shoes and coats, too.

The only reason I knew it was a man was his chest hair. He was face-up, in a filthy pair of denim shorts, hollow eye sockets staring up at the ceiling. And his jaw – of course it was wide open; the lower half rested on his chest! But it was bizarre, because he was wearing a mask. It was dwarfed by the grotesque stretch of the man's mouth, but it was there, dried reddish-brown stains apparent and stretching between his lips.

All words failed me. There were too much that wanted to come, but none that took the leap.

Evan Cromwell leaned over the body and examined the lock mechanism. "Works," he muttered, then stripped off the glove he'd touched the bolt with.

"But it looks like he was trying to get out," Ed breathed. I looked sideways at the man that had become something of a friend, in awe of his ability to be logical, even in a moment such as that. But he was pale and beads of sweat gathered on his forehead and soaked through his mask.

"You say you opened, the door, Tom?"

I shook my head, trying to bring myself back from that place disbelief and horror takes us. "Uh – Molly did, with her front paws. It must have been partially open."

"Why couldn't he get out if it was open?" Ed's voice had taken on a tone of desperation, and it grounded me somehow.

"Let's search the rooms," I suggested, meeting his eyes, and he nodded, his eyes blank again.

We found no one else and were out as soon as it was feasible. Evan was on the walkie to the station straight away, but Ed and I sat on the steps.

"Do you think he forgot how to get out?" Ed still looked bewildered as he pondered the victim's violent end. "I mean, that explains the blood on the door, but what about the state of him? Did you see how he was ripped apart? Did you see his *eyes?* And – and there were scraps of flesh on his hands. Evan said one of his eyes was at the bottom of the stairs, just looking up at him as if to say, *"what happened?"* He smiled, but his eyes were afraid. The effect made me squeamish. "That's not like Brad – that was Miss Mitchell's boyfriend. He – it just looked like he went mad with pain; he stripped down to nothing and lay in the back yard..." he trailed off.

"Maybe it *was* all to do with pain," I tried. "Did you see the bony growths on his knees and elbows? Maybe his reaction was to try and get to it. To destroy it."

"Good insight, Tom," Evan approached, then bent to scratch Molly's head. The pup raised her head from her paws, then went back to sleep.

"I've had some experience," I muttered.

We sat in silence for some time.

"I almost wish we could say an animal did that to him," Ed continued after a while, but quietly.

Evan shook his head, frowning. "There were no signs of anyone but him, Ed. You saw it; there was blood everywhere and no prints." He scratched his head. "Anyway, the examiner's coming herself; he'll be investigated closely. You can go home, Tom."

I shook my head. "I'm going to see Louise-Anne."

"Who?"

"His daughter," Ed's voice was quiet. "But I think he needs to see the doctor, first.

Evan scrutinized my face. "You do look kind of shitty."

"I'm fine." I stood with a grunt, then fought a wave of dizziness.

"Whoa," Evan's gloved hand grasped my shoulder.

"This was just a bit much," I gestured over my shoulder. "I'll be OK."

"You *need* to be in good health to do this position, Tom."

I clenched my teeth. All I needed was to get my work done. And fit my daughter in there. She was at the top of my list for the rest of the day. After seeing what I'd had to see, I needed something good. Something hopeful.

"Don't make me take your badge."

I inhaled sharply and was seconds from releasing the diatribe that streamed from a brain too used to acting on anger when Ed's hand gripped my opposite shoulder. "Come on, Tom. It won't take too long; I'll come with you."

I shook my head. "You don't understand. If Eva Pendleton gets hold of me, I won't get back out -"

"Who?"

I looked between the men. "She's head of a study – they found something in my blood – an anomaly -"

"That's why she's been calling us," Evan and Ed exchanged a look. "Sorry, pal. You're going in," Evan took hold of my elbow and steered me toward the cruiser.

"She called you?"

"Both of us," Ed muttered as he steered me to the car, whose cherries still flashed lazily.

I protested; I know I did, but I was looking back for Molly, too. I needn't have worried about leaving her behind, though. She was jumping into the back as soon as Evan opened the door.

"Molly always knows where to go, doesn't she?" Ed chuckled.

I laughed. "She can't go into the hospital, Ed. What about *that?*"

"I'll take her for a long walk," he answered calmly as Evan pressed my head down and my body responded out of long-buried habit as I sat in the back.

"I can't stay in there," I yelled as Ed moved to shut

the door. He peered down at me, compassion softening his features. Tears were suddenly running down my cheeks, my frustration mounting and threatening at panic.

"Tom, I promise we'll make it clear that you need to be out. We won't let them admit you," Ed nodded reassuringly. "Whatever's going on with your blood – well, that's one thing – but we need to get you examined, too. I don't like how you look."

The man's logic and supporting kindness never failed to sooth. It was magic. Yep, I'll say that even now.

Evan rounded the hood slowly as Ed closed the door.

"OK?" Ed nodded toward Evan, who gave him a thumbs-up.

I recalled a panic attack I'd had as a child when I'd gotten stuck in an elevator with my case worker. My heart tripped and then thudded into high gear. "I can't – I'll give them whatever they want: blood! I'll give them whatever I don't need; I just have to get to my daughter. I have to see her."

I remember Evan peering over his shoulder to share a look with Ed before he went to his car. Evan's was a question. Ed's was a confirmation.

I remember feeling Molly's snout in my palm.

And then I passed out.

CHAPTER 39 – HARVEST

Eva Pendleton frowned at the monitor. "Stop," she said.

I slowed as she lowered the speed on the treadmill, trying to smile. "Isn't this supposed to be one of those tests that go on and on until you *wish* you had heart problems so they'd tell you to stop?" She gave me a look that had me mirroring her frown. "Oh."

"Tom, after everything we've done, I can tell you've already had one heart attack at least, and you're quickly headed for another."

I shuffled from foot to foot, images of that dark dream with its rivers of lava and crushing chest pain filling my mind's eye. I stepped off the machine. "I'm going to sit," I said, only peripherally aware of the trailing monitor cords.

"We need to admit you."

I looked up at her, already shaking my head. "Not today."

She pulled a chair closer and sat facing me. Our knees nearly touched. "It's critical that we do more tests, Tom. I think you need surgery."

"I need to see my daughter."

She laughed, then shook her head. "You don't get it, do you? Your blood could hold the answers we're looking for!"

"But it doesn't yet, right?"

She sighed. "We need to do more tests. We *were* able to replicate the results; your blood *does* carry different antigens!"

"But?"

"But – it's like there's a piece of the puzzle missing. It's just – the only way I can describe the results we're getting is to say it's not a complete picture. We need to keep looking. We need *you*, Tom."

"Fine. And I'll give you blood. Take more now! But I'm going to see my daughter today and I have two friends that guaranteed it."

"They probably don't answer to the Prime Minister directly though, do they?"

"You telling me the big guy himself is ordering me to stay here?"

She pursed her lips.

"Just let me have the day."

"And if you have a heart attack?"

I held my arm out. "Take my blood. Store it. Freeze it – whatever. Then you'll have it in case I die or – something."

She sat back, folding her arms. "Do you think your daughter would come here, instead?"

"No way."

Her eyebrows furrowed.

"I can't ask *anything* of her, OK? Maybe if I go see her and things go well, I can ask her to come see me here, but -"

"I mean, do you think she'd donate *her* blood?"

It came over me in a rush: the reminder that she was sick. I put my face in my hands as my pulse escalated. I needed out. I stood, which resulted in the headrush of a lifetime, and then the doc was holding me steady. "I have to go."

"Mr. Wall? Tom! The leads! You're still attached to the machines!"

I started peeling the wires off, my hands shaking. "I need to see my daughter."

She took them one by one, both hands open to my frantic peeling and tossing. "You act like it's the end of the world if you don't see her today!"

"It *is!*" I couldn't help it; I shouted, and Pendleton was taking a quick step backward. "I'm sorry," I reached out a bit, then let my hands fall. "She's sick, OK? She's sick and I haven't seen her since she fit in the crook of my arm! And she's *letting* me come see her! I don't deserve it, but she is, and if I'm going to die again, I need to go now!" I'd been gesturing wildly, and I let my hands fall again with the reverberation of the last of my diatribe. "If I'm going to die," I said, dropping the 'again'. "I'm sorry," I said once more, fighting the urge to just run.

The doctor seemed paralysed; her eyes on me for several moments that felt like eternity. She had her hands out, palms facing me, and she let them fall, as I had. "She has the virus?"

I nodded; it was all the lump in my throat allowed.

She sighed, absently gazing toward the monitor. "I was really counting on you staying," she said quietly, then raised her eyes to mine. "You do understand how important you are?"

I laughed. It was the phrasing. I'd *never* realized anything of the sort.

"You are the only person we know of that's given us anything hopeful, Tom. I do understand your need to see your daughter, and if she wasn't sick, I'd tell you that waiting until we fixed you up would be smarter...but as it stands, all I can do is put my faith in you, Tom. Faith that you'll come back."

I nodded, but the bald trust in her words had given me pause.

"When? Tomorrow? After you see your daughter?"

I nodded again.

"One more thing. Will you agree to wear protective equipment, like you do at the hospital?"

I inhaled to protest, but she cut me off.

"It's as much for her safety as it is to protect you!"

Me: their asset. I shook my head. "This is crazy."

"I don't know what would happen if -" she looked as though some serious gears were turning behind her eyes. "Huh. I wonder if the anomaly isn't the result of -" she frowned, "- you haven't – how do I say this delicately?"

"I've never needed delicate treatment," I chuckled.

"Something tells me that's not true, but I'll just come out and say it; have you engaged in unprotected sex in the last six months or so? Used intravenous drugs? Received a blood transfusion?"

I tried to laugh, but it came out as an awkward, "Ha!"

"See? It's a delicate set of questions, but I think they bear asking."

I frowned. "I answered those questions on the sheet before I had blood taken the first time."

She nodded. "Right. No to all three."

I nodded.

She looked blankly at the monitor again. "It was a long shot. Anyway, the equipment - will you wear it?"

I rolled my eyes, but then a thought occurred to me. She must've seen my face light up, because she scowled.

"What?"

"I'll wear it there on the condition I can wear it on the

way back, too."

Confusion crossed her features and for a moment, she was very nearly adorable.

"At the Gatineau Hospital," I finished.

Her eyes widened. "Why? I mean, I know you know people there, but – it just seems an odd thing to prioritize when you know what's at stake!" The lines between her eyebrows were back, and she was her old self again.

I told her it was exactly as she'd said. I wanted to see my friends and the staff I had gotten to know, just in case I wasn't back for a while. I wanted to tie up some loose ends. I insisted on it. And then I reminded her I *didn't* know what was at stake. Nobody did!

But I was thinking of the sixth floor. I was thinking about the growing number of sufferers phasing into psychosis in the end and wondering if the two were related.

"And then, I'll be back," I said. "By tomorrow, dinner-time, so make sure I'm on the list of patients." I grinned, then held a finger up. "And if there's a choice of meals, I'll take whichever has mashed potatoes and gravy as a side."

She looked mildly amused.

"It's the one thing hospital kitchens can't screw up."

"What about Jell-O?"

I shrugged. "And possibly Jell-O."

She nodded decisively. "OK."

I grabbed my jacket. "Cool."

"Whoa! Hold on there, cowboy."

I turned back, but only halfway. My thoughts were already on Ed and Molly, on the drive to Wakefield, on what I'd say when I showed up at Louise-Anne's door, and on how

I was going to get up to the sixth floor. And then I knew. I'd take the stairs. *Not with the state of your ticker,* that annoying inner voice said, and I shoved the thoughts aside, focusing on priority number one: Louise-Anne.

"You made me an offer," the doctor smiled.

The blood. I sighed, then opened the exam room door, gesturing her forward. "Lead the way, Madame."

She paused between me and the doorframe opposite, making my skin tense at the rare proximity. "You should know that next time, it *could* be the big guy giving the orders. Come back tomorrow, Tom."

I nodded, but inwardly I was chuckling. *There's no way your "big guy" trumps mine.*

CHAPTER 40 – REAP

Ed was quiet on the drive home, after I filled him in on the visit. I tried small talk, but I'd never been good at it, and quickly settled into silence when it failed to rouse him.

Molly slept in my lap contentedly.

When we arrived at my driveway, Ed turned to me, apparently ready to voice whatever was eating at him. But all he said was, "Do you want me to take Molly?"

I peered down at the pup, who slept on, then back at Ed. "Aren't you going back to work?"

He looked at the digital clock, shaking his head. "I'm going to go home; there's only an hour or so left, anyway."

"Thanks, Ed, but I think I'll take her with me. I'm hoping she'll help break the ice."

He looked astonished. "You're going tonight?"

"I only have a day, Ed."

"Right. Of course. And you want to go to the Gatineau tomorrow."

I nodded but couldn't figure what to say. He seemed... disapproving.

"I'll let Evan know you're taking a few days off, at least."

"I'll be alright, Ed." Molly stretched in my lap, then flipped to her back, eyeing me. "I know what that means," I muttered as I scratched her tummy.

"If you aren't, though –"

I looked up at him. "I will be. I have to be."

He frowned. "Right, because it'll affect far more than Louise-Anne, myself, my family, Evan…all those folks who've gotten to know and admire you. It could affect people all over the world."

I stared back at him dumbly.

"You know that, right?"

I made a dismissive noise. "I don't know anything. Not yet. Nobody does."

"You could hold the key to a *vaccine,* Tom! You could save hundreds of thousands. More, even. You could," he threw his hands up, "your survival could mean the survival of the human race, man! And your death -"

I shook my head. "I gave the doc a nice, big bag of my blood before I found you and Molly on the grass outside the Center, Ed. That's what she needs. She doesn't need me."

He looked at me as though I was a cracked nut. "You don't *get* it!"

I mirrored his look, now.

"They need that blood to study. *If* they find answers, they need more to start building a vaccine. The *first* iteration. And there'll be many, no matter how magical your blood is. And *then* they'll need more for replication and to store for emergency use… Tom, you need to *live.*"

"Yeah, so I can be their pincushion." I tried to laugh, but it got lodged in my throat.

"To save us, Tom."

"She said something was missing. Maybe my blood isn't the only part to the key."

"Even the simplest of keys won't work if they're incomplete, Tom. Regardless of whether you're the whole answer or not, you're very likely part of it."

I gazed at my door through the passenger side window. Shook my head. "I can't get my head around it," I said quietly, then looked back at him. "Until a few weeks ago, I'd never been important to *anyone*."

"I'll bet you were to your daughter," he answered without missing a beat, "even if you didn't know it."

Tears sprang to my eyes. I opened the door and set one foot on the gravel before looking back at him. "I have to go, Ed. Don't worry, OK?"

"You're going to go back, right?"

I nodded. "I might need a ride, though. And your family might have a new pet." My voice cracked as I set Molly on the ground.

"We'll keep her as long as it takes for you to do what you need to do. You don't need to worry about that."

I nodded. "And you don't need to worry about me. I have the feeling I'll get back to Hull tomorrow, whether I'm aiming for it or not."

Uncertainty flickered in his eyes and I braced for an extended lecture, but to his credit, he nodded, gave a little wave, and sat back in the driver's seat. "Talk to you tomorrow."

I closed the door. The window was lowering as soon as it shut, though. I leaned down, trying to ignore the irritation that was fighting to take over.

"Good luck tonight," Ed smiled.

I gave the door a pat then stood to watch him go. Molly was rolling in the grass when I turned to find her, carefree and happy. I shook my head. "Come on, Mol." She perked up, rolling to her front. One of her ears remained flipped over backward, giving her a dishevelled appearance. But her glossy coat and pretty, open-mouthed grin made her into a diva just awake from bed instead of a goofball grass-roller. "You're a funny girl," I muttered, and she was up and running, wriggling all the way to me. "Do you want to go meet someone with me?" I squatted and she stood on her hind legs and jumped like I'd seen circus Dachshunds do, her paws flopping at her chest. I laughed and took her up, then carried her to the door. "Pitstop, first."

It was a short one; I fed the pup and refilled her water, then headed to the bathroom. By the time I was done and heading back to the kitchen, I was rubbing my (severely diminished) belly with a fierce sort of hunger. It had been a long day. An overripe banana, a granola bar and a long drink from the tap later, we were both sated and on the way out the door.

It was a thirty minute drive, but I had enough on my mind that it passed by in what felt like no time, and suddenly we were parked in front of the address Carroll Krull had given me. And I was panicking.

The only thing I hadn't considered on the drive over was what I was going to say to the daughter who was a stranger.

If she answered the door.

CHAPTER 41 – WILT

It took one look from her to know that words would mean everything.

She'd answered on the third knock, with a preceding shuffle toward the door and some nonsensical muttering to boot. "Oh," she said when she saw me. Her face going blank.

It was like looking at her mother. The clear, silvery-blue eyes, the wild hair, the porcelain skin. I'd forgotten that about her mother, and being confronted by the stark reminder in our offspring shook me to the core. I'd loved that woman's skin; it was something unmarred and beautiful on a soul who'd gone through far too much in her lifetime, already.

My daughter seemed to settle into the realization that I was there. She stood back a bit and slouched. The comforter she had wrapped around her sagged, but she seemed too weak or uncaring to gather it up again. "I take it you're not the nurse," she said, eyeing my protective gear.

"I – I volunteer with the patients at Gatineau," I rushed to explain the getup, mortified I might offend her. "Plus, I – well, I need to watch out; I'm – I'm – uh, participating in a study," I rushed on, feeling desperate. Wanting all at once to tell her everything and to take her in my arms and bury my nose in her hair, inhaling deeply to try and find the one thing I remembered about her that would, of course, be gone.

She waved my words away. "OK. Whatever."

My heart fell. It was a term I'd grown to loathe while

I was locked up... or whenever I dealt with fellow shit-disturbers, really. "Whatever" meant "I don't care. I don't, in fact, even care enough to *say* I don't care."

"Thank you for seeing me," I said, and was ready to give her the speech I'd settled on in the car; the one that echoed my letter. *I'm sorry, I'm a terrible human being, I love you, I wish I'd been there...*tempered with, *I'm so sorry you're sick, what can I do? Do you need something? Anything?* But she spoke first.

"I don't want you to come in." She chewed restlessly at a lip already dry and scabbed over in several spots.

I took a step back. "It – it's OK," I said, before she felt the need to explain. It was devastating, but not entirely surprising. "I understand. Can I come back, maybe?" I remembered my promises and added, "Uh – tomorrow?"

She averted her eyes, working her jaw absently, but in a way I knew too well. I took the moment to notice other signs of the monster that ravaged her – the exaggerated slouch, the perhaps too-sharp cheekbones. And what appeared to be a small, lone horn in the center of her head, just back from her hairline.

She caught me, and her fingers went to the protrusion. "I know," she muttered. "I'm a unicorn."

It was what I'd been thinking. Not unkindly – just, that she was different. Special, even in her illness. I took in her face again and smiled. "You look like your mother," I said, then.

"You have to go," she said, meeting my eyes again, "and I don't know when I'll be ready to see you again. Maybe tomorrow, I don't know. But Carroll has your number – oh!"

I followed her gaze to find the pup a few feet behind me. Molly'd refused to climb up the porch steps with me, disallowing me to carry her, even, but she was behind me then, wriggling in that funny way she had, her liquid eyes on Louise-

Anne. "There you are," I said, then reached for her, but she skirted around me and went to my daughter, instead.

"Huh!" I feigned a huff, but was smiling. "Louise-Anne, this is Molly. Molly, Louise-Anne."

I watched the girl that was my daughter squat carefully, wobbling so that I caught my breath and readied to help her up. But she ended up on her knees anyway, as Molly gave her an enthusiastic greeting.

"Aren't you sweet?" She looked up at me. "It's just Lou-Anne," she said. "It's easier, you know?"

I swallowed hard. "It's after our mothers," I mumbled, more to myself than anything.

She looked up again. "I know."

"It's all I knew about my birth mother," I went on, chastising myself inwardly; I hadn't planned on saying anything about my own past. I'd only wanted to ask her about hers.

She focused on the pup, who was flagrantly unashamed of the pleasure she took from Lou-Anne's attention. "The kids have always wanted a little dog," she said.

It was an odd sensation to watch the two most important creatures on earth - to me - enjoy each other, neither needing anything from me at all. I felt awkward. Unwelcome... and I was, wasn't I? She'd only just told me to go. 'I'll bring her back tomorrow," I said, hoping she'd agree without considering. When she didn't answer, I kept on. "Do you get to spend any time with them? Uh – the kids?"

She looked at me critically.

"I'm sure it must be hard, being sick...I'd love to meet them. Of course, I'd never dream of it unless you were comfortable with it. Which you're not, I'm sure, because you're not even ready to see me! But -"

She went back to petting the pup.

"Uh – anyway, I guess we'll go. How will I know when – oh, yeah, you've got my number. It's just – after today, I might not be as free. Well, after dinnertime tomorrow, more accurately."

She stood, and she was laughing. *Laughing*, with her beautiful eyes and gorgeous smile and my God, I could see something else in there, too. Something familiar, because I saw it in the mirror every day, but it was made beautiful through her. Like it was meant for her, always. "Here's your sweet doggy," she said, and handed her to me.

Her comforter had stayed on the ground and through her thin pyjamas I grazed the bones of her arm. Felt her thinness. Saw the sickness again as her laughter faded.

"Are you – I know you're sick, but – how are you doing with it? Are you eating? Keeping hydrated?"

She stretched her jaw again. "I'm doing the best I can," she whispered.

"I wasn't saying – I mean, of course you are. Is there anything I can do for you?"

She met my eyes with tears in her own. "I got your nose," she said.

I nodded. "Good thing I've got a cute, pointy one. They were always telling me I had a girly nose in -"

She watched me silently.

"You're beautiful, Louise-Anne. *Lou-Anne* - sorry."

She shook her head. "I need to lay down," she kicked at her comforter and I bent to retrieve it, letting the squirming Molly down at the same time.

The pup sat beside Lou-Anne's slippered feet, looking at me expectantly.

"We can't stay," I whispered, scratching her behind the ears. She pressed against my fingers and I knew she still loved me. "Here," I handed Lou-Anne her blanket as I straightened, and she took it gingerly. "Come on, Molly," I said, turning to go. But the dog stayed put. I turned back on the stairs. Lou-Anne was looking down at the dog and wiping a tear from her cheek. My chest hurt. I tried to laugh, but it stuck uncomfortably in my throat. "You want to stay, girl?"

Molly barked.

I looked at Lou-Anne, hopeful. "She likes you."

Molly barked again.

"Come on, Mols."

Lou-Anne seemed to have lost her hold on her emotions entirely; she was unabashedly crying into her hands.

"I could leave her with you?"

She inhaled sharply and looked at the pup over her fingertips, and then me. "The kids would love to see her, even over video chat, but I couldn't – I don't want to ask you to -"

I held my hands up. "You aren't asking. I'm offering. She's a wonderful companion, and it just so happens I have somewhere to go. Now, I can get it taken care of tonight instead of tomorrow."

She nodded. I couldn't read her expression.

I looked at the dog. "You going to take care of Lou-Anne?"

"Thank you," my grown child whispered, and something inside me filled up. Filled up so I'd never be empty again.

I met her eyes. "I owe you."

She put her face in her hands again and I went down the stairs, afraid to look back, or I'd break, too.

"You can come get her tomorrow," she called after me,

and the words sounded distant. Surreal.

I turned. "Really?"

She nodded. Molly barked.

"Thank you," I said, and then it was bubbling up and I knew I couldn't stop it.

She nodded, her face red and tear-streaked.

"You're so beautiful," I said, and the tears came, and I was laughing and crying and I told her I loved her and she cried harder and waved, backing into the house with the pup and closing the door.

And I drove to Gatineau Hospital, my tears emptying out and my heart feeling full all the way there.

CHAPTER 42 –
WITHER

I sat in the nearly-deserted parking lot of the hospital for a bit, checking my eyes in the mirror and taking deep breaths. I felt weak and for the first time in my life, it felt appropriate. Thankfully, I didn't give a shit what anyone thought.

There wasn't anyone watching, anyway. I guessed there never had been. *Anger clouds everything,* I thought, and then I *was* a little embarrassed, because every probation officer I'd ever had had said something to that effect, only to receive cynicism and/or laughter from my end.

I was so stupid.

I looked less like a drunk when I checked the mirror again, which was good, because there were no volunteers allowed on the floors after seven P.M., and I'd be scrutinized no matter *what* excuse I came up with for being there.

But maybe there'd be nobody to scrutinize. If I was *really* lucky, the protective gear would get me to the elevator without a hitch, and I could try that option again. And if or when it didn't work, I'd go to the stairs, which were more likely to be deserted than anywhere else.

The place was quiet. I went in the side door, which took visitors through the lobby and straight to the different departmental exam rooms and skipped the emergency room altogether. It was almost eerie walking through the place after hours, especially in a scratchy paper suit and a full face shield. I moved slowly so I could hear over the sound of my legs rubbing together.

I came upon the first set of elevators and switched out my foot coverings as I waited for the *ding!* There were bootie, glove and mask stations at every elevator on every floor. Convenient when you've been sitting in your car and walking outside in your gear. When the *ding!* came, though, it was for the staff elevator, and at first, I folded my hands and waited for the regular one to arrive. Like always. But then, I wasn't there for anything *regular*, was I? I jumped into the car just as the doors began to shut and, to my dismay, the staff elevator reacted to my request to go to the sixth floor just as the one I'd taken from the third had; it asked for a key.

Disappointed but unsurprised, I hit three. My mind raced. I could try the stairs from third; at least if I was confronted, I could say I was there to say a temporary farewell to patients before going into the hospital myself. But another idea occurred to me as I exited into the dimly lit halls of the third floor: there were *separate* staff elevators on the other ends of the third and fourth floors, both. I'd never paid them any attention after first noticing them; not only was I lacking the title to use them, but I'd never seen anyone else use them, either. It would be a risk – what if it was a warehouse elevator meant for transporting equipment? Those had limited access. Regardless, the stairway entrance was on that end of the floor, which would serve as a convenient Plan B. Without deciding, I started toward the opposite end.

I padded carefully in my papery gear, mindfully averting my eyes when I passed open doorways. I slowed as I approached the nurse's station, then held my breath when I saw there was someone there – someone I didn't recognize. But a few quiet moments of observation later, I exhaled. He was sleeping. *Must be the new guy,* I thought, recalling

Jenna's wistful statement earlier. I watched him breathe open-mouthed as I passed the desk. He was young. A textbook lay face-down on his lap. A student, likely.

When I passed Jeremy's door, the urge to glance in nearly overwhelmed me, but I fought it. The kid was getting better; that had to satiate my fatherly feelings for the time being.

I was elated to reach the end of the hall and stand confronted by two doors: that of the staff elevator and that of the stairwell. I considered my options again, clenching my jaw at the sense of urgency that pressed upon me.

What are you going to do?

Why do you need to see the sixth floor, anyway?

Is this even important?

The myriad of alternate activities I could be spending precious time on flitted through my mind. My chest tightened uncomfortably. I pressed the elevator button in a spasm of impatience, and it dinged within seconds. I hurried in, every cell tingling on alert after the sound reverberated down the hallway behind me.

I was faced with a panel very much like those of the other elevators. *Good.* That and its regular sizing ruled out the warehouse elevator possibility. But the bad news was that, also like the other cars, the sixth-floor button had the key symbol on it. But there *was* something different – a small set of keys dangled from the keyhole. My heart leapt. *Someone forgot their keys!*

"Uh – hello?" A male voice echoed down the hallway and I froze, my eyes going to the figure that leaned over the nursing station counter.

Shit.

It wasn't the tightest spot I'd ever been in, though, and I seemed to have retained my "cool head in tough situations" skills from my past life. I raised my right hand in a wave while my left depressed the sixth-floor button. "Just headed out!" I called reassuringly.

"I wasn't sleeping! Just – uh – closing my eyes for a minute after checking the patients!"

The kid's worried he's in trouble, I thought, incredulous. The doors begun to close. I gave a thumbs-up and exhaled.

"Are you a doctor?" he yelled, perhaps only just thoroughly waking to the point that he'd thought to ask the *right* question.

I nodded, but then the doors were shut, a strained "Jesus; I'm trying to *sleep!*" coming from a nearby patient's room and drowning out anything else the young attendant may have said.

I couldn't help but laugh, albeit nervously, both at the angry cry of the patient, and at my stroke of luck at the keys having been forgotten. But then I tried to remove them and they stuck firm – perhaps they'd been jammed. Or maybe someone had gotten lazy, and the keys had been left so long in the spot, they'd stuck there. Regardless, it was without keys in my hand that I exited the elevator when it stopped. *I'll have to use the same one, that's all,* I thought as my heart thudded in my chest.

Sixth floor was not like third and fourth. That was apparent from the start. The atmosphere was charged. The tiny hairs on my arms stood on end as I paused to survey what I could see of the hallway. Unlike the other floors, the doors of all the patient rooms appeared to be shut - and locked from the outside, which was a stark contrast, indeed. And though the nighttime lighting was the same, the jumbled sounds of crying and moaning were new. Muffled sounds of beeping machines came at me from both directions, and I could hear hushed voices from the left-most hallway.

I headed right.

Heart pounding, I rounded the corner and pressed myself against the wall. My chest had that tightness to it again; the feeling that had been more difficult to ignore in the preceding days, but in that moment, it was all there was. A constriction around my torso, with the pulling point focused to the left of my sternum.

I knew time was running out.

One of the already-dimmed lights was flickering. I squinted into the dark, working to find a break in the walls. An end – but the nursing station must've been on the other side, for the only anomaly I could spot was a "caution" sign announcing the wet floor.

I put my hand to my chest. Breathed slowly.

Wondered what the hell I was doing, again.

A chilling scream ripped through the floor and I gasped, immediately shaken to the core. A door flew open halfway down the darkened hallway, then footfalls thundered down the hallway opposite. I flattened myself against the wall, though the doctor who'd exited the room was headed in the opposite direction. More subtle sounds of a door being unlocked followed along with raised voices and shouted orders. Another anguished cry split the air, unmuffled that time by a closed door.

I pressed my palms against the wall and pushed myself off of it; whatever was happening on the other side of the floor had drawn the attention of the staff, so if I was going to look around, that was the moment. I was only a few short steps into it, though, when someone else exited the room the doctor had burst through moments earlier.

But that time, it was a patient.

My first look at a sixth-floor resident left an image in my

mind's eye that I fear will never fade. It had been a woman; that much was apparent, as the gown she wore hung from her bent and twisted form much as useless sails on a windless day. She faced opposite me, exposing deformities in her spine like none I'd ever seen. Her left shoulder drooped; a typical indication of localized rubberization, and she was bent in an exaggerated fashion at the waist; a bony protrusion from her left hip holding her gown away from her on that side. It also draped low from the near ninety-degree angle of her lean to the right, which had her catching herself on the floor every few seconds. Her breath was raspy, like Pax's had been as he'd rattled his last.

As if on cue, she began to hack; massive, dragging coughs that had me catching my gag reflex. But then she turned slightly to her right and so that her profile was to me, and my horror deepened as she begun to fight for breath. Her jaw fairly *dangled* from her face; I could see as much through clumps of stringy hair. And then she hacked again, and from her gaping maw flew a glob of something, which landed with a sickening *splat* on the floor beneath her misshapen face.

I made a sound of disgust. It was involuntary; as surprising to me as it was to her. She turned on a pivot, her extended right arm acting as a support, and regarded me with sunken eyes.

If it had been lighter, or if I'd been closer to her, I may have found the spark of humanity I instinctively sought. But as it was, being observed by it – by *her* – inspired nothing but panic in me.

I thought to run, but my feet failed to comply. My bladder, however, threatened immediate release. But then she made a sound, and though it was unintelligible, it was full of a sadness I could feel.

I wondered if I should say something, but only for a moment. Then everything I had was spent on watching as her eyes slid from me to the wet floor and she bent low, her left leg rising in a precarious balancing act, and then licked the shining tiles with a dangling tongue.

I recoiled in disgust, but quickly realized it was the moisture she was after – the floor *had* just been mopped. And as surely as she was suffering from MARS-21, she was dehydrated.

I observed, mortified, as she ran a useless lower jaw and tongue along the slippery surface until she fell, landing face-first with a terrible *crunch*ing sound that had me gasping. I rushed forward before I thought about it, something primal reacting in a purely physical manner.

She was sobbing pathetically between rasping breaths when I reached her. Her dark, sunken eyes were on me, beseeching but somehow empty at the same time. Her jaw was twisted in such a way that, in my mind, rendered it unfixable. Even if not, her ragged, torn cheeks surely were.

I stood over her, images of the dog Molly and I had come across coming back to me; the way its jaw had scraped at the ground.

So similar.

"Who's there?"

I whipped my head up to find a figure at the end of the hallway; it appeared to be the doctor that had only recently flew from the twisted woman's room.

I backed up several steps, my feet sliding a bit on the wet tile.

"Dr. Enstan?"

"I – I'm sorry," I glanced once more at the puddle of a woman on the floor – she was back to trying to lap up some of the water – and then ran, skidding on the first few steps like the pursued did in cartoons, and then gaining my footing.

I was at the elevator before she cried, *"Stop! Somebody! Stop that man!"*

And there were thundering footfalls again, but I was well-ensconced and the lobby button was depressed and I made it out, just barely, but I did, tearing some of the protective gear from myself as I went, dropping pieces of it along the path of my escape, thoughts of the crisis that faced the world, or the worsening crisis, as it were, racing in circles in my head, with questions about dogs and deformed people and of blood winding their way into the chaos of my mind that threatened to break me.

But the last thought stuck and repeated, layering over and over until all else was gone. Thoughts of blood.

My blood.

Which was *maybe* something. But also, which was *missing* something.

And had I shared any needles lately?

Or had unprotected sex?

Had a blood transfusion, maybe?

No.

But I had pricked my finger on a thorn in the woods and it had bled.

And I'd done it while rescuing a pup who had an injury of her own.

And by God, her owner had been sick.

And dogs could get it.

And, holy shit. Maybe Molly was a survivor, too.

CHAPTER 43 – PRUNE

Considering the urgency of my escape, I lingered in the parking lot for far too long. But I couldn't move; I felt I was on the precipice of something, and if I just stayed, wavering there, I'd fall in the direction fate had planned.

I considered my options.

I could go to Hull immediately; just find Eva Pendleton or have someone contact her with a message: *I think it's the dogs. I think the missing piece is in a surviving dog. Like my Molly.*

I ruminated on the circumstances, still uneasy that I couldn't piece it together completely. I'd assumed my "different" blood had been the result of my rejuvenation, my new "purpose." Certainly, everything else that had changed of late could be explained by it. But what if there were others – maybe similar to me in some way – who also carried the unknown antigen? But – like me *how*? Other ex-cons with a proclivity for mayhem?

I watched the side door suspiciously; why hadn't anyone come to look for me? *Probably have other priorities,* I reasoned, shuddering at lingering images of sixth floor.

My thoughts raced. Or maybe other carriers shared something more basic, like age or existing conditions... a history of substance abuse... maybe they, too, were male, or had the same blood type. My eyes widened. My blood type was rare - AB negative. The rarest.

My fingers itched for my phone.

Do dogs have different blood types? I wondered, then satisfied my urge to grab the phone, but I didn't dial Ed or Evan or even Dr. P; instead I Googled "dog blood types," then glanced at the side door again. Still deserted.

"Huh," I muttered aloud. Dogs had at least twelve blood groups.

I stared out the window. *That could be it.*

Philosophizing further would be pointless; the good doctor and her team would test that, and many more hypotheses much more efficiently than I could – but it was enough to satisfy my need to know for the moment.

I started the car.

I had promised to return to Hull the following day; it suddenly seemed stupid to give up the time I had between then and now. So, I pulled out of the parking lot and went to the only place I wanted to be.

Lou-Anne's windows were dark when I arrived again in Wakefield, which was no surprise, and given the narrow chance I'd won to return the next day, I was pleased enough to sit in the car, my eyes on the door that stood between my daughter, my dog, and I.

Eventually I realized I'd never fall asleep in the car, so I removed what was left of my protective gear just outside the driver's side door, carefully folding it before stacking it on the driver's seat. Something fell from my jacket pocket when I grabbed it, thinking of sitting on Lou-Anne's porch for a while, but a bit wary of the crisp, damp nighttime air of autumn. When I stooped to retrieve it, I was overwhelmed again – it was Linda's note. I'd stuffed it in my coat that day and then forgotten about it, but if there ever was a time I could've used a comforting voice, it was then.

I read it by the light of my phone, which promptly died

once I was finished – yet another small miracle of timing – and then I fell asleep there, leaning against the siding of my daughter's home.

CHAPTER 44 –
CUT BACK

Dear Tom,

It is with a huge sense of excitement that I write this. A bed at the Hull Center has opened up and apparently, I've qualified to snap it up.

I'm on my way to full recovery, Tom.

Many would have (and some did!) discounted the possibility. Even I did when my jaw stiffened up and then froze. In my mind, that was it – a death sentence. I was quite literally working on being OK with dying.

But then, there was you.

You always seem baffled when I thank you, Tom, and I know that's largely a result of a troubled past and perhaps a lack of direction or support. I don't say that to demean you; I say it to empower you. From what you've told me, you've only recently taken some pride in how you live your life, and I get the feeling the past still weighs heavy on you. How could it not, when you aren't aware you can change that?

Just like I wasn't aware of the chance to live.

So please, let me return the favor. Though it may not mean something as weighty as the difference between life and death, I hope it affects you in a positive way.

You can choose, Thomas Wall. You can live your life in a

brand-new way. Sure, you can make the changes you need to in order to rectify some of your past decisions. You already are! But let the goal be something fresh and new. A clean slate.

It took me very little time to learn I had a choice to beat this monster of a disease, but we're different people! This particular lesson may need more time to be realized. But I will be your friend until then, and after.

I hope this helps you, Tom.

Finally, I want to say that our differences mean little when I consider how to live my best life. I choose to live with my new friends – no longer alone and wallowing, but with like-minded people to share each day with. Your young friend Jeremy is moving in with me; did he tell you? It's such a relief to know we won't be alone.

And my dream of a new beginning includes you, too! You are family, now.

I hope I see you often when home is an option again.

Until then, thank you, Tom. Thank you for lifting my heart by going into the trees to rescue an injured puppy, and giving me hope when you took the extra steps to take care of me.

To show me I could survive.

You are a good person.

With love and thanks,

Linda

CHAPTER 45 – REST

I knew immediately that the dream was different than the others. I was in an alley, the sounds of car horns and voices announcing the very near presence of people, but somehow cut off from all that life. Blocked by bricks and mortar only, and just a step off their path, but I was in a dark and stinking crevasse commuters easily chose not to see.

There were muffled shouts from above; I gazed up and beyond a rusted fire escape to discover filthy windows that separated me from the dwellers within. They didn't see me either. After a while, I imagine they forgot they could look. Or maybe some of them were like me – dwelling in between dwellings and just visiting the windowed rooms to get something. Or give it.

Drugs.

Sex.

I thought of the levelled building of past dreams and wondered where that alley sat between the layers. Maybe alley-dwellers brought their solitude with them in death – maybe they were always unseen there, too.

I scanned the length of the dark place in both directions, then moved a bit to explore further. Rubbish crowded the walls – piles of papers and food wrappers, a discarded old TV, and two shopping carts. Something moved beneath the mess and I jumped, then exhaled as a mouse poked its nose out, then scampered toward the end opposite me, where what light there was beckoned weakly.

I felt it, then – the presence of the one who'd brought me back. A pressure on my back. "Look," it said.

And something moved beneath the junk again. Something bigger. I stepped toward it before the presence pushed – because I knew it would - my eyes on the shuffling papers. But it stopped as I approached. I moved the junk around with my foot, balling my fists in anticipation of a confrontation – yes, even with a mouse.

But there were two, that time, and they jumped and squealed when I pushed the garbage around again, then ran, one in each direction. My heart raced. I pressed my palm to my chest, willing myself to breathe, but couldn't manage it just yet, for a swarm of bugs followed the mice, rising from the gap in the detritus as the single entity of a buzzing cloud.

"What is this?" I muttered, breathless, and the presence did push, then, but just a little.

I shuffled the stuff around again, grimacing at what arose on that final attempt: a terrible, but familiar, odour.

I backed away. "Someone's dead under there," I said under my breath, and the truth of the words made my skin tighten with goosebumps.

And a woman stepped up beside me from around my back.

I screamed and jumped back, hitting the brick wall so hard I saw stars. When I regained my vision she was still there, observing me blankly.

"Who are you?" I cried, my voice shrill.

She laughed.

That old shame flooded back – the shame that accompanied any teasing at all – that accompanied, in fact, any real emotion I displayed. Inspired first by foster families and by school kids who knew I had no one. Who knew I was easy to anger. I was entertaining. How young had I been when I stopped seeing the beautiful things? Stepped on the fuzzy caterpillar instead of picking it up and moving it to a tree? Watching the clouds? Imagining a future with people who would care about me?

I'd chosen to pre-empt the shame and scare them rather than be their target. It seemed the only solution. All because having them laugh at me was worse than having them avoid me. I already knew I was unworthy of love – of family – and being teased seemed too harsh a punishment to stack atop all that.

So instead, I'd fought.

But when that woman laughed and that shame flooded in, it was like everything had come full-circle, and I had to choose again.

And things were different. I felt better, and I liked it. So, instead of shouting or storming off, I watched her. Maybe she laughed because she, too, was afraid. "Who are you?"

Her mirth ebbed. "You don't know?"

I frowned. My heart stuttered to a new high. *What if it's someone I wronged? Someone I hurt? Oh, God – what if it's my mother?* I gulped, and the woman laughed again. That time I watched as her throat moved, her tendons standing out from sallow, scabby skin. The sores trailed up her neck and along her jaw, which caved at her cheeks. I could see the hollows at her gums where teeth should be, and her eyes sat in dark, sunken spots as well, the skin there papery and yellow-tinged. "What's wrong with you?" I breathed, next eyeing greasy, tangled hair, which was clumped in spots on her scalp where more scabs had been created, then worried at until they were wounds in their own right.

The woman straightened, suddenly, and changed, morphing into someone younger. Her cheeks filled out and her tone brightened, her hair lengthened and shone. A smattering of freckles ran across her cheekbones and over her nose. I was transfixed. She pointed, then, to the piles of garbage from which the mice and bugs had run, and said, "This is where I met my end."

A wind picked up at the mouth of the alley and blew down it, swirling whatever was strewn about in all directions and uncovering the lump of something that the mess had hidden. And to my horror, it was indeed a woman. It was *her*. Not someone I'd known or wronged, but apparently the one who'd rescued me from death.

The smell hit again, but I fought against reacting. I peered at the young woman beside me, instead, then back toward the pitiful body that had lain for who knew how long after her demise, just beyond the streets. Between the visible places. "That's *you?*" I whispered, and the woman changed again, morphing back to the body ravaged by abuse and addiction and finally, death, but she didn't stop there.

She became dim, fading, but then emerging as a glow, which moved from my side and to my back again and I knew it *was* her – I'd finally seen the one who'd found me trapped in my living room, frowning down at my ruined body and seemingly stuck between spaces.

"It's you?"

"Yes." The voice was back to being unidentifiable by gender or any other contributing factor, but it was at my ear and I could feel her there, solidly, at my back.

"Why?" I asked. "What happened to you?"

"That isn't important now. What matters is that now, I am different. I, too, have a new purpose."

And without warning, we were whisked into that dark place of earlier dreams. I recognized the levels in front of me and shook my head. "Not this again. Why can't you just tell me? Am I doing the right thing? And by the way, how come I'm suddenly supposed to save the whole fucking world? That wasn't part of the bargain!"

The presence laughed. "I don't know. I just do what I'm told, and trust that how it evolves on the physical plane is orchestrated, just so, for a reason."

I shook my head. "I want to wake up. Apparently, I have some pretty serious heart issues, and I want to see my daughter before it's too late."

"All will happen as it is meant to."

I gritted my teeth. "If you're not going to tell me something new, why bring me here? Why show yourself and then fade again? Why show me how you died – or where you died, I guess?"

"Would you rather know me in my past form?"

I remembered how her skin had sagged and sunken and gathered at the sores. "No."

"I show you in order to make a connection – so you know I, too, suffered in life. And that now, I have a purpose. Now, I choose differently."

"Right. And I already know I have a purpose!" I cried. "Am I not doing it right? Because for the first time I can say this and mean it: I'm trying my best!"

"You have one more thing to do, Thomas. You hold the key to it all, and yet you hold it to yourself while people suffer and die."

I was stunned into silence.

"You still must learn that sometimes, even when doing

the right thing is often much harder than doing wrong, it is still right."

I struggled between the urges to laugh and cry, "But, I've made progress! Everyone I've met – they've all said as much!"

"Yes! That much is true, but that final thing…everything depends upon what you do, Thomas. What you choose."

Before I could reply, we were flying toward the levels so fast that my breath was stolen from me, and stopped just as abruptly, a forest scene before us. I squinted through the trees and the perspective changed; I could see a flowing river running through the place, and a man in waders fly fishing in the middle of it. A man that was me.

"Are you telling me that if I sacrifice my relationship with my daughter, this is my – destination, or whatever?"

"I cannot tell you that, Thomas. But it *is* possible."

Visions of the lower levels flashed before my eyes. The molten river, the unyielding darkness, the crushing pain.

"Choose well, Thomas."

It had been one of the first things the presence had said to me, but something in me still fought against it.

"You keep saying that, but I feel like a lot of my ability to choose is gone since I came back. After all, I was brought back by *you!* Given my new purpose rather than finding it and realizing it on my own! And the one thing – the only thing I *want* seems held out of my reach!"

"You say words that do not match what you know."

"What?"

"You chose it all, Thomas. From then to now. It's all been you."

"I -" I stuttered the beginnings of a retort. Of denial. But when I thought about it, it was all true. I'd chosen to return. To change. To do better...*be* better. "You could've let me have more of a choice when it came to the booze," I muttered, completely deflated.

"We have always been short on time. As for the rest – would you have had it any other way? Because everything is not set in stone. You *still* have choices."

I shook my head immediately, knowing suddenly that taking responsibility for my choices had to be my choice, too. "No. You're right. Let me go back."

"All you must do now is choose how many flights of stairs you are willing to climb to reach your level, Thomas."

I nodded, though the fullness of the statement is *still* revealing itself to me. "OK."

The sunlight filtered through the trees and I was distracted by the beauty. I watched myself cast the fly. Saw the fish beneath the surface and wondered if the bait was right.

"We will see you soon."

I gulped. "I know."

And with that, I woke up, but I was falling backward, too. My back and head hit the floor and I cried out, reaching for something to steady myself with and finding nothing. But then, all was still, and when I opened my eyes, I was halfway in the kitchen and half on the porch, and Lou-Anne regarded me from above, her face an upside-down scowl that would have been comical if I hadn't been so disoriented.

"I saw you through the window," she stated matter-of-factly.

Suddenly Molly was there, her paws on my chest, wriggling and whimpering and licking my face. "Hey sweetheart," I muttered, scratching the dog's head and gazing up at my beautiful daughter.

She crossed her arms over her chest. "You're not wearing your getup."

"Oh, shit," I mumbled, remembering the small, neat pile of protective gear on the driver's seat of the car. But with what I knew, I doubted anymore that it was needed. "Are you OK with that?"

She frowned, then nodded. "Want to meet your grandchildren?"

My heart leapt and I sat, ignoring the dizziness that followed. "I'd like nothing more."

CHAPTER 46 – OVERWINTER

It was perhaps the most fulfilling few minutes of my lifetimes. My grandchildren – named Jessie and Mads, the second of which being a German name, after his father's heritage – and even my ex son-in-law were surprised and pleased to meet me, even over video chat.

All had questions, and I tried my best to answer them. I was honest, even if it meant they would like me less in that moment. And Lou-Anne seemed pleased... And there was something else about her that I couldn't quite put my finger on during the conversation.

Molly sat on my lap while we talked with the kids, making everyone laugh by licking my tears off my cheeks before I knew they were there. I'm pretty sure the kids fell in love with little Molly right away. It would take some time for them to love me, but I was satisfied, at least, that now there was a chance. Even if they learned more about me when I wasn't around to tell them myself.

After we hung up, I thanked Lou-Ann.

"I don't want you to assume you'll be a big part of their lives – or mine, for that matter. I want to be in control of how much you're in our lives, and in what manner."

I nodded, my heart thudding at the mere possibility of *something* with a family I wanted so badly, but didn't deserve.

We both jumped when the creaking sound of metal hinges split the air. She rolled her eyes, laughing. "It's just the mail."

"I'll get it." I started to stand, but she stopped me.

She made a face. "It'll just be bills I can't pay."

I frowned.

"Well just one, really," she looked down at the tabletop, rubbing her jaw absently, and it hit me: the thing that was different about her.

"Hey! You seem to be moving your jaw better today!"

She smiled, and there it was – her beauty. Her spark. My stomach did a somersault. "It's really strange, but I started feeling better last night." She fairly glowed with barely contained joy. "I – for a while there, I was sure -"

I put a hand up to stop her but couldn't say anything. The relief was palpable, rolling over and between us in a glorious wave.

"I think it was her," she motioned toward Molly, who was so excited at the recognition she was up from my lap and making her way to Lou-Anne across the table before I could think to stop her. Lou-Anne laughed as Molly licked her face enthusiastically.

I regarded her chapped and scabbed mouth with interest. "Maybe it was."

She frowned between kisses. "What?"

I waited until Molly was settled into her lap. "What blood type are you?"

She seemed momentarily taken-aback, then answered quietly. "Mom said my blood was my connection to you, because it's so rare. She talked about it like it was a curse." She chewed at her lip. "Sorry. But did you know that AB negative is the most sought after for bone marrow donation?"

"The universal donor," I whispered, something firing up in my gut.

She snickered. "Totally useless when it comes to blood donation, but I guess it all balances out. I wish it could make me helpful against MARS, but -" she shrugged. "It's weird; I've always felt the need to be of service to people. It's why I do what I do, but now…"

I took note of her casual cynicism, and how she always mitigated it with a positive, like I did, but I did it in the background. I was suddenly filled with a new sense of urgency. I had a job to do, and in the space of the preceding thirty second conversation, I'd been hit full-on with the gravity of it. I fixed my gaze on my daughter's. "I want you to know that from the moment I held you in my arms, I've known you're the best thing I've ever accomplished."

Her expression registered surprise. Molly was suddenly bounding across the table to me again. I took her easily into my arms, my gaze still on Lou-Anne. "And I've thought of you that way every day – every second! – since, even when I was too sick or stupid or ashamed to reach out."

"I -"

"Is it the house?"

That time, confusion took over her face completely.

"The bill you can't pay?"

Her face cleared. "Uh – yeah."

"I have a house. No payments. It's yours." I stood, and kissed Molly on her silky head before lowering her to the ground. Her heart fluttered against my hand.

Lou-Anne watched me cross to the door, flummoxed, then cried, "Wait!"

"I need to call the lawyer about the house, and then I need to make a call that will render me useless." My breath caught in my throat. "I don't know what will happen after that"

"What?" She stood, but had to catch herself on the counter.

I turned back to her. "You've made my life complete. Just by letting me in a tiny bit. Letting me see you."

She walked toward me. "Make your calls in here. Please."

I'd done so little for her in all the time I'd had, so I did what she asked in the little time I had left. I sat at the table where we'd chatted over a video call with my grandchildren, and I dialled the lawyer from a card in my wallet. It was as easy as instructing him to put the house in Lou-Anne's name. She could finalize the paperwork anytime.

Things had changed after MARS – even the formerly time-consuming processes that necessitated lawyers.

And then, I stared intently at my phone. Who next? Who could I trust the most? The phone trembled in my left hand as a bolt of pain shot from my shoulder to my fingertips.

"What's wrong?" Lou-Anne asked.

"It's happening," I muttered. I switched hands, then dialled Ed.

"Tom? Oh, I'm glad to hear from you. That doctor – Pendleton – she's been calling us, trying to get us to herd you over to the center."

"I'll bet," I smiled. "Never fear; I'm about to call her. I just wanted to talk to you, first."

"Oh." He sounded unsure.

"I want you to know that Lou-Anne and her kids are going to take care of Molly, but your family can see her any time after this is all over."

"Why are you telling me this, Tom? What's wrong?"

Lou-Anne's eyes echoed Ed's concern as she watched my left hand clench into a ball with another shot of pain. That time, though, it was accompanied by a monstrous pressure on my chest.

"I just want you – your family – to meet mine," I gasped. "Thank you for giving me a chance, Ed. Over and over again, you saw something in me other than the man I used to be."

"Tom – are you in Wakefield now? What's the address?"

I let the phone drop without deciding to. Molly whimpered from the floor and stood, her wise eyes on mine and her front paws on my knees. Lou-Anne was talking on the phone; I heard her rattle off her address, and then she was beside me, her hands on my arm.

I collapsed to the floor; I remember bolts of pain shooting from my knees to my lower back when I landed, but not caring. Lou-Anne was beside me, and that was what mattered. "I'm sorry to leave all this with you," I said between shallow breaths.

"I'm getting the Aspirin, and Ed's calling an ambulance. You're not going anywhere just yet, Tom." She pressed her fingers lightly to my forehead and added, "Dad."

I grimaced at a simultaneous burst of joy at the term and the crushing pain on my chest.

"Hold on," she said, but it was distant. And oh, how I wished I could. Instead, I gripped her hand in mine, needing her to hear the last I had to say. Needing it to be just then, because I was feeling lighter somehow, even as the pressure suffocated me. "You have to tell them it's my blood and Molly's blood together, somehow," I grunted.

"What? What is?"

"The cure – the key to everything. I think Molly had it, too and survived. That's the missing piece." I panted, needing to say more but lacking the strength for a moment. "And you have to tell them you're AB negative, too. Please."

She shook her head, but she was fading – my vision was darkening around the edges like a picture thrown into the fire.

"You *are* meant to help, Lou-Anne." There was no breath, but I squeezed out the bit that was more important than anything else, regardless of my purpose or any other factor: "I love you."

She cried, leaning to rest her head on my chest. Somehow the pressure of it lessened the other, darker weight that was there. And Molly was there, too, licking the tears off my cheeks again. I tried to tell her I loved her, too, but I don't know if it came out.

I think she knew, though. She was a pretty smart pup.

And then everything was fading, even the pain. Even as a siren wailed closer. Even as Lou-Anne squeezed my hand and spoke into my ear, saying *I'm so grateful. Thank you. Thank you so much.*

CHAPTER 47 – SLEEP

I packed the last of a makeshift picnic – egg salad sandwiches, potato salad and stuffed sweet peppers – into my pack, throwing a checked blanket in at the last second. I thought of the kids and added the brownies Dad had made himself. I shook my head as I did it, marvelling over how things with my father had changed since the cure. It was like he emerged from a fog when the new, successful treatments were dispatched and the vaccine was sent to quick trials.

And I realized I'd been trying to find the man for years, but the haze of his fear, his worry, and his sometimes misguided actions hid him from me. From everyone.

But as the burden of MARS-21 began to lift, so did the shroud that had ensconced my father so completely.

And I was surprised to find it bittersweet, because even as I regained a father who'd always been physically there, my dearest love had lost a father who'd only just appeared.

Funny how people's lives twist around each other; by the time we think to look back at how we've arrived at our destination, we're shocked to realize that in some ways, our loved ones fade in and out of our lives and hearts regardless of their physical presence.

I've learned so much from all of this. From cooking for seniors who could be alternately crabby and gracious, from watching the person I was always meant to be with fade and then return, with a hail-Mary gift that would potentially save mankind, from taking the reins on the business so that my father could do what he revealed to be his lifelong goal: travel the world with loved ones. From so much more... but perhaps nothing as profound as loving a woman and her children as my own family. Oh, and Molly too.

Where would we be without that silly dog?

I say that lightly, but she and I were best friends by the time I was driving her and Lou-Anne to their weekly visits to the team at the Center in Hull. I think Molly was best friends with everyone, though.

And our Center became the model for Centers around the world, and we taught them to find the antigens in the rare human survivor with AB negative blood and in surviving dogs with, as it turned out, *any* of the blood groups. And then mix them – and that was a miracle, too, because no special methodology needed sussing out; something as simple as mixing saliva, or blood, or any type of bodily fluid from either subject would produce the antibody that would cure MARS-21 sufferers the world over.

But it wasn't all easy – the surge in psychosis cases nearly proved the cure to be too late. Crazed humans and canines alike brought a brand of chaos the world had never experienced before the disease was fought back with the new human/dog genetic weapon we'd gained, thanks to Tom Wall and Molly the Dog.

But that's another story entirely.

I put the pack in the car and headed to Aylmer, where Lou-Anne and I would picnic with Ed LaFrance and his family. After Lou-Anne proved so instrumental in finding the cure, her mortgage problems disappeared – which was ideal for her and the kids; Lou-Anne wanted to get back to the Home as quick as possible, and from Aylmer it would've been difficult. But Tom's gift of his home was far from wasted; it turned into a meeting place for people wanting to connect. Ironic, considering the lonely life Tom seemed to have lived, up until the end, when he seemed to have made the closest connections he'd ever had. And in honour of him, and his late, but not *too* late efforts to restore some connection between people, we meet in his home. We have meals, watch the dogs frolic in the tall grass, watch TV, and generally do the things families and friends do together.

And despite the lessened population, the number of folks who gather there is growing.

Some have even started a large garden in the back, the fruits of which are free for those in need.

I don't know if Tom would be pleased with what's been done there – I didn't know him well enough – but I can say that his efforts to help people lasted far beyond the last days of his life. We still live better because of him. Ed's whole family, in fact, was saved by him, in a sense.

Ed always talks about the day he met Tom as something so seemingly random that turned into the salvation of his family. I don't exaggerate - apparently, he'd started feeling sick only days before Tom had his final, massive heart attack, and testing proved he, his wife, and his children had all contracted the disease. They were among the first to test the cure.

And all those initial tests were successful. All of them.

Sure, there are still debates over how it was administered. Really, the only outrage was due to the fact that the critically ill – especially those in late stages of physical deformity and/or psychosis – were *not* among the first to receive the treatment. You can imagine the ethical dilemmas around that one. And the rare ones in those extreme cases that did survive – whether they were given the cure or not – were often so disabled that their quality of life was severely compromised.

But nothing is ever perfect, is it?

And I've gotten off track. I was headed to a picnic.

CHAPTER 48 – WATER

It's not all fly-fishing and sparkling waters, nor happy reunions and gained closure. It's true my mother greeted me the second time I died – holding a hand out to me and smiling, saying *I'm Louise, Thomas. I'm your mother* – but to say my heaven was the end of all my pain and suffering, or even my final resting place, as is traditionally said, would be a lie.

Remember my savior? The dead junkie-turned-supernatural presence who brought me back to life? Well, that's Edie, and she was there to greet me the second time around, too. And despite my inclination to be done with earthly work, it turns out there's still a lot for me to do, and Edie's my trainer, so to speak.

It's a small price to pay to be fishing in cool, reflective waters rather than in a dark void with a river of lava. To have the privilege of looking on the ones I've left behind with joy and pride rather than forgetting they exist as my world is swallowed by a preoccupation with what is happening to me.

I may sound trite. I apologize for that. I'm still not perfect.

And there are still mysteries.

Like who *Edie's* boss is, for example.

Maybe those enlightened ones on the higher levels are blessed with the answers we all crave in our physical lives, but my level is more about restoration and redemption than enlightenment and – whatever else goes on up there. I imagine some sort of cosmic research and development lab where beings greater than myself – than *us* – endeavor to make things better. Or different, at least.

Don't get me wrong – I'm not ungrateful. Just regretful that my life only truly started after I died. But that's on me. I'm determined, too. Now that I know there is more to aspire to, apathy has no home in me. I envy those who are endowed with a faith in life that doesn't have to be proven... but I know, too, that those perks aren't free.

So, I won't say I know *nothing.* And at least I know there's much more to learn than I already know – that in itself makes me better. But I still flounder. I still work. *Hard.* But there is one thing I know now beyond all doubt: I'm not done yet.

There's always more, whether you believe you want it or not. Whether what comes matches your expectations, or your dreams or nightmares, whether it's your first time around or your fifty-first. And while we're there, on the physical plane, where we forget and there are things that require no faith, things like death and pain and abandonment, it becomes easier to make our choices based on the tangible.

But there are things like love, too. And touch. And kindness. Connection.

Puppies.

And we can choose to see more of the beautiful things, and maybe even the intangible things that do require faith, like a destination greater than the physical form.

We all choose. We all have the power to affect what happens next.

So, make it good.

BOOKS BY THIS AUTHOR

Rose's Ghost - The Trilogy

Viktor and Rose Maplestone built their house in the woods as a hideaway, but their safe haven became a prison when those left behind failed to join them, proving to be lost or killed. When Rose and Viktor join those who've gone before, there is one left to solve the puzzle of his ancestors. But Greyson isn't alone; he has help from living friends and the ghosts of family.

Rose's Ghost

She just wanted her baby back. Rose's Ghost is the first book in a series of three about a family's connection with a tormented ghost, still desperate to gain back the child she lost. Rose remains tethered to her family's property, beseeching those who reside upon or around it to help in her quest. But somewhere between her death and the haunting of Maggie Ridgewood's family, Rose's reality has become darkly skewed, and her efforts to find her child threaten to alter the lives of those whose help she enlists – or end them.

Heather's Grave

Rose is at rest, but the haunting of the Ridgewood family continues in Heather's Grave: Book 2 of the Rose's Ghost series. Maggie is relieved to have found peace in the Ridgewood family home, having solved the mystery of Rose Maplestone. But with the onset of new adventures as she and Jack prepare for their new addition comes more ominous change. Max is forced to admit his anxiety stems from more than regret over his role in saving Alice Ridgewood from Rose's ghost. His body is sick, too. And the tragedies of the Maplestone family didn't end with Rose, for after all, the child she lost was a secret in life – her existence unrecorded and unacknowledged - except by those who'd witnessed it all. And as her desperation to honor her child grows, Rose determines to help Maggie in the strangest of ways – raising questions around her intent. Does Rose mean to help, as she's vowed, or do her methods force an ultimatum instead, wherein the life of Maggie's child depends on the finding of hers?

Dmitry's Shadow

Greyson is grateful for the peace he's found with the help of his friends, but all is not yet well; the questions of his ancestry remain. Why did Viktor Kotova flee his home country? Who was left behind? Amidst rumours of a family connection with the mafia and the suspicious circumstances surrounding his grandfather's death, there are ghosts that linger, insistent on the solving of the Kotova family puzzle. So, Greyson and the property of his family home - once abandoned and then demolished - remain haunted, and like his mother before him, he enlists the help of those who reside upon it.

But Max and Maggie are fighting demons of their own, and Charis finds her world rocked by the dark patches in her vision. Will they be able to pull together and face the truths of a buried past? And will the answers they find bring long-awaited closure to a man whose life is just beginning at the age of seventy-four?

Asylum

From the creator of the Rose's Ghost series comes another thrilling tale: Asylum proves to be a ghost story that stands on its own.

We follow Bailey O'Connor on an exciting urban exploration trip across the border to discover the secrets of a long-abandoned institution for mentally and physically handicapped children. But there's more than just mystery darkening the crumbling buildings they discover, and Bailey finds herself lost within them with the help of those who linger.

The search for her is mounted during the day while her own search takes place in the dark. Are the rumors true? The whisperings of experiments performed on the innocent and vulnerable? What secrets lurk within the few impenetrable buildings on the site? Most importantly, can the truth be uncovered before the property is leveled and its secrets are buried forever?

Told in Dale's unique voice, readers both familiar and new will appreciate an engaging cast of characters and a compelling story that is hard to put down.

Constance & Enzo's Tea Time With Peyton

From the author of the Rose's Ghost Trilogy and Asylum comes a thrilling new tale featuring familiar characters...

Peyton's come a long way from the awkward twelve-year-old girl we met in That Summer, but her incredible gift is still wreaking havoc with her life. In her ongoing quest to find others like her, she's unknowingly left a trail of breadcrumbs to her front door – for commiserating friends and desperate souls, alike.

But she couldn't have predicted the lengths one visiting stranger would go to take advantage of her ability to talk to the dead. She's never been good at predicting the actions of people, dead or alive, But this time her weakness - combined with the all-encompassing need of her captor - results in her disappearance.

Her advantage? Those who love her will do everything they

can to find her and bring her home, including the recruitment of two uniquely qualified women. Will Margot - a pioneer in the world of science and the supernatural, and Charis - a sometimes reluctant, but highly gifted psychic - succeed in using their own special talents to see clues the police simply can't?

Chrysalis

In Chrysalis, we explore the quiet underworld of an ultra-conservative Canadian city. Our unlikely hero, Trey, is an energy-seeing, cross-dressing sex worker on the precipice of a life or death decision, but when a friend goes missing, he finds himself distracted from the business of self-destruction.

Desperate to find his missing colleague, twenty-four-year-old Trey finds himself part of an unusual group, from a deranged kidnapper to a devoted cop, all focused on a missing girl. And when confronted with these Canadian people, dealing with both human and Canadian issues, we find ourselves suspending our judgement on characters we'd often prefer to look past.Through it all, we witness Trey's chance at transformation – will he be able to set himself on a new direction in life as he finally begins to understand that being different doesn't necessarily mean you don't belong?

Spirit Talker

The first book in a new series from the author that brought you the Rose's Ghost Trilogy and Asylum.

Shya's no stranger to events of the paranormal sort – the women in her family have passed down their strange gifts for as long as they know. But the early loss of her mother has meant far less guidance for Shya than they'd both hoped for, and now she finds herself floundering as she faces darker elements of the spirit world.

She's grateful for her friends in The Seers group... at least they take her seriously, and even provide insight she couldn't have gleaned herself, thanks to their incredible collection of supernatural gifts. But none of them are prepared for the fight that looms ahead, and it's not only a possessed child's life that hangs in the balance – the demon wants Shya most of all.

Will The Seers succeed in saving both souls when Shya's gifts are turned to work against her?

Join Shya and The Seers on an adventure that will have you in its grips and leave you wanting more.

Soul Seer - Book 2 Of The Seers Series

Dawn prides herself on her strength as a leader, and her confidence hasn't let The Seers down... until Shya's possession, which every member of the group blames themselves for, Dawn included. But the confrontation of her own weaknesses uncovers more about her past – and the present! – than Dawn was prepared to face.

As they all travel to Shya's family home again, uncertainty seems to be the only constant they can rely on. Mel and Ed are absent, the twins have a terrible secret they've yet to share, Sheila is riddled with anxiety, Dawn seems to be the vessel through which Shya sends her cryptic messages in the form of poetry, and the world is suffering the effects of the portal ripped in the boundary between the living and the dead.

Can they close the portal and save Shya, too? As the group falls victim to the demon's trickery, their faith is badly rattled, and Dawn hasn't a clue how to make it all better.

Bird With A Broken Wing

A fourteen-year-old girl living in a rural community of Nova Scotia, a group of neighborhood kids, and hours spent exploring or just hanging out in the woods and on the train tracks along the river.

Bird With A Broken Wing brings us back to a time when the best thing about evenings and weekends was heading outside to find your friends - but there is nothing typical about Margot's new friend, Wren. And the new family at the bottom of the hill knows why.

Just as she tries to accept her feelings of being perpetually left behind, Margot discovers some of the different faces of love in the most unexpected way.

That Summer

Twelve-year-old Peyton is dealing with an Asperger's diagnosis and a summer spent away from her parents. Everything changes for her that summer, but it takes some new friends - live and ghosts alike - to get through it all. In the end, she not only learns that being herself is her best option, but that she can make a positive difference in the lives of others, too.